THE SERIAL KILLER'S SISTER

After completing a psychology degree, Alice Hunter became an interventions facilitator in a prison. There, she was part of a team offering rehabilitation programmes to men serving sentences for a wide range of offences, often working with prisoners who'd committed serious violent crimes. Previously, Alice had been a nurse, working in the NHS. She now puts her experiences to good use in fiction. *The Serial Killer's Wife*, *The Serial Killer's Daughter* and *The Serial Killer's Sister* all draw heavily on her knowledge of psychology and the criminal mind.

THE
SERIAL KILLER'S SISTER

ALICE HUNTER

avon.

Published by AVON
A division of HarperCollins*Publishers* Ltd
1 London Bridge Street
London SE1 9GF

www.harpercollins.co.uk

HarperCollins*Publishers*
Macken House, 39/40 Mayor Street Upper,
Dublin 1, D01 C9W8
Ireland

A Paperback Original 2023
3

First published in Great Britain by HarperCollins*Publishers* 2023

ISBN: 978-0-00-856221-2

Typeset in Sabon by Palimpsest Book Production Limited, Falkirk, Stirlingshire
Printed and bound in UK using 100% Renewable Electricity at CPI Group (UK) Ltd

For Emily.
The best daughter-in-law I could hope for.
Thank you for giving me such a beautiful
granddaughter. And for reading my books!

Prologue

'Do we have to go inside?' The boy, small for eight, stops walking before reaching the flaky green gate and looks up at his sister, his large, brown eyes begging.

'We're already late. You don't want another whipping, do you?'

'No.' His lower lip wobbles, and the girl sighs and turns to him, putting her backpack on the pavement. With both her hands firmly on his shoulders, she stoops to look into his eyes.

'Come on. I'll sneak you in and straight up the stairs. Then I'll make us Dairylea sandwiches.'

'Can we eat them in your special tent?' As he asks, he dips his head, and a chunk of sand-coloured hair falls over his right eye. The girl pushes it back. There's only one year and eleven months between them, but already she's far more grown up; she's had to be.

'Course,' she says.

He smiles, then, and takes a deep breath. 'I'm glad I've got you.'

'I'm glad I've got you, too,' she says. And she means it.

The smell of stale fags, alcohol, and what she guesses is pee hits her as she cracks open the front door and pops her head around to see if the coast is clear. She had considered trying the back door, but that needs WD-40 and squeals like a hundred mice, so they could never have snuck past *him*, no matter how drunk he is today. He always senses when they're home. He smells them, like the giant in the sky in Jack and the Beanstalk.

It's not him the girl glimpses, though, and she allows the air in her lungs to escape with a low hiss. Maybe they got away with it this time. The woman, dressed in a grubby, oversized t-shirt, with skinny legs clad in patchy grey leggings, lies on her back on the stained beige two-seater sofa. One arm dangles off it, the hand open and an empty wine bottle on its side beneath it. Crushed beer cans scatter the floor, making the pattern of the carpet almost invisible. A waft of sick rides on the air and the girl screws her nose up before pinching it tight with her thumb and finger. She notices lumps of undigested food mixed in a gravy-like liquid on the side of her mother's face, spreading over the edge of the sofa.

Her breath hitches. Is she dead? The girl moves to block her brother's line of sight. She can't let him see. 'Go on,' she whispers, pushing him behind her back towards the stairs.

He barely gets his foot on the first step when the voice bellows.

'Where the fuck have you two been?' He's standing at the top; must've just got out the loo. The girl pulls the boy back to her and they both recoil, slamming hard against the wall. If they could disappear into it, they would. 'You better have got my stuff?'

As he descends the stairs, she slips the backpack off her shoulder, undoes it and with a shaky hand delves inside. The man jerks forward, yanking the bag from her grip. He pulls out the bottle of whisky, then throws the bag back at her. The metal zip catches her square in the face. She yelps, touching her fingertips to her bleeding nose. He snorts, then pushes past them. Just as they think they've escaped the worst of it, he turns and rushes at the boy.

'Pathetic wimp. Bet you got your sister to steal this, didn't you?' He whacks the bottle against the boy's chest. 'When I was your age, I'd be getting my old man whatever he fancied. No questions. No big sister to do it for me. You need to grow a pair.' He makes a grab for the boy, one large hand squeezing hard between his legs until he cries out. The man laughs. 'Just like I thought. No balls.'

Hot tears run down the boy's cheeks, which makes the man laugh even harder.

The girl launches at him, smacking his arm. 'Leave him alone!' she yells. 'I'm going to call the police.'

'Oh, really? Where's this come from, eh, kid? What are you, seven?'

'No, I'm ten and you're not our dad, so you don't belong here.' The warm, tight ball that began in her stomach, like a knotted piece of string, grows bigger and gets hotter. It rises up until it explodes out of her mouth like a firework: a fizzing, burning Catherine Wheel, making

3

a high-pitched squealing noise. The boy's hands cup his ears, and he cowers in the corner as the girl's scream goes on and on.

It's not until the front door bursts in, wood splintering like gunfire, that the screaming stops.

And they are saved.

The large, wooden double doors of Finley Hall Children's Home open wide, as if they're the entrance to a magical castle. For one hopeful moment, they stand in awe, mouths agape as their faces turn upwards to the ornate ceiling.

That split second of optimism – the feeling that they've escaped their awful life, managed to find a safe and secure place to grow up – ends abruptly with a harsh shriek. Their pale faces watch as a man drags a boy across the hall in front of them, his feet barely touching the stone floor tiles as they scramble to find purchase.

'What are you waiting for? Get here!' A woman dressed head to toe in black, her hair wild and straw-like, appears from a room to their right. 'Don't take any notice of Frank. If you do as you're told, you won't have to meet him.' She turns on her heel and goes back into the room. The name *Miss Graves* is written in black on a silver plaque on the door.

The girl gulps down her fear, turns to her brother and plasters on a smile. 'It's you and me, always, right?'

'Cross your heart?' The boy's voice quivers.

'And hope to die.' She makes a quick cross on her chest with her forefinger. The boy steps in front of her, preventing her from moving.

'Stick a needle in your eye,' he says, coolly.

She sighs, looks down at her brother and declares, 'Stick a needle in my eye.'

Then she clasps his hand in hers, and together they walk into their new home.

MAY 9th

Four days to go

Chapter 1

The stench of smoke invades my nostrils and burns my throat, but I continue to draw deeply as I lean on the glass balcony balustrade, watching the seagulls swooping over the rooftops heading to the sea beyond. My silk dressing gown flaps gently in the breeze, offering a coolness to my thighs as the morning sun competes, its rays warming my face. I close my eyes to savour the moment.

'Inhaling the sea air would be preferable, surely?' Ross comes up behind me. I can't sneak a ciggie past him – he probably smelled it from downstairs. I haven't had one for over a year, but I remembered where I'd hidden the remaining few (for emergency purposes only).

'Caught me.' I don't turn around. I'd rather not see the disappointed look he's bound to have on his face.

'Remember when we first moved in and we spent hours sitting on this balcony overlooking Ness Cove, being hypnotised by the whispering waves?' he asks, snaking his arms around my waist.

'Yes, and I still love it. But today, the salty air on my lips isn't a match for this.' I needlessly hold up the cigarette. 'Nicotine does more for my nerves.'

'Ahh, right. Inspection results today?' His arms slacken.

'Yup,' I say, stubbing out the cigarette and pushing the end down into the peat of the pansies. There's a neat row of terracotta plant pots and an aluminium planter running the length of the balcony. It's the only garden we have to speak of – the easiest to maintain. 'I know we've had them loads of times before—'

'But each one manages to make you doubt yourself,' Ross says. 'I know. I remember you being like this last time, too.'

That time, the night before the report was due Ross had helped take my mind off it with a surprise meal out at our favourite Italian restaurant in Teignmouth. The Colosseum is where we've celebrated each wedding anniversary, and the owners are always so warm and friendly that it's a real comfort place for me when I'm feeling overwhelmed. I probably should've predicted how stressed I'd be waiting for the result and booked a table myself this time.

'Sorry,' I say. 'I'm not the easiest person to live with when I'm under scrutiny.'

'Don't be daft,' Ross says. 'It's because you care. If you were nonchalant, I'd be worried.'

He's right. I worked hard to get this teaching position. It's at an independent school in Staverton, a nearby village, and initially I felt guilty for working with children whose parents could afford the luxury of an exclusive, private education, so far from the one I had. I'd been adamant I'd do something extraordinary for disadvantaged children, helping make a difference to their lives; just as I'd always prayed someone would do for me and my brother. Then the crippling doubt began to sneak through me like a poison, the utter fear of failure overpowering me. How could I risk letting another child down as badly as I had been? I realised that the possibility of me being the only person standing between a child's life of misery and a happy future was too great a pressure and if I didn't get it right, I'd never forgive myself. I'd be crushed by the responsibility.

I met Serena, a teacher at Seabrook Prep School, at just the right time. She gave me a way to have the opportunity to make a difference as a teacher, while also managing to take the easy way out.

Ross wraps his arms around me again and I relax back against his chest.

'You have literally nothing to be nervous about. You're an amazing teacher and those kids are lucky to have you.'

'I hope so. I love them like my own—' I cut myself off abruptly as I feel Ross's muscles tense, ever so slightly, but enough to be noticeable. I screw my eyes shut, inwardly wincing. For an uncomfortable moment, I think he's going to say something, but then he nuzzles into my neck, breathes me in and kisses me, allowing my brief moment of panic to ebb like the tide.

'I'll make you a coffee,' he says, pulling away from me. 'Or would you rather a vodka?' His deep, throaty laugh reassures me that he didn't take my flippant comment to heart. Reigniting the issue of children after we put it to bed last year isn't something I want to do.

'A coffee will suffice, thanks. I'll save the hard stuff for this evening.'

After one final gaze towards Ness Cove, I back away and close the balcony door, giving the usual thanks to the universe for everything I have. It's a far cry from where I grew up, even further from the future I was so sure I was destined for. The only one I believed I was worthy of.

It takes several attempts to button my sleeves, but finally, having taken some diaphragmatic breaths and given myself a calming self-talk, I stand back and check my appearance in the full-length mirror. Smart, sassy and classy. That's what I see looking back. It's a third true; I am smart at least. The rest might well be an illusion – a distortion of reality – but as long as it's what the parents, the head teacher Mr Beaumont, and the school inspectors believe, that's a job well done on my part. I have lived by the 'fake it till you make it' principle since I was about ten years old, and it hasn't steered me far wrong. I smile at my reflection as I pick a stray thread from my red top and then smooth both hands down my black pencil skirt. Ross is right – there's no way I could receive anything other than a good report.

'Poached eggs?' Ross asks as I enter the kitchen. His suit jacket hangs over the back of a chair and his white shirt sleeves are neatly rolled up as he cracks eggs over the boiling water. I shake my head, nausea gripping my stomach at the thought.

'Thanks, but I'll grab a bagel from the bakery on the way to work.' I won't, but he doesn't need to know that. He gives me his one-eyed-squint look that confirms he's well aware of my lie. I half-laugh. 'Wow, I can't slip anything past you today, can I?'

'Can you ever?' There's a slight edge to his tone, and

I frown. I'm about to go deeper into his comment when the doorbell rings. I give Ross a quizzical glance.

'Might be Yasmin,' he says. 'She mentioned dropping a new property portfolio by for me this morning so I can bypass the office.' He leaves the kitchen and I hear the front door open. A man's voice rumbles through the hallway. Not Yasmin, then. Ross's estate agency business in Shaldon, The Right Price, only employs four staff and I've met two of them: Oscar, the silent partner, and Yasmin, who helps out in the office. The other two are agents who Ross is yet to introduce me to. I bend to place my mug in the dishwasher and give a small gasp as I straighten and see a large-framed man, smartly dressed in a suit that makes him look very much like an estate agent.

'Oh, hi. You must be a colleague of Ross's?'

I note Ross's tense expression as he peeps around from behind the man, and realise he isn't.

'Good morning, Mrs Price. I'm Detective Inspector Walker from the Devon and Cornwall Major Crime Investigation Team.' He stoops to clear the low beam of the ceiling then stretches one arm out, presenting an open leather wallet containing his ID badge. I stare at it before taking his other proffered hand and shaking it; it's large, square, and mine is completely enclosed in its firm grip. My heart gives a little jolt, as if warning me of what's to come.

'Is there something wrong?' I say, my pulse quickening. He's looking at me specifically, not Ross. But, I deduce, if someone was hurt or had died, there'd be two of them. That's how it works on the telly. And besides, I'm no one's next of kin other than Ross's, and he's safe. Then my legs tingle.

13

I *am* someone else's though, aren't I.

'Can we take a seat, Mrs Price?' DI Walker's tone is authoritative, his words not really posed as a question, more of an instruction.

Ross jerks into action, he too having been momentarily stunned by the unexpected arrival of a detective.

'Is your colleague coming in?' Ross asks, and my heart tumbles in my chest. If there are two of them, then my theory doesn't hold. I look out into the hallway, but I don't see anyone else hovering. Then, spotting a blur of movement out of the corner of my eye, I glance out of the kitchen window, at the people dressed in black and yellow walking past. It takes me a few moments, as if time has slowed, to register that they're police. Once this fact settles in my brain, a mix of intrigue and suspicion flares.

'No,' DI Walker says. 'She's conducting door-to-door enquiries with the rest of the team.'

'Right, sure.' Ross makes a face at me before skipping around DI Walker and pulling out a chair at the kitchen table for him. My feet stay planted as my mind wanders. *Door-to-door enquiries.* Okay, that's not so bad. It's not just me he's seeing. Maybe he's here because of a local burglary or something like that. The voice in my head doesn't buy that, though – they wouldn't send a senior detective for that type of crime, would they? The activity outside suggests something bigger. I swallow down the lump in my throat and take a deep breath as I finally take in the man's fresh-faced appearance, then, without thinking, say:

'You seem young to have made detective inspector already?'

Ross shoots me a wide-eyed glare, while DI Walker gives a tight smile that offers the only evidence of ageing skin by causing a slight crinkling at the corner of his eyes.

'I get that a lot. I think it must be the police equivalent of doctors these days looking like teenagers,' DI Walker says, drily. I mentally kick myself; offending him before I know why he's here isn't the best start. I'm sure he's worked hard to get to his position, and having people question it must be irritating.

'Sorry, I think I watch too much crime drama.' I force my muscles to move, and sit down next to Ross, opposite DI Walker. I immediately jump back up. 'Oh, I'm so sorry. I didn't offer you a drink. Tea? Coffee?' I sense the weight of Ross's stare, and avoid his eyes.

DI Walker juts his arm out, releasing a watch from beneath the cuff of his crisp white shirt, and checks it.

'Not for me, thank you.' He places a small electronic notebook on the table and gives a cough, readying himself to communicate the reason for his visit. I thud back down in the chair. Wild fluttering in my stomach combines with my increased heart rate to provide me with an adrenaline-inducing cocktail. I slip my hands under my thighs to hide their tremor.

'What can we do for you, Detective Walker?' I smile.

His azure-blue eyes look directly into mine, and they're so intense I lower my gaze, a strange feeling washing over me. What is he about to say? The room closes in on me, the air sucked from the atmosphere as I wait with my breath held.

'We've been trying to track you down for a while, now, Mrs Price.'

My mouth dries. Is this it? The moment I've been

dreading for so long? But would that warrant an entire team of police? I swallow, painfully.

'Oh, really?' From the corner of my eye, I catch Ross straighten in anticipation. I wish he'd left for work before the detective arrived.

'Your name is Anna Price, previously Lincoln, yes?'

The sound of my pulse pounds in my ears. 'Yes, that's correct.' I stare unblinking at DI Walker.

'I'm sorry to be the one to inform you . . .' DI Walker's eyes flit from mine to Ross's and back to me and I swallow my frustration together with my words: *Get on with it, tell me he's dead!* 'Your brother, Henry Lincoln,' DI Walker's features begin to blur; my blood pressure must be sky-high right at this moment, 'is wanted . . .' – *not dead* – '. . . for the murder of multiple women.'

'What?' I push back from the table, standing so abruptly that the chair topples to the tiled floor with an ear-ringing crash. Ross leaps up and drags it back to its position, then places a hand on my shoulder.

'Anna, breathe,' I hear him say. And I do. My chest heaves with the deep breaths I'm gulping in.

'This must come as quite the shock. I'm sorry.' DI Walker gives me a concerned look. 'Do you want to take a moment? Or maybe sit somewhere more comfortable?'

'The lounge,' Ross is saying. 'That would be better, I think.'

I'm manoeuvred to the sofa, where I plonk down heavily, the wind from my sails well and truly taken. I was prepared for *dead*. Not for *murderer*.

Henry – a killer? This can't be for real.

Chapter 2

Ross's hand takes mine, gently pulling it away from my mouth. I feel a sting, then the bubble of blood oozes and drips down my chin. I hadn't realised I'd been picking the skin on my lip – a childhood habit left over from the anxiety and stress I suffered while at the home. I've tried hard to eradicate it. I dab it quickly with the tissue Ross has whipped from the box on the table.

'Are you okay for me to continue?' DI Walker asks. I nod, while inwardly screaming *NO!* 'Your brother is wanted in connection with five murders—'

'Five?' I blink rapidly, shaking my head. '*Five?*' I repeat.

'Yes, I know it's a lot to take in.' DI Walker leans forward and rests his elbows on his knees. 'They've all taken place over a two-and-a-half-year period, with one female being killed on two specific dates each year. The fifth occurred a few months ago.'

A serial killer. Henry is a serial killer. The words, spoken in my own voice, loop in my head over and over like an

17

annoying earworm. The earworm continues to drown out the voices of Ross and the detective and the dizzying sensation it's creating makes lying down the only good option. Not here, though. I need to go to bed. I bend forwards, readying to stand, but Ross's hand firmly pushes down on my thigh, preventing my escape.

'They were committed in different counties, which is why it's taken a while to link them,' DI Walker says. I'm vaguely aware this isn't the beginning of the conversation – I've missed a chunk of it, and I try to gather myself so I can focus on what's going on. 'The evidence we've gathered shows they are connected, though; we're not disclosing it for obvious reasons, but each murder shares the same signature.' It's as if I'm on a mobile phone going through a tunnel; the words are crackling, fading in and out; fragmented like a Dalek's voice. I draw in air through my nostrils, but the nausea creeping through my gut only intensifies. I haven't seen Henry in years. We didn't part on the best terms, but despite it all – despite everything we went through – him turning out to be a serial killer feels a step too far.

'I – I don't . . . I can't.' I shake my head, but the fog doesn't clear. 'Why are you here, telling me this?'

DI Walker smiles thinly. His expression softens and he leans closer to me, like he's about to explain a complex idea to a child. 'We hoped you'd had contact with him. Knew where he might be.'

'That would make things easier,' I say. DI Walker gives a disappointed nod, aware my answer means I don't. And I really don't. I've heard nothing from him, and I've not tried to contact him. There's simply been no need.

'One of the dates your brother has committed murders

18

on is the fifteenth of February.' DI Walker's eyes are on my face, watching for my response. It's immediate; a reaction I'm unable to control. My eyes widen and every muscle in my body tenses.

'That's my birthday.'

'Yes.' He purses his lips. Nods again. When I don't offer anything else, he checks his notes. 'The other is the thirteenth of May,' he says, raising his eyes to meet mine.

My heart stutters, but thankfully my outward reaction is masked by the previous shock.

'Four days from now,' Ross adds, helpfully.

'We don't yet know the significance of this other date and we're running out of time, Anna.'

I can't breathe. My lungs are paralysed; no air seems to be able to enter them. I push Ross's hand from my leg and get up. Dizziness instantly overwhelms me, the room spins, and DI Walker and Ross blur into one before my eyes close and there's nothing but black silence.

Chapter 3

'Anna, baby. Anna. Open your eyes. Come on.'

My cheek stings. I put a hand to it, opening my eyes. Ross's face is close to mine.

'What . . .?'

'You fainted.'

I've experienced some truly stressful situations, but never come close to passing out.

'I'll call the doctor,' Ross says, already scrolling through his mobile.

'No. No need. Please don't make a fuss.' I swing my legs off the sofa and push myself into a sitting position. DI Walker doesn't appear to have moved from his spot. I wonder how many people he's broken news like this to in the past. I'd hope not many, but if his demeanour is anything to go by, he's certainly not fazed. He shifts now, and his dark eyebrows knit together to create a long, caterpillar-like line. I get the impression that he thinks my reaction has only served to waste his time. 'I'm sorry

21

about that,' I say. Heat rises up my neck and I rub my fingers over it, making it worse.

'As I say, I'm sure it's come as a shock. But I really do need to ask some questions. Like your husband said, we have four days until Henry is likely to strike again. Any assistance you can offer will be greatly appreciated.'

'Of course.' I glance at the time on my phone.

'I'll try not to keep you long,' DI Walker says, his voice clipped. 'I'd hate to make you late for work.'

'Oh, I'm . . . it's not . . .' Great. Now he thinks I'm not taking the threat to a woman's life seriously enough – that I'm more bothered about getting to work on time. 'As long as it takes, Detective Walker.' I force a smile, pushing my shoulders back. 'Ross, darling,' I say, turning to him. 'Maybe you could make us all a cup of coffee, please.'

Ross hesitates but nods and gets up. I wait for him to leave the lounge before speaking.

'You say Henry's wanted in connection with murders from the past three years. What about previous years? I mean, why has he started now?'

'I was hoping you'd be able to enlighten me on that score.'

'Henry hasn't been in contact with me for . . .' I screw up my eyes, trying to calculate the time, '. . . I don't know, must be fifteen, sixteen years, maybe more. I honestly thought you were here to tell me he'd died.'

'The fact is, he's killing on those specific dates for a reason. His sister's birthday is meaningful to him and I suspect he's sending a clear message by committing murder on that day.' DI Walker cocks one eyebrow. 'As in, I think he's communicating directly with you.'

'Most people pick up the phone. Or email, or something.' I laugh, awkwardly.

'Unless . . .' DI Walker pulls at his tie. 'I don't mean to alarm you, Mrs Price – but I think we need to consider that you could be in danger. If you say you're estranged, it might be he didn't know where you lived, or how to get into contact with you before.'

'Well, if he's keeping an eye on the investigation, he'll likely know now, won't he? You've led him straight to my door.' My tone is heavy with accusation, but I don't care. How stupid to come here if that's what he thinks. Unless that was his intention, of course.

Ross walks in and sets three mugs on the coffee table. 'Led who to our door?'

'Henry, obviously,' I snap. Ross quickly lowers his gaze from mine. 'Sorry, babe. But this is all mad. I can't believe it's happening.' I pull my fingers through my hair.

'I can assure you we've been meticulous in our investigation so far and if Henry has found out your location, it's not through us.' DI Walker picks up his mug and I inwardly wince as he takes several large gulps of the steaming liquid. 'The records at the children's home in Sutton Coldfield where you and Henry were resident were destroyed before it closed its doors for good. It took us quite some time to work out Henry had a sister, and of course, you've since married and changed your name. It's safe to say Henry is already a number of steps ahead of us – he likely knew where you lived prior to this morning.'

'Oh, God,' Ross says, sitting down. 'You think my wife is in danger from her own brother?'

'I'm not ruling it out, is what I'm saying.'

I frown, my mind latching on to an obvious flaw in his

23

thinking. 'But, as my birthday's already passed this year, surely I'm safe?'

'That's a possibility, yes, but I'm afraid we can't assume that,' DI Walker says. 'There's nothing to stop him targeting you on the other date.'

I lock eyes with DI Walker as I respond. 'And that's why it's important for you to know the relevance of the other date – because it would shed light on his motives? Maybe point you in the direction of his next victim?'

Even as I'm saying these words, my mind wants to reject the notion that we're talking about victims – about *murder* victims – in relation to Henry. Maybe it's a huge mistake and the detective will return later to apologise for the misinformation, saying they got it all wrong and it was a terrible mix-up. A case of mistaken identity.

'Yes. If we knew what significance it held for Henry, we might stand a chance of catching him before he takes another innocent woman's life.' He falls silent, looking suddenly weary. Maybe the case is taking more of a toll on him than he's letting on. He moves closer to me; so close I can feel heat coming off him. I shrink back, the proximity uncomfortable, but he's still close enough that I can smell the coffee clutching to his breath as he speaks again. 'It's not a date you recognise? Your parents' birth dates—'

'I can guarantee you it's nothing to do with *them*,' I say, cutting him off.

'Oh? How can you be so certain?'

'You must know *some* of the background, surely?'

'We know Henry had a difficult time at the home, was in numerous scraps with other children, some of which resulted in minor criminal charges being brought against him. Your mother is listed as deceased, having died from liver disease—'

'Yes, thank you for the summary. She was an alcoholic and drug user who'd do anything for a quick fix of either. She had no clue where our father was, or even who he was, and she'd sleep with anything with a heartbeat. She neglected her own children, put bullying, abusive men ahead of their wellbeing. She let them suffer. Henry neither knew, nor cared, when her bloody birthday was. So, like I said, the significance of the thirteenth of May has nothing to do with them.'

Years of compartmentalised outrage bubbles beneath the surface. Every now and then something triggers a memory of my childhood, dredging up the trauma of how we were treated, but I'm careful to push it away, not dwell on it. If I give any tiny seed of anger room to germinate, there's no telling how rapidly it'll grow; how much damage it'll do. I wonder if Henry allowed his to take root and take over. Maybe I shouldn't be so surprised about what I've just learned.

Broken people can do broken things.

DI Walker lets out a long sigh, then stands. 'I'll want to speak with you again, Mrs Price. The police station would be more appropriate – and given the urgency, sooner rather than later. I'll get my DS to arrange—'

'No, I don't think so,' I say, standing. I swallow hard as thoughts I haven't had in years begin swarming into my mind. Surprise registers on both the detective's and Ross's face. DI Walker narrows his eyes and I realise I need to give a valid reason. 'If Henry is keeping an eye on the investigation, don't you think it'd be best not to make it clear to him that you're involving me? He isn't going to try and make contact if he keeps seeing police here, or realises you've taken me to the station, is he?'

DI Walker looks at me. He's difficult to read, but I sense he's weighing up what I've said. 'Fine. For now, I'll let you get on.' He reaches into the inner pocket of his suit jacket and pulls out a small, white card. 'Here are my details. You must call if you hear from Henry or if you're worried about your safety. And if there's anything else that comes to mind, however irrelevant you think it is, and even if it's two in the morning, call. I want to know.' He presses the card into my palm, then locks his gaze on me. 'I don't want to be knocking on someone's door in four days' time telling them their wife, mother, sister or daughter has been brutally murdered.' The intensity of his voice sends a shiver down my back.

He nods towards Ross, who blinks rapidly before shaking himself free of his trance.

'What are you going to do? About Anna, I mean. Will she have protection?' Ross's voice is filled with panic.

'We'll be keeping a close eye—'

'That's vague,' Ross says, his voice sharp. 'What does that even mean?'

'Ross, love,' I say, laying my hand on his arm. 'If Henry had wanted to harm me, he'd have done so already.'

DI Walker is at the front door, but he turns to offer a reassuring smile. I'm not sure it's enough for my husband.

'But he said you could be in danger.' Ross directs his hissed words to me. For some reason, I'm not feeling as worried for my safety as Ross is. Is it the shock? Maybe I'm numbed by the news. A part of me doesn't believe what the detective told me – surely it's not possible that

Henry could kill five women? How sure is he that it's the *same* Henry Lincoln they're after?

'I strongly suggest you remain alert, observe your surroundings at all times and report anything out of the ordinary. Like I said – call at any time. And if the resources are available, I'll get an officer posted outside.'

I open my mouth to question this, given what I've just said, but DI Walker pre-empts it, adding, 'Covertly, obviously.'

Placated for now, Ross shows the detective out.

I stand in the doorway, my muscles rigid as I watch DI Walker speaking to a group of uniformed officers directly outside our house. What are they talking about? Me? Henry? Is Detective Walker asking them to remain stationed right there on the pavement?

'Let's get back in,' Ross says, disappearing from my side. DI Walker finishes whatever he's saying, and I follow his progression until he walks out of my line of sight. A policeman catches my gaze and before I think it through, I stomp towards him.

'Do you have to all congregate here?' My tone is unintentionally sharp, so I offer a smile to soften it. 'Only it's likely to attract a lot of attention, surely?' The policeman I'm aiming my question at merely shrugs, but a woman steps through them and approaches me. She's dressed in plain clothes, like DI Walker, so I assume she's a detective too.

'Sorry, ma'am,' she says. 'I'm Detective Tully, part of the investigating team.' Her smile is warm and genuine; she exudes compassion and I wish it'd been her who'd delivered the bombshell about Henry, not DI Walker. 'We've been carrying out door-to-door enquiries but we're almost done in this area so the officers won't be here much longer. I realise this all must be very unsettling.'

'Yes, it is, quite,' I say. 'I know you're only doing your job, but as I said to Detective Walker, Henry isn't likely to show his face with all this police presence, is he?' I cast my gaze around, as if I might see him lurking among them.

'I'll move them on, ma'am, don't worry.' She gives me a nod, then turns to address the officers and like a swarm of bees, they gradually progress down the street and begin to disperse to their various vehicles.

Once I'm satisfied they're gone, I stride back inside, go back to the kitchen and look at the card the detective gave me. The thought that all the activity is because of Henry causes pins and needles to prickle my fingertips. If what they're saying about Henry is true, I cannot afford to become embroiled in whatever mess he's created – I need to stay as far away from this investigation as possible.

I press the lid of the pedal bin and place the detective's card into it.

Chapter 4

Even the car radio blasting out the usual upbeat tunes on Heart FM can't drown out my thoughts as I drive the route to work. I hit red light after red light; it's as though even they are working against me. I'm lucky to be out of the house, though, having escaped another lockdown; this one was threatened by Ross, as opposed to the government. His reaction to DI Walker's announcement that Henry is a wanted serial killer wasn't initially over the top. Most people would, no doubt, react similarly: shock, uncertainty, worry. Expected responses. But when DI Walker left, Ross flipped and tried to make me stay home from work. I can't – but more importantly, won't – allow this to affect my day-to-day life by hiding away. I have an important job that I love and, as I pointed out to him, I'll probably be safer surrounded by staff and pupils at the school than I would be at home anyway. Still, in my mind's eye, I see the fear etched on Ross's face, pinching his features in such a way that he looked unrecognisable.

I grip the steering wheel until my wrists hurt. 'Why, Henry? And why now?'

A blaring horn snaps my attention back to the road. I'm sitting at a green traffic light. I put my hand up in apology to the car behind me and accelerate, the speedometer soon nudging fifty as I take the approach road leading to the dual carriageway. I was already uptight about today – awaiting the report has had my nerves jumping. Nothing compared to what they're doing now, though. Every tiny muscle in my entire body is on edge: twitchy, agitated, tense.

Ross knows that I had a crap childhood and he is aware of how hard I've fought against it to get to where I am today. He knows I have nothing to do with Henry. But what he doesn't know is why. Not the real reason.

My mind drifts as I come off the carriageway and slow down. I head through the lanes towards Seabrook – a journey I can do without thought.

I never considered Henry to be a truly bad person. Misguided, yes. As he grew up, he had a mean streak – he made mistakes. But this? If what DI Walker says is true, then Ross is right to be worried. Secrets are always a risk. But a serial killer knowing your secret is a whole other level. As I conjure Henry's face the last time I saw him, my blood chills in my veins. To save a future victim, am I going to have to share why the other date is significant? If I do that, it won't just be my marriage that I risk.

'Jesus!' I slam both feet down hard, the emergency stop causing a screech of tyres as I am flung forwards against the wheel. The little girl, mere centimetres from the front of my car, freezes. She stares at me, her eyes wide as saucers, her mouth fully open in a silent scream. I unclip my seatbelt, fly out the door and rush up to her. 'You stupid girl! Why did you cross? Didn't you *see* me?' Blood is pumping so hard through my body it feels like my heart will erupt through my chest. I'm about to grab her by the shoulders, the urge to shake her into awareness overwhelming, when other peoples' voices ground me. I look up. I have an audience.

And then I see it. The black and white stripes. Shit. It's a zebra crossing. All power leaves my body, and my legs tremble.

'I'm . . . sorry, Mrs Price.' The girl, who I now recognise from Seabrook Prep, stammers the words, close to tears. I put my hands to my face, take a deep breath. It's me who's the stupid one. Driving without paying attention.

'No, no. It was my fault – *I'm* sorry.' I lay my hands gently on her shoulders and guide her to the pavement, trying to ignore the alarmed and angry mutterings of the onlookers. Most of whom are parents of the pupils.

Well done, Anna.

I make sure she's all right before getting back in the car, but the damage is done. The image of her frightened little face will be forever burned into my retinas. I keep my eyes averted from the onlookers, shame burning my face, then very slowly drive on, my focus dead ahead.

I'm still shaking by the time I park up, but it's guilt that's replaced any shock. The girl's name came to me after I drove away from the crossing. And now, as I get out of my car, another memory hits me and my stomach clenches. During one of my playtime duties Isobel had come up to me, slipped her hand into mine and asked if she could stay with me because she'd fallen out with her best friend. Oh, God – what must she be thinking of me now?

31

I reach my classroom just as the bell sounds. No time for a much-needed second coffee. I smack my briefcase down on the desk and watch my kids file in. They're silent as they walk to their tables, but Mikey sneaks me a cheeky grin. He's come on leaps and bounds this year with his social skills and it melts my heart to see his confidence growing. These kids might have opportunities far beyond those whose parents aren't able to pay for their education, but their willingness to learn and overcome personal challenges never fails to amaze me.

I break into a smile as I look at them, standing behind their chairs awaiting my nod that they can sit. I pause for a moment, considering the predictability of this everyday occurrence. A small, banal detail – a rule that all the children follow without question. And they wait for a gesture from me; I possess the power to say if they can sit or not. Granted, it's not control at a grand level, but I do hold the ability to dictate certain behaviours. As a teacher that's a given. Am I any different to those who controlled me, Henry and the other children at Finley Hall? I've adapted, learned, and now *I'm* the one who has control over others.

I guess Henry adapted too.

By breaktime I'm gagging for a coffee and I'm first in the staff room. Thankfully, I'm not on playground duty today, so I can hide away in here for the next fifteen minutes. The room overlooks the rolling fields of Staverton, and on certain days you can spot the steam train winding its way along the track to and from Totnes, puffs of smoke swirling into the sky like huge, fluffy clouds. Ross and I took the steam train to the butterfly farm when we were first going out and he showed me some of his favourite places along the route from when he was growing up. I still remember the twisting feeling of jealousy when he talked about his childhood – his memories of his family. I'd love to be part of a big family like Ross is used to, but we've decided we're better off just the two of us.

Ross remains close with his mum, dad and brother – their relationship is unlike anything I've ever had, so I don't fully *get* it. I'll always be an outsider looking in, which has caused some friction in the past. They've tried so hard to welcome me into their family, knowing I'm lacking in that department, but it's not easy, and so avoiding family gatherings is my way of managing the situation. I think Ross would prefer it if I spent more time in their company – his regular attempts at hosting a murder mystery night at ours have thus far been unsuccessful. I have the feeling after this morning's visit from DI Walker that he might well stop trying, now there's an actual murderer in the midst.

The staffroom door swings open and snatches me out of my thoughts.

'Morning, hun.' Serena, looking whimsical in a boho dress, flounces in, heading straight for the cupboard. 'How come you weren't at the rendezvous point this morning?' She stretches up, then rummages inside. 'Thank you!' she whispers, removing a packet of chocolate digestive biscuits. 'I had a bad feeling Beaumont had found my hiding place.' She turns, twisting open the packet, and smiles as she dunks a biscuit into my cup.

'Hey!' I shake my head but let her do it. A trail of brown drips follow the biscuit towards her mouth. 'I was running a bit late. Sorry.'

Serena swallows, then shrugs. 'Never mind. I was just itching to give you the lowdown, that's all. I was going to call you, but by the time he left it was almost midnight and I didn't think you'd appreciate it. Seeing as you're in bed by ten these days.' She flashes me a wide grin, bits of biscuit still visible between her teeth.

'Are you mocking me?'

'Moi? Of course not.'

'So? Did he exceed your expectations?' I ask, trying to sound as enthusiastic as usual. Serena's love life is more entertaining than any soap opera and I look forward to the daily instalments. But I feel as though I've already lived my own episode today, so I'm not as eager. I don't let that show, though. I live vicariously through her these days – the excitement of new love, like getting high from drugs, is addictive; but I've forgotten how it feels now. After eight years, mine and Ross's relationship seems to have settled into a gentler, slower and more comfortable groove. It would be different again if we had children.

'It was . . . interesting,' she says, a coy look on her face.

'Interesting in a good way? Or interesting in a *weird* way?'

Serena dips another biscuit in my mug, then slowly puts it in her mouth, prolonging the suspense. 'In a *different* way, I guess.'

I get the sense she wants me to ask more, but I don't know if I want to hear the sordid details of her sex life right now. I stare into my mug, feeling slightly nauseous at the sight of the floating bits of soggy biscuit, and when I look back up, Serena is standing with her hands on her hips and peering at me curiously.

'You seem a bit . . . distant,' she says. 'You're not worried about the report, are you?'

'Not really. A bit. Oh, I don't know, Serena.' I cup my chin in my hands, let out a long sigh. She's my best friend. I want to be able to let it all out – tell her what I've been told this morning. Maybe sharing it would help me process it, make sense of it. But what will she think of me? It plays out in my head: *Oh, hey, Serena – guess what? A detective came over to my house and told me my brother is a wanted serial killer. He's murdered five women. How mad is that?* And I immediately know I can't let any of those words leave my lips. Somehow, I'll be guilty by association and my quiet, happy little life will blow up.

What are you doing, Henry? Why punish me now?

'I know you were nervous about the report, but honestly, you'll have come out on top, there's no doubt in my mind. You always do.'

I smile. It wouldn't be entirely disingenuous to let her think I'm worried about how I've come across in the assessment because until the knock on my door earlier, that *was* all I was concerned about.

'You know me,' I say. 'Just want my kids, their families, to have the best possible version of me.'

'You give them your everything. Everyone knows that. If a bunch of assessors couldn't see that during their limited time here, then they're useless and should be fired.'

The staffroom door flies open again, the appearance of the head teacher extinguishing the conversation like water on flames.

'Here you are,' Mr Beaumont says, his cheeks flushed. 'I've been looking for you.' He's not directing his line of sight, or his speech, to either of us in particular but I'm so sure it's me who he's speaking to, I jump up.

'Oh?' I say, my eyes flitting to Serena, whose wide-eyed look makes my pulse judder. Mr Beaumont's tone isn't his usual light and breezy, 'everything is good', one. It's his panicked 'something is very wrong' one, and we both know it. I can almost sense Serena's desire to retract her statement about not having any doubt in me. Was my assessment that bad?

'In my office now, please.' He turns without making any eye contact, a terrible sign, and strides out. Being summoned, or more often dragged, to the office was a regular occurrence for me at Finley Hall. I never thought I'd relive those times as an adult, though. My palms sweat as I head to the door, not daring to look at Serena. As I hurry along behind him my heels clonk across the parquet floor of the hall. He walks so fast I can't keep up, like he's on a mission. A thought invades my mind: I'm assuming he wants to see me about the report, but what if it's not that at all?

What if DI Walker has been sniffing around here? Christ. If Craig Beaumont so much as links me to something so terrible, he'll probably sack me. Having the sister of a serial killer as his senior teacher would not be the image of his precious school he'd wish to portray. And who could blame him? I glance outside the windows to the car park as I pass by, craning my neck to see if a police car is visible. I can't see one, but I suppose he might have already left.

Beaumont's office door is closed by the time I get to it. Bloody power play. He wants me to feel uncomfortable; wants me to stand here uncertain. Should I walk in because he summoned me and knows I was behind him, or should I knock? Irritation makes my muscles twitch as I hover with my hand raised, debating what to do.

I give two sharp knocks and enter without waiting for a response.

He's seated, tapping away at his keyboard, and I stand in front of his desk, my knees knocking beneath my skirt while I attempt to keep my eyes on him. I can't let them wander around because that would make me seem nervous. The room is stuffy, the air within his dark-wood panelled office stale. He never so much as cracks a window. I don't know how he bears it all, trussed up in his three-piece suit. He's all pomp and show. I ball my hands by my sides and try to slow my breathing down. I can't lose this job, it's everything I've worked for. These kids are my life. I won't let Henry take this from me.

'This isn't the conversation I wanted with you today,' he says, not looking up. 'Well, not any day, of course. But specifically not today.'

His pause doesn't mean I should speak, so I allow the moment of silence to expand. I must let him fill in the gaps; I need to learn how much he knows. I have to ascertain what I can get away with here. He shakes his head, steeples his fingers in a way that makes him seem much older than his thirty or so years. The fact he's reached this position at such a young age is something of a mystery, and despite our best detective skills Serena and I haven't managed to prise this information from him yet. But the rumour among some of the other teachers is simply that the previous head was his uncle and pulled some strings. I'm more inclined to believe that because Mr Gally left so abruptly six months ago, they had little opportunity to advertise and then interview a suitable replacement. Beaumont was in the right place at the right time, so they got him into position quickly to prevent the governors kicking up a fuss.

His eyes haven't left his computer screen, which is unnerving – I want to lurch forwards, grab a hold of his face in my hands and force it upwards. He can't even look me in the eye. But then, since the Christmas party he's not been too strong on eye contact. I shudder as I remember how he'd stared at me the whole night, making me feel uneasy, then just before the evening ended, I called him out on being 'a bit letchy', in front of the entire staff. So I probably shouldn't read too much into how he's avoiding my gaze now.

He closes his eyes. I want to sigh, or shout at him. *Get on with it, man!* And then he swings the monitor screen around so I can see it. A fluttering inside my stomach grows rapidly into a violent beating of wings as I recognise what's on the screen. The image is paused, and in a particularly unflattering moment as the woman's mouth is wide open in mid-yell – teeth bared like an animal on the attack. Her hands are poised and look as if they are about to land on the small, terrified child's shoulders. I gasp. The woman on the zebra crossing looks manic, deranged, almost unrecognisable. Almost.

'If I hadn't seen this footage with my own eyes, I wouldn't have believed it for a single second. But, Anna, it's here. In black and white.'

'Footage?' I gulp down my unease. Bad enough to think this was a photo – but if there's more. . .

'Yes. I think you should watch it. Seeing as so many others have already.'

My heart pounds as he elaborates; his words flow into each other and blur. But I get the gist. This piece of footage first found its way onto the parents' WhatsApp group before being shared on Spotted Staverton's Facebook page, and he's had call after call from concerned mums and dads. He hits the play button and I watch in muted disbelief as the woman who looks like me leaps from the car that is identical to mine and lunges towards the scared girl. I'm stunned at how angry this person is. My mind tries to reconcile the features of the woman I see on the screen with myself. It's not me. Yet, of course, I know it is.

'Oh, my God,' I say, shaking my head. The video footage stops abruptly and I look to Mr Beaumont. 'Where's the rest? This isn't all of what happened.'

'This is all that was uploaded. There is no more.'

'Well, it's making it out to be worse, Mr Beaumont. I mean, look!' I rush around to his side of the desk and play the last few seconds back. Just before the video cuts off, I've got my hand raised as if I'm about to strike her. 'I do not hit her. I *did not* hit Isobel. This makes it look as though I'm about to attack her.'

'Yes. That's exactly how it appears, Anna. So, you can see why so many parents have demanded I do something about this.'

'What?' The single word is barely audible, spoken in astonishment. Fear. *Do something about this?* The words ricochet off the inside of my skull and my blood runs icy cold inside my veins. If I leave the office now, go back to my classroom, carry on as though nothing has happened, I wonder if this whole incident would somehow erase itself. But the weight of what's to come is already heavy in the room – Beaumont's expression foreshadows it.

'I'm going to have to ask you to take leave, Anna.' And there it is. A tingle begins at the back of my nose and I know tears aren't far behind. I hang my head. 'For a week at least,' he says. 'Until I can gather the relevant information for a full misconduct case review.'

My head snaps up. 'Who recorded it?'

'*That's* all you have to say?' He gives a disbelieving sigh together with a shake of his head.

'I have the right to know.' I'm barely holding it together, my frustration leaking from my clipped words – any moment now I'll lose the ability to keep my anger harnessed.

'It was posted anonymously.'

'Of course. I don't even get to know who the hell is trying to ruin my career.' Maintaining composure is something I'm usually good at, and until today I've not uttered a single contemptuous word while in my teaching role. Certainly, I've not given Mr Beaumont cause to question my standards or my integrity before. Now both are under fire.

'You have to realise how this looks, Anna? You're a senior teacher at a highly respected private school. And there's evidence of appalling behaviour. Based on this footage, the parents of the pupil in question have every right to take legal action . . .'

Legal action. The words instil a sense of despair and blood rushes to my head, making my face burn. 'I didn't touch her, Mr Beaumont,' I say, firmly without shouting. 'You have to believe me. There were witnesses. Not one of them will say I laid a finger on her.'

'A parent has come forward, actually, Anna.'

'Good, good.' Relief washes over me. 'So you'll know this is being blown out of all proportion.'

'The parent saw your hands on her shoulders.'

'Well, yes. I laid my hands on her to reassure her, Craig. I wanted to make sure she was OK.'

'Mr Beaumont, Anna. Let's keep it professional.'

A surge of hot anger rises inside my stomach and it's all I can do not to explode. But that would play into his hands. And those of whoever has started this. I can't let that happen.

'Fine. Have it your way, *Mr Beaumont*. Thanks for the vote of confidence. I assume you've got cover for my class.'

'Yes, Serena will step in. She is more than capable of taking two classes for today until I organise someone to cover your period of suspension.'

I nod, lost for words as the phrase 'period of suspension' rings in my head. A few hours ago, everything was ticking along as usual. My only concern was an Ofsted report. Now, I have to worry about a serial killer who might be targeting me, a potential assault charge, and losing my job. With my eyes to the ground, I walk briskly back to the classroom, grab my bag and leave without uttering a word to the class, or Serena.

Tears don't even come as I sit behind the wheel of my car and replay the events that have occurred this morning. I'm numb, like I've been immersed in a bath of ice. How the hell do I fight this?

Chapter 5

Suddenly, I'm back at home, the car in its usual position in the road directly outside the house. I have zero memory of the journey – not even driving across the bridge into Shaldon, where I usually slow right down to glimpse the boats on the glistening water. It's all just one big blur. Worrying, when I consider what else I could've done while my mind wasn't focused on the road. Isobel's face, frozen in panic, flashes in my mind as I sit with my forehead against the steering wheel. How could I have let myself get so angry at a child?

The big question currently burning a hole in my mind is: who posted the footage? I only learned about Henry about an hour prior to the zebra crossing incident, but could he have somehow had a hand in taking or uploading the video? No one could've foreseen me almost hitting a pupil, though, let alone have anticipated my reaction. Surely this has to be separate. Or, it *is* linked in that someone has grasped the opportunity I so helpfully gave them and run with it. I simply played into their hands. So, the next question has to be *why?*

A splatter of greyish liquid hits the windscreen, bringing me out of my thoughts. I spot the offender, sitting on the telephone post, and I swear the seagull is laughing. I burst from the car, slamming the door and stand with my hands on my hips.

'Don't think you're alone in the shitting-on-Anna-Price department, mate,' I shout up at it. A man I don't recognise walks past on the opposite pavement and looks up in the direction I yelled, then turns back to me.

'Afternoon,' he says with a nod. And then he offers a smile that smacks of sympathy, even pity. I mutter a quick hello and dart up the path, my face flushed.

Inside, I fling my bag on the sofa and run upstairs. My laptop lies open on the dressing table-cum-desk and I fire it up. With the inside of my cheek firmly between my teeth, I find the offending footage on the 'Spotted Staverton' Facebook page and while biting the end of a biro, watch it again. This time, with no one else scrutinising my reaction, I take my time and study it frame by frame. The angle tells me that it's from a CCTV camera, not someone's mobile as I first assumed. How did someone get hold of it so quickly?

I slam the chewed pen down on the table. This changes things. It *has* to be connected to this morning's visit from the detective; the timing is too coincidental. I go back downstairs to the kitchen and dig the card out of the bin. Before I can talk myself out of it, I dial the number. It rings several times and I'm about to hang up, but then the tone alters. There's a pause; silence for a moment, and I begin to think no one will speak. Then I hear the deep, hypnotic voice I was expecting.

'Detective Inspector Walker; how may I help?'

For a split second, my voice freezes. Earlier my gut was telling me to stay clear of this investigation, yet here I am calling *him*. What am I doing? But I need answers – so instead of ending the call, I clear my throat.

'It's Anna Price,' I say. There's a moment of hesitation on his end, so I add helpfully, 'You came to see me this morning about Henry Lincoln.' I hear a noise, like a muffled laugh through a covered mouthpiece.

'I hadn't forgotten, Mrs Price,' he says, and I can tell he's smiling. Despite not being visible, I'm embarrassed, and my cheeks burn. 'Have you heard from Henry?'

'No, no. I'm calling about something else, actually. I'm not sure why, really . . . it doesn't seem feasible that it's got anything to do with it,' I say, my words all hurried. I already regret making this call. I'm going to sound paranoid. Or worse, I'll come across as hopeful. Like, if I can somehow blame my behaviour and subsequent public downfall on Henry, I'll be able to feel better about myself or get out of trouble at work.

'You sound upset, Mrs Price. Would you prefer to speak face to face?'

I consider this for a few seconds. He is more likely than me to be able to get to the bottom of the zebra crossing footage. Especially now I'm aware it's from a CCTV camera.

'I'd appreciate that.'

'Great. I'm at Newton station – you know where that is?'

'Oh,' I say, my stomach dropping. 'I . . . really don't want . . .' I should've expected this after he was keen to get me to the station earlier to discuss the murder cases.

45

I try to think on my feet. 'I don't mind talking with you, Detective Walker, alone. But if I'm to help, I'd prefer it if my involvement is kept low-key.' There's a pause and I imagine him glaring at me down the phone, shaking his head, thinking I'm being deliberately uncooperative. I bite my lip as I await his response.

'I can be at yours in fifteen.' His voice is clipped, and I'm about to thank him, but the phone line goes dead. I assume it's because he's so keen that he's grabbed his suit jacket and is immediately heading over to me. I check the time. If he's coming, he'll be here by three.

Not long before school ends, I think. A stabbing pain grips my stomach. I should be with my kids, sending them off with some interesting homework for the evening. I guess Serena will check my teaching plan and set the required work. She must be beside herself worrying about what's gone on. I'll give her a call later. Of course, she might have gleaned further information herself by now, and if not, she definitely will at home time. No doubt it'll be the main topic of discussion with the parents at the school gate. I groan and rub my fingertips into my temples – a tension headache is starting. I go to the cupboard to get some paracetamol.

'For Christ's sake, Ross.' How many times do I have to tell him it irritates the hell out of me that he uses the last of the tablets and puts the box back into the medicine tub? I throw it across the worktop, then pull out a fresh box, stab my nail into the silver foil of the pill packet – the popping sound is strangely soothing – and push two tablets out onto my palm. As I tilt my head back to swallow them, the doorbell sounds. Here we go.

DI Walker is at the door, rigid, like a soldier standing

to attention. I wonder if he used to be in the military. He looked young this morning, his face having an air-brushed quality about it, but now he seems to age in front of my eyes. His longer-style hair, which had been gelled and neat earlier, is now somewhat messy. It's peppered with grey, which I hadn't noticed before, giving him a Keanu Reeves quality. And although his eyes are still as bright as this morning, the skin beneath them is puffy.

'This was on your doorstep,' he says, handing me a large, white envelope. I take it without looking. The post person generally leaves anything bigger than the postage stamp itself on the doorstep because the letterbox is so tiny.

'Will be for Ross, no doubt.' But as I cast my eyes down, I see my name printed on it. No stamp, though. My fingers tingle, and I immediately flick my eyes to DI Walker in alarm.

'You're not expecting anything, then, I take it,' he says, eyebrows raised.

The lump in my throat is so huge no words will pass it, so I just shake my head.

'Don't touch it anywhere else.' He turns, striding back to the pavement as I freeze, holding the envelope as though it might explode. He unlocks his car – a black Audi – then returns with a pair of latex gloves. He deftly snaps them on and takes the envelope back from me. 'Shall we?' He jerks his head towards the hallway, and I step back inside. He follows me into the lounge and we retake the same seats we'd been in only seven hours earlier.

'It might be something personal,' I say, defensively. I don't know why, but the fact he's taken over – is about to open *my* mail – irks me. I've no clue what's inside. But if it's from Henry, as he clearly suspects, it might hold something I don't want anyone else seeing. I inwardly curse. If only I'd gone to the door before he got here, I could've opened it in private, decided if it was something I wanted, or needed, to share. Now it appears I have no choice in the matter. I brace myself as he turns it over in his hands.

'Could you get me a knife, please?' His attention is fully on the white envelope as he scrutinises it, so he doesn't catch my miffed expression at him taking over when it's my letter. But I do notice him flinch slightly at my sigh as I reluctantly get up and go to the kitchen, my mind whirring, trying to find a way I can see whatever is in the envelope before he does. But nothing comes to me.

If it is from Henry, what could possibly be inside? Is he about to reveal the one thing we both promised we'd keep secret? My skin fizzes, with every nerve ending jumping. I need to have some kind of story ready, just in case. I take a knife to DI Walker and while he slowly inserts the point beneath the edge of the envelope, I hover over him, holding my breath. I have the urge to close my eyes tight too, delay the inevitable, but I force them to stay wide. The saliva in my mouth dries up, causing a choking sound as I attempt to swallow. It's the only sound in the lounge right now; I could literally hear a pin drop.

And then it's open. And DI Walker is gently extracting what looks to be a page from a newspaper.

'What is it?' My voice is creaky, like it needs lubricating. I should've got a glass of water while I was in the kitchen. I stand with my arms crossed, my head tilted to try and decipher the words on the page as the detective, his eyes narrowed in concentration, carefully unfolds it.

'A newspaper page,' he says, without taking his eyes from it.

'Well, yes, I can see that.'

'With something written over it.' He looks up at me now, with an intensity that makes my breath come in shallow bursts. He leans forward and places it on the coffee table, flattening it with his gloved hand. My heart hammers against my ribs as I stare. My eyes aren't focusing; I have to blink several times before the words, written in red ink across the newspaper print, become clear.

Each one has been different but part of a whole.
Each one I take is a window to your soul.
Each one tells a story but hides within it a clue.
Each one has been bringing me closer to you.
Middle for diddle, that's your lot.
Choose wisely, now off you trot.

I feel winded, like I've been punched in the stomach.

'Mean anything to you, Mrs Price?'

'I don't do riddles, DI Walker,' I say, not meeting his eyes. 'And just Anna is fine by the way.'

'Okay. Well, I guess we'll be spending some time together over the coming days, Anna.'

There's a weird moment of silence as this statement settles. I haven't even had the opportunity to tell him what happened to make me call him yet, but he's already assumed I'm involved now this envelope has turned up. Henry has found out where I live, has come here and left this bizarre, and freaky, message that heavily implies that everything he's done up until now – every murder – has brought him a step closer to his end game. To me.

49

Is his end game to *kill* me?

I baulk at my own suggestion, my head shaking involuntarily. This whole situation is utter madness – the Henry they're searching for must be someone different. They've got it all wrong.

But the riddle . . .

'Hang on, there's something else.' DI Walker has turned the paper over. I sit down beside him, not trusting my leg muscles to hold me up. Fainting for the second time in front of the detective would be embarrassing.

I frown as I realise what I'm seeing. Stuck under some Sellotape is a needle.

'What on Earth?' I mumble.

DI Walker sits back, his hands in his lap. He's got a faraway look on his face, and I imagine a thought bubble containing an ellipsis in the air beside his head as his mind ticks over. I don't speak, allowing his process to continue as he tries to work out what the riddle and the needle might mean.

'The first victim was left in . . . well, let's just say, a particular way.' He turns and leans in, so our faces are close. His eyes stare into mine, unblinking. It's as though he's testing me; deciding if he should share information. I suppose it's against police rules, or policy, or whatever, to divulge details of an ongoing case with a civilian. But then he's already hinted that we'll be working together – because let's face it, time is running out and I might well be the police's best source – so he might have to tell me certain things in order that I can properly assist the investigation. He takes a deep breath, and, seeming to have made his decision, begins to speak.

'She was posed.'

I suck in a sharp intake of air and DI Walker pauses, a worried look passing over his face. 'Sorry,' I say, giving my head a shake. 'It's okay. Go on.'

His jaw contracts – the skin taut along the bone. His hand goes to it, two fingertips massaging the muscle in a circular motion. 'The most noteworthy thing was her mouth,' he says. 'Her lips were sewn shut.'

'Oh, my God.'

'It was a statement.'

It doesn't take a psychologist to decipher that much. Or maybe the meaning is obvious to me because I'm suddenly certain that it's directed *at* me.

'He's silencing the victim,' DI Walker says. 'Like I suspect he wants to silence you.'

My lips stick to my teeth. I run my tongue between to moisten them, but don't say what I'm thinking: that the sewn lips have a slightly different meaning. It is about not speaking, but it's not about silencing me.

Our lips are sealed.

I think DI Walker is mistaken. I'm not sure that Henry wants to kill me. He wants to play with me. Taunt me.

This is a game.

And it all started at Finley Hall.

Chapter 6

FINLEY HALL CHILDREN'S HOME

'Can you help me, Anna?'

'What's up, buddy?' Anna lays a hand softly on Henry's shoulder, but there's an edge to her tone that belies her gesture. Kirsty tuts and rolls her eyes, clearly annoyed that they are being bothered by Anna's pain-in-the-arse brother yet again. Anna turns away from Kirsty's disapproving glare, her tummy twisting. She's torn between her love for her brother and her need to please the first real friend she's ever had. Henry's eyes plead with her, and she closes hers so she can't be swayed. It's been six months, yet he still seeks her support almost every day. He may have grown an inch, but he's still small in comparison to the other boys his age, and his level of confidence is even smaller.

'It's them.' Henry tilts his head back, indicating to the group of kids behind him. 'They won't let me play. They just call me names.'

'I'm sorry. I know how hard it is to make friends,

Henry. It took me weeks to build up the courage to even talk to Kirsty. But look at us now.' Anna looks to her friend, and Kirsty high-fives her, their identical bead bracelets clanking together. This reassures Anna that she's said the right thing to please Kirsty, and the resulting warm feeling she gets allows her to be a bit firmer with her brother. 'You have to try a bit harder,' she says. Anna's eyes fill with tears as Henry's bottom lip wobbles, and she blinks them away quickly before Kirsty spots them.

'I *have* tried, Anna.'

Henry scuffles off towards the small kids' playground, his head bent so low it looks like he might topple over.

Kirsty watches him. 'God, brothers are the worst. Why couldn't we have sisters.'

Anna's nostrils flare as she takes a deep breath, then she swallows hard before responding. 'Yeah, but then we'd have to *share* stuff with them. And I don't mind Henry – he's sweet.'

Kirsty narrows her eyes and shrugs. 'Is he? The way he stares . . .' She gives a shudder but doesn't finish her sentence.

'Maybe you could get Dean to hang out with him, that way we'll get some peace. They're the same age, so it'd make sense.'

'You don't think I've asked?' Kirsty nudges Anna. 'But you know he won't do anything to help me if he thinks someone might *see* him doing it.'

Anna gives a nod to show her agreement. 'Not long before we have to go out to school. Then we'll be apart from them.' Anna says it to make things better with Kirsty, but really the thought makes her tummy tie up in knots. How will Henry cope at Finley without her?

'Yeah, your brother does need to learn to stand on his own two feet if he's gonna survive Finley when you're not here every minute of the day. He'll only see you after school and in the holidays.'

Anna's mind drifts, her not-so-distant memories flooding in. 'It'll be weird. It's always been me and him, you know? I don't like to think of him upset – he's been through enough. He's not even nine yet.' Anna watches as Henry kicks a stone around the playground, keeping a good distance from the infant kids. He wouldn't want the bigger boys thinking he was playing with them. 'Look at him,' Anna says, her voice filled with pity. 'He's so sad.'

Kirsty gives an exasperated sigh. 'Go play with him then. I'll catch you later.' She turns to walk away, but Anna pulls her back.

'Hang on. I've got an idea. I know it's babyish, but we used to play games before we came here to take our minds off stuff. His favourite was called 'The Hunt'. I could set him a task, and that way he'll be busy, and we'll be left alone.'

'You're too nice by half, Anna.'

'Ah, come on. You'd do the same for Dean.'

'Nope. I really wouldn't. But then, he's not likely to want to hang around with me anyway.'

'So, you up for it?'

'Oh, go on then. Is it like hide and seek?'

'Sort of. I hide something – usually stuff it inside some-thing, or maybe bury it – then I leave a trail of clues for him, or sometimes I make up a riddle.'

'A treasure hunt then.' Kirsty pouts her lips and looks skyward, distinctly unimpressed. 'Fine. But make sure they're hard clues. Don't want him doing it too quickly, eh?'

'Yeah, yeah. Right, come on. We need to sneak back inside, go to his dorm and find something to hide.'

'You're actually taking something of his?'

'Well, yeah. It has to be something important to him, or what's the point? He'll give up too easily if it's something dumb.'

'Good point. Maybe you're not quite as nice as I thought, Anna Lincoln!'

Chapter 7

'Are you all right, Anna?'

DI Walker's words seem far away; muffled. I hear them but I'm unable to respond. My mind is back there. At Finley Hall. Where this unfolding nightmare began.

'Anna? Anna!'

I snap back to the here and now and stare at the detective, all wide-eyed and startled. 'Sorry. Was thinking.'

'Do you want to tell me what's going on?' DI Walker's face is uncomfortably close to mine – if I lie to him, he's going to see it. I read somewhere that starting a lie with the truth makes it more convincing. And I'm not actually going to *lie*. I'm just not going to give him the full story.

'I think you're right about Henry coming after me,' I say. DI Walker's eyebrows raise, but he doesn't speak, so I take a breath and carry on. 'But I'm not so sure I'm going to be his next victim. Well, not a victim in the sense that he intends to kill me.'

DI Walker's face scrunches up in confusion. 'What makes you think that?'

'Because this,' I point at the newspaper article on the table, 'is a game. One that we used to play a long time ago. And all this is his way of drawing me into it.'

'Why?'

'That, I don't know.' I force myself to keep eye contact with him. I consciously prevent myself from blinking, swallowing hard or fidgeting because those tells will expose me. 'But he's made his first move.'

'Like chess?'

I hesitate. I know I should explain more about The Hunt; how and why it started at the children's home – what it became – but the instinct to hold back this information until I know Henry's full intentions myself is too strong.

'Something like that, yes.' I push myself off the sofa, slowly so as to test my legs, and then retrieve my laptop. 'And there's something else.' I pass it to him.

'What's this?'

'The reason I called you,' I say. 'I'm not sure how it's possible, but I think what happened is connected.'

'What do you mean, what happened?' I sense frustration in DI Walker's clipped tone.

'Just . . . watch.' I lean across him and hit the button to play the footage. I pay close attention to DI Walker's expression, silently picking at my fingernail while the CCTV of the zebra crossing incident plays out. When it stops, the detective looks up briefly, frowns, then watches again. And again. My nerves can't take this, I begin to pace.

'So? What do you think?' I say, when his silence becomes too much to bear.

'About your behaviour? Or about the fact someone has been able to access the CCTV?'

My face burns. 'It cuts off at a moment that makes it look a lot worse than it was. Had it played for longer, you'd see that I calmed down and I *gently* put my hands on her shoulders; it really didn't happen the way it looks here.' I'm rambling, I know. My attempt at convincing him is, I'm well aware, more of an attempt to convince myself.

'I rather imagine that was the point. Clever.' He looks at it yet again, this time pausing it frame by frame. 'The date and time stamp has been cropped out. What time did this occur?'

'It was around eight forty. I left here about ten minutes after you left.'

'You were followed, then.' He says this so calmly it makes me stop my pacing.

'What?'

'You said you weren't sure how it could be connected, but if they were following you and witnessed it, they might well have used the opportunity to their advantage.'

I'm about to argue against his theory – it sounds ludicrous. But then I remember how preoccupied I was and realise I wouldn't have noticed if a vehicle was tailing me. Still, why not just record it with their mobile phone? It's easier and less time-consuming than tracking down the exact piece of CCTV.

'Doesn't explain how they got hold of the CCTV footage so easily.' I verbalise my thought.

'Leave that to me.' DI Walker gets up. 'I'll get on to digital forensics, see if they can help.'

'Will they be able to trace who posted it?' I watch as

DI Walker's mouth turns down at the corners while he seems to think about his answer, and I bite the nail of my index finger because his pause is too long.

'Given that he knew how to hack it in the first place, I'd be surprised if they could. He'd likely know how to make himself untraceable. But you never know.'

My shoulders slump. 'What should I do?'

'Figure out what this clue means.' DI Walker takes a photo of the riddle and then folds the paper up and places it in an evidence bag. 'The solution will lead us to whatever he wants you to find. As much as I loathe games, I can't see another way. You have to play, Anna. It's our only chance to find him. Stop him.'

'If he's been here, though, and evaded capture by you and your team . . . what makes you think following this clue will get you any closer to catching him?'

'Now he's left the envelope, he'll know we're onto him. It's very unlikely he'll turn up here again. No. My bet is that he'll be close to wherever that clue takes us. He'll be watching.' DI Walker takes off the gloves and stuffs them into his jacket pocket.

'That makes sense.' Bile burns in my stomach. The thought of Henry watching me this morning, and now waiting for me at the location he's set, is terrifying. What does he want?

'The other date is key. Have you had any further thoughts about May the thirteenth?'

'I've racked my brains, but no.' I shake my head. 'I could dig out my old diaries . . .'

'That's a great idea, yes. It's clearly a significant event and it would seem highly plausible that it should be a date from his past. Maybe from your childhood prior to the children's home, or an event that marked a change for him at Finley Hall.'

'I'll get on it.'

'Thanks.' DI Walker gives me a nod, then asks for my mobile number.

He takes his phone and taps a few buttons. 'Right. I've sent you the image of the riddle. Don't show anyone.' He doesn't wait for a response. Turning away, he stalks towards the front door. 'Anna,' he says as he's on the threshold, 'make sure to call me the second you think of something. Anything. I can't reiterate just how crucial it is we figure this out as soon as possible.'

'Yes, DI Walker. I fully understand the urgency.'

I watch the detective fold himself into his car and keep my eyes on the Audi as it goes down the narrow road and disappears around the corner. Then, after a wary glance around to check if anyone is there, I rush back inside and lock the door.

I don't have any diaries from my time at Finley Hall. I burned them all.

But I don't need them to work out the clue. The location was obvious to me the moment the riddle mentioned the words 'middle for diddle'. Ross is due back any minute, so I won't be able to leave right away. With my mobile in my hand, Google Maps open, I pace from the lounge to the kitchen and back, staring down at the screen as I try to formulate some kind of plan. It says it's a three-hour drive from here; I'll set off early in the morning, before Ross gets up. That way I can avoid any awkward questions. With luck, it'll also mean I can avoid detection from the police, because I can't afford for DI Walker to be with me when I find what Henry's left for me.

61

Chapter 8

My lips are sealed and a promise is true:
I won't break my word; my word to you.

FEBRUARY

Two years ago

He'd moved her with ease to begin with, her limp body sliding off the bed onto the floor, then he'd pulled her across the carpet like a huge slithering snake, through the door to the landing. But then the adrenaline waned, and his muscles ached with the exertion; he'd had to stop and rest.

Now, sweat dripped into his eyes. He swiped the back of his hand roughly across his forehead, muttering under his breath.

'Fucking bitch.'

After a few moments' break, he grabbed hold of her again, dragging her by her arms to the stairs, his breath heaving with the effort. Backwards, he took a few steps down, then yanked on her arms so that she followed. While her head remained off the ground, her legs banged against the wooden treads as he descended them. At the bottom he let her go, her body collapsing in a heap, and he leaned up against the wall to recover his breath. He was fit, but he hadn't anticipated the true strength he'd need to carry this out.

It would get easier, he told himself.

By the time he was ready for *her*, he'd be so well-practised he'd be able to do it in his sleep.

And with less conscience than now.

Her skin was pale like porcelain, and appeared smooth like it too. He couldn't help himself; he removed his glove and, bending forward and down, he ran a fingertip over her cheek. So soft. Warmth still clinging to it. It would take around twelve hours before it cooled, but rigor mortis would start after three hours, so he had to get a move on; he would struggle to get her into the right pose once that happened.

Finally in the lounge, he hauled her onto the sofa and laid her down on her side. Standing back, he examined the scene. He shook his head and went back to her, lifting one leg and angling it so her thighs were open. Then he draped one arm so it hung close to the carpeted floor. That was better. Taking the kit from the table where he'd left it when he was upstairs dealing with her, he removed the needle and cotton.

After some roughly laid stitches, he stepped back and whispered, 'My lips are sealed and a promise is true: I won't break my word; my word to you.'

He ducked down and grabbed one of the other props he'd brought. He wrapped her fingers around the neck of the wine bottle and pressed them into the glass to keep them in place. Here, the rigor mortis would come in useful. But it didn't really matter if the bottle dropped from her dead grasp, because that would add to the authenticity. She might not ever get to see his handiwork, but it was important to him to be true to the memories. He took the front page of one of today's newspapers and laid it on the arm of the sofa.

He was pleased with his work, but it needed one final touch.

Every serial killer had to start with one murder. And every serial killer needed a calling card.

Chapter 9

There are three missed-call notifications on my mobile – all from Serena. I'd turned it off while DI Walker was here so as not to be distracted, but now I know I should return her call or she'll worry and likely drive over to check up on me. I don't want her getting mixed up in any of this. The police might well believe that Henry wouldn't be stupid enough to hang around my place now, but I don't want to chance it in case they're wrong.

'Sorry, Serena. I didn't hear my phone.'

'Thank God for that! I was in full panic mode after the third try and so I called The Right Price to speak to Ross—'

'Oh, really?' I screw up my eyes and silently curse my friend for caring so much about me that she'd call my husband at his estate agency. *Please have been out conducting a viewing.* 'Was he there?'

'No . . .'

I heave a sigh. 'Good,' I say, without thinking.

'. . . but he came into the office just as Yasmin was

67

about to hang up, so . . .' Serena falters as I give an audible groan. 'Er . . . should I *not* have spoken to him?' Bafflement spills out through the words. I rub a hand over my forehead. Damn. I should've foreseen someone telling Ross, and pre-empted it by calling and explaining the situation immediately. I think it's too late now . . .

'What did you say to him?'

'I only said I'd been trying to get hold of you, but of course, he was confused as to why I wasn't with you, given the time.'

'Please tell me you didn't mention the suspension. I haven't had a chance to talk with him.' Like a child, I cross my fingers as I wait for her response.

'Not in so many words,' she says, slowly. I can hear guilt in her tone. 'But he might have got that impression.'

My stomach dips. 'How?'

'Well, I had to say something about why I was worried, didn't I? So I did imply that you'd *had* to go home early . . . like, against your will.'

I hold my sigh in and count to three to calm myself. 'It's fine, I don't expect you to lie for me, Serena. It's my fault, I could've dropped in to see him on my way home. I was just in the worst mood and stupidly thought it'd be better if I waited until he got back from work.'

'Probably best not to air your laundry in public anyway,' Serena says. Her falsely light and breezy voice takes on a heavier, uneasy tone. 'Although, that ship might well have sailed.'

My heart plummets. 'He hasn't seen the footage, has he?' Now it's my turn to be in full panic mode. It really needs to come from me, with me controlling the narrative as much as possible. Limit the damage somehow.

'I'm sorry, Anna, I think . . .' She's speaking, but the words are no longer reaching my brain, or at least my brain has stopped paying attention, because the sound of the key in the lock has superseded them.

'Got to go.' I hang up and head straight for the door. Ross's face is pale, startled, as I leap at him the second he walks in. Not wishing to give him a chance to get a word in first, either, I plant my lips firmly on his and kiss him hard. He pushes me away.

'Ow, Anna.' He presses his fingers to his mouth. 'Jesus.'

'Sorry, just pleased to see you. Been a hell of a day.' I place my hands on his cheeks, offering a smile. He squints.

'Yes. So I heard.'

'Let's sit, shall we? I'll get the wine.' And before he can decline, I rush towards the kitchen. I slam around for a bit, collecting two glasses from the dishwasher before snatching the already opened bottle from the fridge. My hands shake as I pour the remaining liquid almost equally between them. I add a little more into mine, swig a mouthful, check it's equal, then take the glasses into the lounge.

Ross isn't sitting.

'Here.' I give him his glass and take a seat on the cuddle chair by the window. There's a chill in the air, but it's a warm May evening so I know it's nothing to do with weather and everything to do with atmosphere. 'I have a few things to say.'

'Me too,' he says, taking a sip of wine.

'Can you sit with me?' I pat the space beside me, my stomach tensing as I watch his face. We've been good together lately. Our bumpy patch from last year seems like a distant memory. Or it had done, until this moment.

Now, as I await his reaction with trepidation, that patch comes hurtling to the fore once again. Our discussions about the future of our marriage, *my* resolution that we shouldn't bring children into this world even though it was at odds with my yearning for them, were some of the hardest conversations we'd ever had. We made it past that test, though; put our arguments behind us – laid them to rest – after Ross came around to my way of thinking and we moved on. But now, with this new challenge, the old issue feels like it's bubbling just under the surface, threatening to expose itself. Nothing is ever truly buried.

'Look, it doesn't matter what spin you put on it . . .' Ross sits down, but not beside me, and he keeps his eyes averted. 'You should've told me straight away, not let me find out in such a . . . a . . . *humiliating* way, Anna.' He's keeping me at arm's length, preventing physical contact.

'Humiliating? You think *you* found out in a humiliating way? Try being dragged into Craig Beaumont's bloody office and being forced to watch it in front of him!' My face is hot, about to burst into flames, my entire body's volume of blood seemingly squashed into it at this moment.

'I'd take that over a client, someone who's known me and my family for years, being sent a video link on her mobile phone while I was trying to close a deal, Anna.'

'Bit rude to look at a video while having a meeting.'

'That's not the point and you know it. She opened it, watched with her mouth agape, then stared at me as though I was a serial killer—'

'That's not funny.'

'No. And neither is seeing my deranged wife about to attack a child, Anna.' His eyes bulge, the vein on his

70

temple throbs. I haven't seen him this angry. Ever. 'What were you thinking?'

I stand up and begin to pace. 'Obviously I wasn't thinking, was I? I was reeling from the detective's visit. My mind was all over the place. But whoever posted that video did it to make me look bad—'

'They didn't have to try very hard.'

A deep ache pulls at my stomach as the contempt in his voice hits me. 'It didn't happen the way it looks. Honestly.' I suddenly feel so tired, and sit back down, head in hands.

Ross huffs. 'The camera never lies.'

'Well, actually, that's not true. But anyway, it's not that – the footage was abruptly stopped, Ross. Just at the point it seemed like I was going to lay my hands on her. If it'd been allowed to play out, you, and everyone else, would've seen that I didn't hurt her, I was apologetic and helped her back to the pavement.'

'You're not getting it are you? Even if what you say is true, you'd already scarred that poor girl with the way you launched at her.'

'But . . . like I said, I apologised . . .' My words sound feeble now, and as Ross shrugs and averts his gaze, I fear I'm wasting them.

'If that's the way you treat kids, Anna, maybe it's a good thing we're not having them.'

My jaw slackens and I have to fight back tears. Great. He *is* still holding a grudge about our agreement not to have children. All these years working hard to create this life, and within a day, it's gone to rat shit. How can something that's so challenging and difficult to gain be so easy to lose?

MAY 10th

Three days to go

Chapter 10

It's still dark when the vibration beneath my pillow stirs me. Groggily, I reach a hand under it and silence the alarm. It's not as though I need the wake-up call – the night has been long and almost entirely devoid of sleep. Even the hypnotic sound of the waves has been no match for the thoughts crashing around in my mind.

The bedroom is oppressive; the darkness is not yet diluted by the sun. It's four-thirty, an hour before sunrise. Ross used to think I was mad when we first moved here and I'd regularly get up, pull a pair of joggers over my pyjamas and take a travel mug filled with coffee to Ness Cove Beach to sit on the wall and watch the sun slowly peep up over the water. Peace like that is hard to find.

He came with me a few times, and we snuggled together safe and warm in each other's arms as we enjoyed the stunning colours and revelled in how wonderful the natural world was. After last night, if I were to suggest he join me for sunup now, Ross would definitely decline the offer.

I turn my face towards his. Soft, snuffly breaths escape his pursed lips and I lean closer, touch mine against his in the lightest of kisses. He's a heavy sleeper and even a full-on snog wouldn't disturb him, but I daren't risk it now.

I creep out of our bedroom into the spare room, where I laid out my clothes before going to bed. I quickly dress and go downstairs to make up a flask of coffee. I grab the lunchbox I packed last night and stuff it, along with everything else I'll need, into my old backpack. Tiptoeing unnecessarily, I make my way to the front door and open it a crack, then pause, my heart thumping. Will Henry be somewhere outside watching the house? Waiting for me to make my move? My fingers tighten around the handle until they lock, as though they're attempting to stop me leaving.

'Don't be so ridiculous.' My whispered words sound loud in the dark, quiet hall. A squirming sense of dread pushes through my veins; the word *stay* repeats itself inside my mind. I could be making a huge mistake by following Henry's clue, yet the risk of not following it is significant, too. I have no choice, and he knows it.

I open the door fully, checking up and down the road. There's no one about that I can see. No strange cars parked nearby with silhouetted figures inside them, keeping watch. A surge of unidentifiable emotion fills my stomach and stops me in my tracks. I think it's a mix of relief and disappointment. I'm grateful I'm not being observed by Henry, but I would've thought the police – DI Walker – would be keen to make sure I was safe. Seeing as they were the ones who alerted me to the danger I might be in, that I might be the next victim. DI Walker was quick to reassure Ross that he'd post a police officer outside if possible, but clearly I'm not worthy of the resources.

Perhaps they *want* me to be the next victim. One way of flushing Henry out is to make me the bait.

I shudder, but before I can allow my negative thoughts to sabotage my plan, I step outside.

A narrow strip of light is visible on the horizon, the inky sky smudging into a deep blue. With a gulp of fresh morning air, I take the few steps to the pavement and climb into my car. Not allowing myself to hesitate any more than I already have, I start the engine and move slowly off, beginning the three-hour drive to my past.

Nerves consume me as the miles on the road signs become single figures, and the countdown is really on. Nine miles. Five miles. Three miles. The roads are now vaguely recognisable, and my hands begin to slip on the steering wheel. I pull over on a quiet roadside, run my palms down my trousers and get out to stretch my legs. Or that's what I tell myself I'm doing, but really I know it's because I want to prolong the inevitable. The last time I saw Finley Hall I swore I'd never get within spitting distance again. Now, I'm allowing Henry to force me back there. It's why he chose it, no doubt. He wants to make me uncomfortable. Wants me to suffer; make me as vulnerable as possible. Wondering what else he has in store is another reason to put off going there. A voice that sounds very much like DI Walker's screams inside my head:

> *A woman's life hangs in the balance.*
> *A woman's life is in your hands.*

Potentially my own.

'Fuck.' I get back in the car, pull away from the kerb, and keep my foot to the pedal, even though I've got every alarm bell imaginable ricocheting around my skull telling me to stop the car, turn around and go home. The female voice from my satnav calmly instructs me to make turns, but I don't need her now – muscle memory has taken over, despite it being seventeen years since I was last here and I didn't drive then. I guess some things are imprinted on the brain. My mouth waters as I approach the final corner, nausea threatening. When I turn, the upstairs of the home will be visible above the high wall. *God, what am I doing?*

And there it is. The old, brown-brick building looms ahead.

A large mass, heavy and dragging, sits in my lower abdomen as I steer into the driveway. The posts look the same as they did, but the wrought iron gates are different; they no longer have the words FINLEY HALL on them. It's now The Grange – an old people's residential home.

As I approach, my heart in my mouth, I notice a newer building set to one side, part-obscured by trees. It looks like a summer house, but I imagine it's where the caretaker lives. I crane my neck to see inside as I pass, half expecting someone to come out and stand in my way; stop me, ask who I am and why I'm here. Am I visiting a relative? I should get a cover story ready before I try and gain access – I can't very well say, 'I used to live here as a child, so please can I come and look around?' I don't want to leave such a clear trail. If I had DI Walker with me, of course, gaining entry would take a simple flash of the badge, no questions asked.

Gravel crunches as I manoeuvre to the signposted car park. Back when my brother and I were brought here, this area was all laid to grass; there was only the sweeping driveway and space for about five cars right outside the main building. Not many visitors came to Finley Hall. If it were possible to sneak around the side of the building to reach the back gardens, I could perhaps bypass the questions and instead get to where I need to be without drawing unwanted attention. The high walls and padlocked side gate prevent that option, though, and I can't see a handy ladder anywhere.

I run over my story again in my head. My legs are wobbly as I make my way to the entrance. The large, black wooden doors that once brought a sense of dread have been replaced by modern, glass, automatic ones. An intercom is screwed onto the wall to their right. Great. What if I can't even make it past the threshold? I'm surprised now that I was even able to enter the gates. I turn back to see them still wide open, another vehicle slowly driving through. Perhaps they are left that way during visiting hours. With my finger hovering over the buzzer, I wonder if it would be a better idea to wait for whoever is in that car to park up. I could sneak in with them.

A voice erupts from the speaker, making me jump out of my skin. 'Good morning. Who are you here to visit?'

Shit. Can't very well wait now. 'Oh, hi.' I bend down closer to the intercom, and my voice is breathy with nerves. 'I didn't make an appointment. I know it's early, but I'm only in the area today and was hoping I could . . .' My mind blanks, my rehearsed story refusing to come to me now I need it. I clear my throat to give me time to think.

Was I going to say that I hoped to look around? Or to speak to someone about getting my mum on the waiting list? Whatever I say, I suddenly realise that if they ask for specific details, I'll be flummoxed.

'The open day has come and gone, I'm afraid,' the female voice says, pre-empting my request. I relax a bit, thankful she's given me a starting point. She sounds pleasant, her tone soft, so maybe she'll take pity on me.

'Oh, my timing is always so bad. I knew it would be a long shot but I thought I'd try my luck while I was visiting Mum.' I'm feeling more confident now, and the words come more easily. I hear an intake of breath, the woman readying herself to give me the final brush-off. 'You see, my dad recently passed, and she's been so lonely. With me living in Devon and all, I haven't been able to get the time off work until today.'

'I'm sorry for your loss. Maybe—'

'Never mind, I understand. Do you happen to know of another residential home in the area? This is the only one that was recommended to me.'

There's a pause, then some rustling. I hear muffled speaking; she must've covered the microphone. I wait, willing her to let me in. The car that drove in passes by – the middle-aged man, smart, alone, gives me a fleeting look and carries on. He doesn't strike me as someone who'd be up for helping me gain access.

'I can get one of our carers to give you a very brief tour,' the voice says. 'But I'm afraid the manager isn't available to discuss packages—'

'That's really good of you,' I say, quickly. 'Thank you so much, I appreciate your help.'

And the door whooshes open. I experience a thrill of

triumph, before I remember what I'm doing here and it turns to dread.

The smell is the first thing I notice. It's not the musty, old people smell I was expecting, but a pleasant, zesty aroma like freshly squeezed orange juice. The entrance hall has the same Victorian geometric black-and-white stone floor tiles, and the wooden panelling that reaches halfway up to the high ceiling, but it seems brighter – not dark and dingy like it used to be. But maybe it felt that way because of what it meant to me; how seeing it made me feel back then.

The woman I spoke to greets me and offers a handshake. All very formal. She's called Georgia and she is the senior care worker on this shift, she tells me.

'If you don't mind waiting in the lounge, Natalia will be with you shortly.'

She ushers me across the hall to the room that used to be the games room. Gooseflesh immediately springs up on my arms, and my legs stop moving. A pool table once stood in the middle, its green cloth worn at one end. If I close my eyes I can see the scuffs as if it were yesterday, remember the times I'd witnessed the arguments over who was allowed to play, watched in horror as Frank stormed in, slamming one unfortunate victim face down against it. I can still hear the cries, followed by the deathly silence as someone was dragged away and made to sit alone for hours in an otherwise empty room, in unofficial solitary confinement. Tears prick my eyes; I blink rapidly to clear my vision.

'Are you all right?'

I nod. Forcing myself forwards, I step into the room. I focus on the chairs lined up by the window and stride to one to sit down. The lounge is empty. I imagine as it's early that maybe the residents are all being assisted in their ablutions. Georgia is staring at me, a concerned expression on her face.

'Thanks again, Georgia. I am really grateful for you letting me in.'

'You're welcome. If you leave your details when you've finished the tour, I'll make sure the manager calls you. I hope it's what you're looking for.'

I hope so, too. When she's gone, I get back up and walk to the far end of the lounge, to the window that overlooks the first-tier lawn. Down some stone steps lies the large area of grass, edged with trees. Or it did. I'm almost afraid to look now in case it's all different. If the trees have been felled, I'll be back to square one. I take a deep breath and look out.

I breathe a sigh of relief. The rows of conifers are dwarfed by the large cedar trees – and I'm transported back to being a child. More importantly, I'm taken back in time to The Hunt. I have to get outside and somehow ensure I'm on my own when I search those trees.

After a whistle-stop tour of the home, I ask to see the grounds.

'Sure,' Natalia says, guiding me through the patio doors at the rear of the dining room. There are only two residents out in the gardens – the 'young ones', as Natalia described them. A married couple in their seventies who were made homeless following a fire last year. Natalie likes to talk, I've found out.

'Very impressive.' My words are forced through tight lips. Being here again after swearing I'd never return feels as bad as I could ever have anticipated, but at least a lot has changed within the walls of Finley Hall – not so much is recognisable. But outside, it's almost identical to how I remember, albeit the shrubs and trees have grown somewhat. But standing on the concrete steps, I can envisage the area filled with children, all running around, playing. Screaming. I want to put my hands over my ears, block out the noise of my memories.

'We're lucky to have such amazing gardens here,' Natalia says, pulling me out of my past. 'The residents enjoy sitting watching the wildlife, or the more able ones love to walk the paths by the lake – there's even a maze,' Natalia says, like an excited child.

'Ooh, I'd love to see that,' I say, widening my eyes with fake enthusiasm. It might be a good opportunity to ditch her and get to the trees. Natalia grins and takes a step down, beckoning me to follow, when an alarm sounds. We both look towards the high-pitched wail.

'Oh, so sorry. Maybe another time.' She jogs back to the door, looking to me to do the same. 'It's a bathroom alarm.'

'I'll be fine here – you go,' I say. 'If you're not able to come back, I'll let myself out.' She hesitates for a second, but as I flash a reassuring smile, she nods and runs inside.

Perfect timing. I wait for the coast to be clear. A few moments later, the young ones disappear into the treeline at the bottom of the grounds where the path leads to the lake. I stride towards the cedar trees. There are three in the main ground, and it's the centre one I go to. *Middle for diddle*. The trunk is thicker, the tree taller, but the hollow knot remains. I check around me. Natalia is still inside; no one else is in sight.

I stand on tiptoe to peer into the hollow. I had to get up onto my friend's shoulders to reach it before. All I can see is a black hole. Damn. I'm going to have to put my hand inside. Every horror film moment where I've screamed at the screen for the character not to do it comes back to me now as I pull my sleeve up and place my fingertips in the cavity, inching my hand in further and tentatively feeling around.

'Please don't let there be a spider,' I whisper.

My hand finds something cold, hard, and I withdraw it quickly, cursing quietly. I take a couple of deep breaths, then shove it in again, grasp the item between my finger and thumb, and pull it out.

My breath catches in my throat. It's faded, the red now a pale pink, and the plastic screen is cracked, but I recognise the old childhood toy instantly.

And just as instantly, I know what it means.

Chapter 11

FINLEY HALL CHILDREN'S HOME

The second Anna's eyes open she knows Henry's been in their room. It's as though over the past three and a half years at the home she's developed a sixth sense. She peeps over the edge of the bed and sighs. It's what she's been dreading. There's a piece of paper folded neatly in half on top of her slippers. She groans, her tummy already beginning to bubble with anxiety.

'Kirsty,' she says, looking over to her friend. 'Hey, Kirst.' Anna swings her legs out and reaches across the gap to give Kirsty a shake. 'Wake up.'

'Whaaaat? Shit, Anna, it's still night.'

'It's almost seven.'

'But it's a weekend.'

'Sorry. But I need you to wake up.'

There must be something in Anna's tone, because with a sudden jolt, Kirsty sits up, palming any sleepiness away from her eyes. Her hair is wild, a mass of brown tangles that mirror Anna's own.

'What's the matter?'

Anna points to the floor.

'Oh, great.' Kirsty stares at the paper and puffs her cheeks out, air releasing like a deflating balloon. 'It's been a while.'

It's been six months since the last one, but that one left its mark. It also almost broke the girls' friendship. The Hunt was a staple game for the first year Anna and Henry were at Finley Hall. Anna did it as a way to try and help Henry overcome some of his problems – his challenges with making friends, with fitting in. He'd come to rely on them – on Anna – just as he had when he was little. But as Anna matured, she slowly felt suffocated and tried to wean him off. She initiated fewer hunts, left Henry to his own devices more, and ultimately cut down the time they spent together. She began putting her friendship with Kirsty first, relishing finally having a strong bond with another girl. In Henry's eyes, Kirsty was taking his sister away from him and so he began instigating the hunts himself, clawing back time with Anna – he wanted things the way they were.

Henry's eleventh birthday saw a change in him – in the games. They became more spiteful. Manipulative. He used them as a way to force her into spending time with him. The Hunt began to invoke dread – the fun they once had was totally stripped away. The treasure hunts became a tool purely to torment Anna; nothing more. No longer were the items personal, belonging to Anna. All she found were horrible things: a rusty mousetrap, the decaying mouse carcass still caught; huge spiders in matchboxes; gone-off apples crawling with maggots. And the last time, he'd set a trap, a brick narrowly missing her head when she walked into the clue room. When Anna refused to report it to the home manager, she and Kirsty had fallen out. It was getting dangerous, she'd said: someone would get seriously hurt if Anna didn't do something about it. But Henry was her brother – she couldn't tell on him.

'What are you going to do?' Kirsty asks, her eyes glued to the paper as if it might scurry towards her, harm her in some way.

Anna inhales deeply. 'Nothing.'

Kirsty raises her eyebrows. 'What? Like . . . ignore it?' She seems shocked, even though she's been begging Anna to do just that.

'Exactly. I'm fed up with his immaturity.' Anna grabs the paper, and without unfolding it rips it down the middle. She bites her lip, her mind teetering between relief and regret. Should she just do this last hunt, then speak with Henry and tell him she's not doing any more? No. He'd talk her out of it; threaten her in some way. She gets up, strides to the wire waste bin under the desk and shoves the torn paper in. 'Screw him. I'm not playing this stupid game any more.' She crosses her arms and gives Kirsty a confident smile. 'I'm not giving him the satisfaction.'

'Halleluiah. At last.' Kirsty leaps off the bed and launches herself at Anna, flinging her arms around her. 'I don't get why you did them anyway. I've told you. You have to ignore him. His nasty games. It's jealousy, that's all. He has to get on with his own life, Anna.'

'I know. Well, today is the first day I'm standing up to my brother. I mean, what's the worst that can happen?'

* * *

87

She's motionless when Anna finally spots her after searching for her for the past two hours, lying in a heap at the edge of the lake.

'Kirsty! Shit, Kirsty!' Anna runs towards the bridge and is across the other side within seconds.

Anna drops to her knees beside her friend, lays a hand on her. Her clothes are damp; she's been there a while. Anna's heartbeat stutters as she puts her head on Kirsty's chest to check if she's breathing. She cries with relief when she feels her chest rise and fall.

'Thank God. Kirsty, it's me. Please open your eyes.'

Kirsty's face looks pale and waxy, and as Anna touches it a coldness tingles through her fingertips. She'd do anything now for this to be one of Kirsty's pranks – it's almost Halloween; it would be typical of her to try and scare Anna by pretending she was unconscious. Last year, she'd bunked off school and at four o'clock had hidden in their shared wardrobe, waiting for Anna to return. When Anna went to change out of her uniform and opened the wardrobe, Kirsty screamed and leapt out at her. Of course, while Kirsty had collapsed in a fit of giggles at jump-scaring her friend, Anna had merely collapsed from fright, taking half an hour to calm down.

This now seems serious, though. Real. Anna shakes Kirsty's shoulders and her eyelids flutter and open. Her eyes roll and she lets out a groan.

'It's okay, Kirst. You're okay.'

'What? Why am I . . .' Kirsty pushes herself up into a sitting position and looks around, confusion crinkling her forehead.

'Did you fall from the bridge?' Anna asks, grasping at the most obvious reason for her friend's current state. If she'd been sitting on the end post and had lost her balance and fallen backwards, it would explain her position.

'I don't . . . I—'

'Here,' Anna says, offering her hand to help Kirsty stand. 'We should get you to the office. Marnie will check you out.'

'I'm not seeing her. Just 'cause she's got some fancy certificate on the wall, doesn't make her a nurse. The woman didn't even tell us about periods until we'd been having them for a year.'

'But you were unconscious, Kirsty. You must've hit your head.'

Kirsty runs a hand over her scalp. 'No cuts.' She shrugs. 'Bit of a bump, mind,' she says, wincing as she touches the back of her head.

'You don't remember what happened?'

'One minute I was walking over the bridge; next, your face is looming over me. I guess I tripped.' This puts paid to Anna's first theory, and instead the possibility of Kirsty taking a knock to the head before collapsing takes its place. With concern creeping through her, Anna looks around to see if anyone else is loitering. It's getting dark, so she can't be sure, but there's no movement, so she turns back to Kirsty. As she does, she spots something lying in the long grass and bends to pick it up.

'Yours?' She holds up a vodka bottle, giving Kirsty a judgemental glance.

'Ahh, there you go. That's what I was doing,' Kirsty says, flippantly. 'I'd only had a few swigs, though.'

'Where'd you get it from?' Anna cocks one eyebrow.

'You know my fake Aunt Linda? She snuck it in on her last visit.' Kirsty huffs. 'At least she's good for something, eh? And look, promise not to mention this to anyone, right?

89

I'm in enough trouble without adding alcohol smuggling to the list.'

Anna's skin prickles with unease; she has a niggling feeling something's not quite right, but brushes it away. It was an accident, like Kirsty said. Anna reluctantly agrees not to tell anyone, but her worry for her friend lingers.

'What if you've got concussion?' she asks. 'Or a blood clot?'

'Oh, Anna. Don't be so melodramatic. I'll be fine. Look into my eyes.'

To Kirsty's annoyance, Anna does just that, and then runs a finger in front of Kirsty's face, getting her to follow its path forward and back a few times.

'Yeah, okay. If you're sure,' Anna says, giving in.

It takes them fifteen minutes to get back to their room, Anna adamant they should walk slowly. In that time, she makes Kirsty say the alphabet forwards and backwards and do all the times tables, just to convince herself that Kirsty isn't suffering from concussion, to feel better about not reporting the fall to the first-aider. She'd feel terrible if something happened to Kirsty because of her.

Anna's brow creases as she pushes the door open.

'Did you leave that there?'

'No.' Kirsty says. The girls stand just inside the room, both rooted to the spot. 'But it is mine,' Kirsty says, pointing to the object in the centre of the floor. 'And isn't that the paper you tore up this morning with it?'

Anna gently nudges Kirsty further in so she can close the door. She casts her gaze around to see if anything else has been disturbed, then takes a few tentative steps to the middle of the room. Anna picks up the paper.

'It's Henry's riddle. But it's been sellotaped back together,' she says. She picks up the toy. 'Here.' Anna hands Kirsty's Tamagotchi back to her.

'What a dick,' Kirsty says, turning it over in her hands. 'He's taken the battery out. He's killed my cat.' She hangs her head, and for a moment, Anna doesn't know what to do. Guilt that it's her brother who has caused her friend's sadness crushes her. If she'd just done The Hunt as usual, he wouldn't have destroyed it.

'I'm sorry, Kirst.' Anna puts her arm around her friend. 'I know you've had it for the longest time.' And this fact suddenly hits Anna. She'd assumed Henry had chosen the Tamagotchi because he thought it was hers, but everyone knew it was Kirsty's – she was always checking it, making sure her cat was fed and played with. Henry was well aware it didn't belong to Anna.

'Your brother clearly doesn't like being ignored.'

'No, I don't think he does.' Anna swallows down bile as an awful thought occurs to her. 'Did you see him earlier? When you were walking to the lake?'

Kirsty's forehead crinkles, then she gives a small gasp. 'I passed by him. He was standing by the cedar.' The girls look at each other, eyes wide with shared understanding. Anna strides to the window overlooking the grounds and scans the area. She doesn't have to look far. Henry is leaning up against a tree, arms crossed, staring up at the girls' window, and if Anna isn't very much mistaken, he has a smug look on his face. She keeps eye contact for as long as she can bear, then just as she's about to break it, she sees Henry cross his chest with his finger, then put it to his eye. She backs away with a shiver.

Placing something of Kirsty's by the discarded clue is more than a sign he's displeased. It's a warning.

Henry was angry with Anna for not playing. She hurt his feelings.

So, in turn, Henry hurt Kirsty on the bridge. It was his revenge. And leaving Kirsty's Tamagotchi here is to show Anna he means business. It's his way of telling her that if she doesn't play, someone she loves gets hurt.

Chapter 12

I clutch the Tamagotchi in my hand. If I don't play, someone will get hurt. Someone I love – that's the deal. That's the message I remember all too well from the last time Henry was ignored. Even though it's now some seventeen years later, I can't afford to see if the same would apply again. What if he targets Ross? He knows where we live; it wouldn't take much to show me what he's capable of.

Tears stream down my cheeks. I let them freefall and drop onto my top, my head bowed. Years' worth of pain, frustration and fear all releasing in this moment.

A hand lays on my shoulder. I let out an involuntary shriek and jump around.

'Sorry, sorry.' DI Walker steps back and puts his palms up.

'My God, don't sneak up on me like that.' I glare at him, taking in his dishevelled-looking, tired appearance. The case is obviously causing strain, but what the hell was he thinking creeping up behind me? I could've lashed out at him and added assault of a police officer to my growing list of offences.

'It appears I'm not the only one sneaking around.' He narrows his azure-blue eyes at me in a playful way, and I relax a little. If he's angry I've come here without informing him, conned my way in to the home, then he's hiding it well – or perhaps he's secretly chalking it up as another mark against me.

I look around him, up towards the doors I'd walked out of with Natalia. There's one lone uniformed officer standing stiffly as his head moves left to right, presumably scanning the area. 'Where are the rest of your team?'

'We're stretched to the limit on this one. Everyone's scattered around, trying to cover as much ground as possible in the little time we have left.'

'Yes, of course.' My only knowledge of murder cases has come from what I've read and seen on TV, but I'm aware everyone will be working around the clock to apprehend Henry. Of course, it also means they could be keeping tabs on me; maybe more so than DI Walker is letting on . . .

'They're not best pleased you gained entry by false means, Anna.' DI Walker gives me a reprehensive glare.

'No, I'm sure they aren't. I considered telling the truth, but . . .'

'Lies are easier?' he says. I'm not sure if this is a trap – getting me to admit to lying now will give him ammunition later down the line. But I have been caught out, so admitting it won't really harm me further.

'Something like that,' I say with a shrug of agreement.

'Like telling me you didn't know what the riddle meant?'

I shift from one leg to another, a tingling sensation making them restless. How long has he been watching me? Did he see me get the toy from the tree? I grip it tightly in my fist, not quite ready to share my find.

'I wasn't sure enough that I was right. I didn't want to waste police time – not when you're so stretched.' Our eyes lock and although it's unspoken, I sense battle lines have been drawn.

'Well, were you? Right, I mean?'

I avert my gaze. 'It would appear so.' Telling DI Walker more about the treasure hunt game isn't something I can hold back any longer. I need to explain it because I know it's key to finding Henry. 'Welcome to The Hunt, detective,' I say, forcing a smile. 'If I don't follow the rules, bad things happen.' I turn away from him, begin walking further down the lawns towards the treeline. I hear his heavy thudding footsteps and then he's beside me, doing a funny kind of side-step so he can talk and watch me at the same time. I wonder what he's thinking – if he suspects I'm holding back.

'Is it possible that you didn't follow the rules before, and that's why he murdered the five women?'

'Oh, wow.' I stop dead. 'You believe it's my fault those women died?'

'No. Not your fault. I'm seeking a reason why he's been doing it. You saying bad things happen if you don't follow the rules strongly suggests a cause; that's all I'm saying.'

I start off again, ducking between a gap in the hedges. I swear it's the same gap we used to walk through before when we were sneaking off for a forbidden cigarette by the lake. Each step I take, the heavier I feel. By the time I reach the bridge, the weight will be too much to bear.

'There haven't been any games since leaving here,' I say, finally. 'And besides, the point of the games was to hide something of importance for the other to find. And when his game was ignored once before, it was some*one* important that got hurt. He wouldn't choose a random person with no link to me to kill. It's not his style. It would have to be someone I loved.'

'Like Ross.'

I shudder. 'Yes, like Ross.'

We're at the bridge that spans the narrowest part of the lake. I sit in the middle of the stone wall and wait for DI Walker to do the same. He hitches his trouser legs up so he can bend his knees easily, then plonks down beside me. We both watch an electric-blue dragonfly hover between us, its wings creating a sound like a tiny drill. This was always my favourite spot to come when I wanted to be alone. Somewhere I could give space to my thoughts and allow them to 'be'. Once I'd acknowledged them, they would leave my overcrowded head and blow away on the breeze across the water. In all the years of therapy that followed my time at Finley Hall, I never found a better way to manage my darker thoughts than that.

It must be the nostalgia of this spot; I hold my arm out to DI Walker now and uncurl my fingers to reveal the toy.

'You'd best bag this.' The pulse in my throat throbs as I watch for his reaction.

'What is it?' He pulls a glove from the inside pocket of his jacket and takes it.

'How many of those gloves do you have stuffed in your pockets?'

He laughs. 'Always be prepared.'

'And it's a Tamagotchi,' I say. 'A craze around the time we lived at this place.'

'Ahh, yes.' He nods, gives a half-smile as he holds it up, examining it. 'I remember these little buggers. Virtual pets. You had to remember to feed them and play with them, or they'd die.'

'Yep. Henry used this one, or one like it anyway, as a warning.'

'How?'

'I found a new riddle one morning and just decided I wasn't going to play any more. Me and my friend carried on with our day. We didn't even look at the clue.'

'I assume you'd never ignored one before?'

'No. I'd wanted to, but Henry . . . well, Henry was persuasive.'

'He didn't like being ignored.'

'He did not.' I turn around and look over the bridge into the rippling water. 'That's where . . .' I take a steadying breath. 'That's where he left her.' I point below and to the side – by the foot of the bridge.

'Your friend died?' DI Walker's eye widen.

'No, no. She was hurt, knocked unconscious.' I suck in a lungful of air, the detective's assumption hitting me hard. 'I guess there's a possibility he'd *intended* to kill her, though. I never thought about it like that. We assumed it was a warning and we never tested him again.'

'Are you still friends with . . . what was her name?'

'Kirsty,' I say, then quickly add, 'we lost contact after this place. Everyone scattered – there was an online group someone started up in the early days, but that petered out pretty quick. She wasn't on there, though, as far as I remember.'

'You didn't ever try to look her up again? Make sure she was okay?'

His question sounds judgemental, like I've done my friend a disservice by not keeping in contact. DI Walker has no clue what it's like – I shouldn't expect him to, but knowing he is judging me is hurtful and I'm immediately on the defensive.

'As I said, everyone scattered. We all had our histories, DI Walker. Had pasts we didn't like to talk about and wanted to run from. She was no different. Some people don't want to be found.' I cough to clear my throat – expel the emotion that's threatening to choke me. 'None of the women, Henry's victims, were named Kirsty, were they?' DI Walker stares at me – through me – and my stomach twists.

'No,' he says, standing and turning to look over the lake. 'Have you thought more about the date – the thirteenth of May?'

'I didn't find anything in my diaries.' I blush, despite my attempt at being blasé. I get up too, hoping he won't notice my lie if I'm moving rather than sitting next to him.

'And it's not the date you finally stopped playing and Kirsty was hurt?'

I don't answer straight away, and he looks hopeful.

'No. That was autumn, leaves everywhere. Cold. We'd been talking about Halloween. So, definitely not May.'

'Why does your brother want to ruin your life now, Anna?'

'That's the question going over and over in my mind, too.' I shift uncomfortably, redistributing my weight from one foot to the other.

'Well, where to next?' he asks.

'I don't know.' We walk off the bridge, back towards the main house. DI Walker is still holding the Tamagotchi in his gloved hand – he hasn't placed it into an evidence bag.

'What's the clue?' he says, turning the toy over.

'It was just that. The same, or at least similar to the Tamagotchi he left in the dorm after he hurt Kirsty. I assume it's him just letting me know it's not over.'

'I don't know. It seemed to me like the riddle was important – like, a starting point. He sent you here because it's somewhere you both know. Seems strange he wouldn't continue his game – send you off in another direction, keep you playing.'

'Perhaps he's watching us now.' I shudder, turn my head this way and that, checking every inch of visible ground. There are no lurking figures that I can see. 'It could be a test, to see if I'd come on my own, not involve the police.' I huff. 'Which I did try to do, but now you've ruined that.'

DI Walker gives an apologetic smile. 'If you'd let me in on it, I'd have followed at a safe distance. Disappearing in the early hours trying to avoid detection makes you look a little guilty, don't you think? I had no choice but to follow you.'

'I didn't see anyone when I left. No car followed me.'

'Kind of the point of covert operations,' he says. Although his tone is light-hearted, almost humorous, I catch a hint of smugness. I'm not going to fall for it and laugh or offer a comeback. I've had enough of games. As DI Walker is finally about to stick the Tamagotchi in the bag, he stops. 'What have we here?' He carefully pops

99

the battery compartment open. 'There's something inside it.'

He takes the toy to a nearby picnic table. With his still-gloved hands he unfolds the paper inside it. 'Here,' he says, pushing his chest towards me. 'Take my notepad out of my pocket.' I do as he asks. 'Write down what it says.'

My hand shakes as I grip the pen. The words of the new riddle swim in front of my eyes and I have to blink a lot to focus.

> *You're not the only one with something to hide,*
> *You're not the only one that's cheated or lied.*
> *You're going to regret being the one who fled,*
> *You're going to end up losing your head.*
> *Tell-tale tit, your tongue shall be slit;*
> *All the dogs in town shall have a little bit.*

My heart gallops as I attempt to write it down legibly, and when I finish, DI Walker bags it along with the toy.

'Your new clue.' He looks at me, excitement evident.

'I don't get it.' I stare at it, read it a few times. Each time it sounds more threatening. My memory, though, refuses to recall anything to help it make sense.

'Come on, Anna. This is important. Think.'

'I am, Detective Walker. Christ. Sorry if I'm a bit freaked out by all this. You might be used to this stuff, but I'm just a bloody teacher.'

'And a good one by all accounts, so I'm told. Logical thinking and emotional intelligence is your thing, and this is someone close to you.'

'I'm not close to Henry,' I say, forcefully. 'Yesterday

morning everything was normal; my life was as expected. Then you show up and throw my world into chaos; I get suspended from my job and now I'm being stalked by a serial killer and the fate of another woman's life rests in my hands. I can't think straight.'

'Okay. Okay. You're right, I'm sorry. I really shouldn't be putting all this pressure on you. I don't want to let Henry create another victim, Anna, that's all. I'm determined to save at least one life in this whole mess.'

'I understand that. Of course I do. The clock's ticking. But just so you know, I don't usually cope well with stressful situations; I'm prone to panicking and making rash decisions.' I don't know why I'm telling him this, but I can't seem to stop. 'If you want my help, I have to put the clues together in the right way. There's no time for me to jump to the wrong conclusion and send you – us – on a wild goose chase. I have to be sure the solution is correct first time. This first one took me three hours to get to. If I'd been wrong, that's a lot of time wasted. See?'

'Yes. Fine. I'll give you some space.'

'Thank you.'

'But Anna?'

'Yes?'

'You have to share everything. No disappearing and trying to figure out a clue on your own. I can't allow you or another woman to be the next victim.'

'Don't worry – I'm really not intending to lose my head, DI Walker.'

'No, but then I'm sure his other victims didn't intend to lose parts of their bodies either.'

I can't hold my alarm back – my sharp intake of breath is instinctive.

'You never mentioned that,' I say, aware my words are wobbly, like I'm in a car driving over a cattlegrid.

'Sorry. I didn't want to give you the gruesome details if there was no need.'

'You told me the first victim had her lips sewn shut. Did she also have something removed?'

The detective sighs, seemingly annoyed at himself for having let that information slip. 'No. That started happening with the second and subsequent murders.'

'Oh.' I massage my throat, trying to dispel the lump of anxiety.

'Look, I'm going to organise protection—'

'No.' I'm shocked at how quick, and firm, my rejection of his offer is, and judging by his gaping mouth, so is he. I give myself a shake. 'Sorry, thanks, detective, but I don't need it. If an officer is posted outside my door, it could stop Henry making contact and I'll be forced to withdraw my co-operation. I'm sure you don't want that, because as you rightly pointed out, we're running out of time.'

'And if his ultimate goal *is* to kill you? That line in the riddle isn't exactly ambiguous.'

'I disagree. But regardless, while I'm happy for you to come to my place alone, I think the rest of the team should keep their distance.' I'm not happy for him to be around me either, but I have to be realistic – it's a murder case and whether I like it or not, I'm involved. I look back to the home and see Natalia emerging, her hands firmly on her hips as she scans the area. 'Er . . . I think we've outstayed our welcome,' I say. I couldn't be more relieved to walk out of this place again. And this time, it really will be forever.

Chapter 13

A secret's a secret – my word is forever;
I will tell no one about your cruel endeavour.

MAY

Two years ago

The tongue slipped between his fingers, and it took a few attempts to hold it still long enough for him to make the first cut. The knife was sharp, but nevertheless it took some hacking to sever it. There wasn't a lot of blood – she'd been dead for half an hour – but he'd come prepared and had ensured there was plenty of plastic sheeting underneath her. He hadn't wanted to chance splattering the area with her blood because the focus had to be on the final, staged scene. He had learned from the first woman that it was easier to kill close to where the staging area was to prevent having to move the body too far. This time, he'd only had to drag the dead weight across the hall to the next bedroom, where he'd erected a kids' tepee tent he'd bought specially for the occasion. It was in the bigger of the two rooms, to give himself space to manoeuvre.

She was smaller than the first woman, making the process so far much simpler. He rolled her off the bloody plastic sheet and wiped her down, then pulled her by her arms. She almost glided over the floor.

'Note to self,' he muttered. 'Rooms with no carpet are better.'

His breath was steady; no huffing and puffing like before as he finished dragging her towards the tent. He set her to rest at its door and, taking a step back, he looked to the tepee entrance and then at the woman, assessing. With a plan in mind, he turned the body so the head was closest to the tent. Then he backed himself into it, grabbed her arms again, and hauled her inside. Posing her would be more difficult than the last. He sat her up, bent her legs so they were crossed, and moved away from her. The top half of her body slumped over. He repositioned it, but the same thing happened.

'Stupid, stupid bitch.' He climbed out, took some deep breaths, shrugged and rolled his neck to loosen himself up, calm down. Then an idea came to him, and he ran downstairs. He gathered what he needed and returned to the tent. He jammed the wooden handle of the broom down the back of her jeans and used the tape to secure it along her spine and around her middle. Now she remained upright. Smiling, he repositioned her clothes, then put one arm in her lap and the other in front of her as though it were reaching for something.

Content with the pose, he retrieved the severed tongue from the other room. It looked like one of those joke shop props popular at Halloween, and for a moment he was transported back to Finley Hall, the memory of past Halloweens spent there like a dark shadow in his mind. He placed the now-cool tongue between two pieces of bread then popped it onto the plate, which he positioned beside the woman's hand.

'A secret's a secret – my word is forever. I will tell no one about your cruel endeavour.'

Only he intended to do just that.

Setting a triangle of Dairylea cheese beside it, he smiled. Just his final touch – his signature item – to add now. He supposed the fact he was posing the bodies, and with the current day's newspaper nearby so that the date he'd committed the murder was clear, could be classed as his signature, but he needed to be sure. It required the extra 'wow' factor. Something that would be meaningful and specific to *her*. Adrenaline surged through his veins as he did it, his breathing coming fast. As before, he moved back to observe his scene from afar – to see how others would see it.

He reckoned it might take a while for the police to link this and the first murder. Being in different counties would slow things, and apart from the victims living alone – which was crucial for what he needed to carry out – they didn't share similar physical attributes. Usually, serial killers selected targets based on physical or personal characteristics – they had an 'ideal'. His choices were more complex.

Detectives would conclude it was the same perpetrator once the different police forces shared information and realised there was a calling card. This would signal to the police that they were dealing with a possible serial killer. After the next one, there'd be no denying it. It's not that he wanted to be caught – although he craved the notoriety, maybe, and the knowledge that he was the one to instil fear and gain revenge. The main thing was that he needed the murders to be linked so that she knew what was coming. Ultimately, he had one goal. Each murder would take him a step closer to her – and to uncovering the truth.

Some promises should be broken.

And some liars should never prosper.

Chapter 14

It's pretty obvious from the new riddle that Henry's intention is to torment me. He's always felt let down, particularly by females – it's unsurprising that women are his target victims. I guess his hatred of them began with Val – 'mother' – then shifted to Miss Graves at Finley Hall. While he was there he was let down by everyone around him, me included, so I can't help wondering if everything he's doing is purely an attempt to regain my attention; my time. He needs to be noticed.

The riddle could relate to any number of things – none of which immediately make sense. I stare at the words, reread the lines, but nothing stands out as being a clue to the next location – not like the first one. Henry's making me work harder this time, adding pressure like a timer on a bomb, hurtling towards zero and the unavoidable explosion. I push the paper away. Obsessing over it isn't helping; I need a distraction. That way, my brain will relax and find the answer.

The laptop is open on the dining room table, its screen blank – like a black hole, and just as deadly. I know within it lies a version of myself I cannot bear to face. Because of the visit to Finley Hall, I put the hideous zebra crossing incident out of my mind, but maybe I should be trying some damage limitation. Get on the school's Facebook page, or at least open the teachers' WhatsApp group to see what's being said there. I can't hide from it, not if I want to retain my professional standing.

I make a tentative step towards it, my heart thrashing like a caught fish on a line, hands gripped into fists by my side. I'm so wound up by the mere thought of what people are saying about me, that when I hear a noise from the back of the house, my first thought is that my eardrums have popped due to the pressure building in my head. But then I hear it again and freeze, fully alert. It's the back door. Someone is trying to force it; break in.

Is Henry here? Oh, God – why did I turn down DI Walker's protection offer? I'm going to look really stupid if Henry carries out his promise of me losing my head. I can almost hear the detective's voice saying *I told her this would happen*.

Act. Do something.

Hearing the creak of the door fully opening, I finally leap into action, rushing to the side table. I grab the lamp, yanking the plug from its socket, turn it upside down and loop the cord around my wrist. Ducking behind the half-open lounge door, I lift the solid-wood lamp base up high, ready to bring it down on the intruder's head as they walk in.

A shadow grows bigger on the wall beside the door. I hear the breath of the person on the other side. *Henry.*

How will I know it's him? I haven't even seen a photo for the past seventeen years. Doesn't matter, though. Even if it's not him, it's someone wishing me harm. Or someone stealing from my home. Either way, this will be self-defence.

As the door pushes open, I let out a huge war-like cry and launch myself at the person entering. I'm about to crash the lamp against his skull, when his equally loud cry stops me.

Ross cowers, his hands over his head protecting it from my swinging lamp.

'Fuck!' he yells. 'Anna, it's me.'

All power leaves my legs and I collapse in a heap on the floor, the lamp thudding down beside me as my grip on it loosens. I swallow hard and try to gulp in air at the same time, causing a weird hiccup to escape. 'Sorry,' I gasp, the realisation dawning that I just almost killed my husband.

'Why the hell did you jump out on me like that?' His eyes are wide, black, his pupils obliterating his irises.

I feel a flash of anger. 'Why the hell are you sneaking in the back door?'

'I . . . I just . . .'

'What?'

'I came from the other way – I'd been looking at the property behind ours.'

'Okay, well you don't usually use that back entrance.' I gather myself, get up onto my knees. Ross gets to his feet first and offers me a hand. 'Thanks,' I say. Neither of us speak for a few moments as we recover our breath. Ross leans back against the wall.

'That was close.' His hand is on his chest. I look into his eyes and see the shock still in them.

'I need to tell you something,' I say, not shifting my gaze from his. 'I'll make us a coffee and bring you up to speed.'

'Sounds ominous.' His face is weary, dark circles like smudges under his eyes. The vertical line between his eyebrows deepens; evidence he's worried. That's one of his tells. Mostly, he's very good at hiding his emotions, maintaining control at all times. Everyone has some kind of expression, or characteristically noticeable thing, though – something maybe only the closest person to them would recognise. I'm sure I have something too. And right now, I'm hoping Ross isn't seeing it as I step away from him and leave the room to go and make the drinks.

'I went back to Finley Hall this morning,' I say as I walk back in with mugs in hand. My pulse pounds in my neck as I see Ross standing over the piece of paper containing the riddle, his face pale.

'What's the matter, Ross?' I put the coffee down and twist the paper around so it's facing us. 'Do you know what this means?'

'No, why would I know?' he snaps. 'I assume it's aimed at you?'

'I just thought . . . well, you looked like it might mean something to you.'

He shakes his head and sits on the sofa, taking a mug. His hands are shaking. 'You drove all the way to the Midlands?'

'Yes, I had to. And this new riddle was tucked inside a toy. Henry has started The Hunt again and wants me to play.' Ross knows about the game Henry used to make me play, how it turned nasty; I told him that much early in our relationship. I'm not sure if the expression on Ross's face is surprise, anger, or disappointment. It could well be all of those and more besides. He opens and closes his mouth, but no words are emitted.

I place the piece of paper on the table in front of us, the same way DI Walker had done with the first clue. I give Ross a brief overview of the morning's events, culminating in how I found the Tamagotchi in the hollow of the old cedar tree which contained this new riddle. I push the paper closer to him.

'So?' I prod.

'So . . . what?' He gives me a perplexed look.

'Does anything jump out at you; make sense at all?'

'No, it doesn't mean anything, I'm afraid. But I don't like the sound of it.' His breath judders and I get a sinking feeling in my stomach which informs me that, for the first time since we met, I don't entirely believe my husband. Is the liar referred to in the riddle actually Ross, and not me? But then maybe all the colour drained from his face when he read the line about me losing my head. Although the 'losing my head' part could quite simply mean me going out of my mind and jumping to conclusions. And what would Ross even have to lie about?

Christ, what a perfect way to drive a wedge between me and my husband. Henry is truly one of the best manipulators – this could be exactly what he's aiming for.

'Right, well, I think I need some fresh air. Fresh perspective. Time's running out and DI Walker is counting on me.'

Ross looks taken aback. 'Really?' His eyes narrow.

'Yes, DI Walker feels sure I can help them figure it out. Stop Henry before he kills again.'

'Oh, does he now?' Ross gives a little *humph* and curls his lip. 'Well, he better have your best interests at heart, Anna. If they're using you as bait—'

'They're not,' I say quickly. Although that's crossed my mind on more than one occasion. 'See you shortly.'

'Will you be okay on your own? Maybe you should stay indoors.' His words, edged with worry, cause a wave of guilt to swoop through me.

'I'll be fine. I've got this.' I hold up the personal alarm I bought years ago when I first moved to the coast. I depress it quickly and it emits a short, high-pitched burst of squealing. 'See?'

'And you've got your mobile?'

'Yeeees,' I say, patting my pocket as I pull on my coat. 'Don't start dinner; I don't know how long I'll be. I'll grab fish and chips for us on the way back.' I slam the front door harder than intended, stalk down the path out into the road, and head towards the Ness.

As soon as I'm alone with my thoughts, Henry swamps them. Why is he trying to spoil my carefully forged life? Is his so bad that he needs to ruin mine now? According to DI Walker, this is the third year that Henry's been killing women, so maybe something significant happened to him that started this off. Or, maybe after I left Finley Hall – and him – behind, his behaviour worsened and he became increasingly sadistic. Just because he's started The Hunt now, doesn't mean he wasn't killing people in the years prior to this latest string of murders. The police might not have linked him to any before. I pull my jacket around me tighter. It's not cold, just a bit breezy, but a chill shudders through me.

I skirt around the edge of The Ness House. The

restaurant appears quiet but no doubt there are locals gathered to drink and chat at the bar end. The warm glow of light seeping through the windows, casting a yellow hue across the grass, is comforting. But I veer away from that and head to the coastal path. It's more secluded; I'm less likely to bump into anyone who wants to give me a hard time over the CCTV footage.

The peace of the evening is calming, the lapping waves so relaxing I almost forget what a mess the past two days have been. But then, as a freak wave crashes against the rocks, the lines of the riddle crash against my skull: *Telltale tit, your tongue shall be slit; all the dogs in town shall have a little bit.* These last lines have to hold the clue to the next location because they're different in tone to the rest. They're part of a childhood rhyme. The last clue was linked to Finley Hall, but I'm not so sure this one is. I don't think he would send me to the same place twice.

Frustration clouds my mind and I let out a strangled cry. Damn Henry. I'd give anything to ignore the little psychopath again. If I were to go about my business, carry on life as normal, it would be like giving him the middle finger – showing him he doesn't have power over me. But that's wishful thinking. He holds all the power, and he knows it.

He could ruin my life.

He could *take* my life.

What's certain is that someone will die, whether I play his game or not.

And I can't have more blood on my hands.

But how can I fight back against an enemy I can't see?

MAY 11th

Two days to go

Chapter 15

With my mind full, I wandered for hours last night, and when I got in and was met with an incredulous look from Ross, I realised I'd forgotten the fish and chip takeaway. He rushed out to the closest one, but it'd closed. We ate baked beans on toast in silence.

Now, this morning, as Ross sits across from me, he appears distant, a sad look plastered on his face. It's like something has happened, something bad, that I have no memory of, and an air of mistrust hangs between us at the breakfast table. It can't be just because I forgot the dinner. As I'm about to get up and leave, unable to bear the lack of conversation, Ross sighs. I look at him, hopeful he's going to open up to me.

'What are your plans for today now that you've been suspended?'

His bluntness cuts, and I have to force myself not to bite, although I can't help but shoot him an equally cutting smile. 'Well, Ross – it's a first for me, so I'm not sure.'

'Sorry.' He blinks a few times, as if to rid his vision of an unwanted image. 'I understand the stress must be getting to you.'

'Stress? Yep, that's one word for knowing a woman's fate is in your hands.' I throw down my fork; it clanks against the plate sending a blob of egg yolk across the table. 'I have to work out the clues, help the detectives find Henry before the thirteenth of May. That's my priority – he has to be stopped.'

'I agree,' Ross says, suddenly animated. 'But it's their job, Anna, not yours.'

'I'm assisting—'

'You're being used.' He drains his coffee and gets up, slamming the mug on the worktop. 'I've got some viewings to do with Yaz. But call me if you're at all concerned, okay?'

'Yes, thanks,' I say, flatly.

'Please don't go chasing clues halfway around the country, either, eh?'

'I can't promise that, Ross.'

His face reddens. 'Fine. Then I can't promise I'll be here to pick up the pieces.'

'Fair enough.' My nose begins to tingle, but I jam my teeth together to prevent the tears. I try to hold his gaze but his eyes won't fix on me. He purses his lips and puts his hands to his face, rubbing his palms roughly over it.

'Are you okay?' I ask, moving towards him. He puts his arms around me, nuzzles his face into my neck. We stay this way for a while. I don't want to be the first to pull away. Then I feel a dampness on my skin and my pulse skips.

'I do love you, you know,' he says. Then pushing himself

118

away from me, he turns and leaves without waiting for my response.

After pottering needlessly about the kitchen, rearranging the mugs in the cupboard and wiping down the already spotless worktops, I go upstairs and jump in the shower. Usually with the jets of hot water massaging the stress away, my mind becomes sharper. Not this time, though. I rest my head against the silver-grey shower panel, my arms limp at my sides. Why can't I figure out the riddle? Where does Henry want me to go next?

And why did Ross act so strangely when he read it? That question kept me tossing and turning last night. I recoiled from my pale, drawn reflection this morning, shocked at how I appeared to have rapidly aged overnight. I've tried to convince my tired brain that I'm reading more into Ross's reaction than was actually there. But just now, he struggled to make eye contact – and he cried. The only time he's cried during the entire time I've known him was when we talked about children. Or, more to the point, when he couldn't alter my stance. When he had finally agreed our marriage was more important than having a child, tears had flowed. We'd cried in each other's arms until we were exhausted and had fallen asleep. The next morning, we got on with our life together. Just the two of us. And we've been great ever since.

Emotion that strong from Ross is a serious alarm bell. So why was he so upset? I think it's more than worry; deeper than the fear of what might happen to me if Henry really is after me. Is it possible that Ross is *involved* in all of this?

'Get a grip, woman!' I massage a dollop of shampoo into my hair, pushing my fingertips hard into my scalp.

It's Ross, for God's sake. We love each other – he's just *told* me he loves me. I can't allow Henry to infiltrate our marriage like this – undermine our trust with a few words on a bit of bloody paper. I continue to punish my skin, rubbing my thighs with the exfoliating mitt until they become red and sore. It doesn't help to relieve the gnawing sensation in my gut, or the creeping dread snaking underneath my skin. I rinse the shower gel off and stand with my head up, the water splashing my face, willing the solution to the riddle to pop into my mind.

Nothing. I bite down on the mitt and scream, tears of frustration and panic mixing with the water and stinging my cheeks. As I turn the lever, ceasing the pounding water, the doorbell sounds. I freeze, one leg in, one leg outside the shower cubicle, a steady drum of water dropping onto the bathmat matching the speed of my heart. Who's that? My leg wobbles, and I step fully out then wrap a towel around me. I wait. Did I imagine it?

It rings again.

I blow out a slow stream of breath, forcing myself to be rational – it's probably just a delivery man. I'll leave it. Any parcels are taken to the neighbour if we're not in; I'll just pop around and get it later.

The bell rings again.

And keeps on ringing.

Clearly this person isn't going to go away. I curse quietly, pull on my dressing gown and hurry downstairs, adrenaline coursing through my veins. Henry surely wouldn't ring the doorbell – especially not multiple times. It would draw too much attention.

He's a serial killer, Anna – he wants to be noticed.

My hand hovers above the handle, then I think *sod it*,

120

and fling the door open. There's no one there. I stick my head out, but I can't see a retreating delivery person. And on the doorstep lies another envelope.

'Where are you, you coward?' My yell seems to bounce off the neighbouring houses as I bend to snatch the letter from the step, echoing my fear back at me. Then with the envelope gripped in my hand, and fuelled by rage, I stomp barefoot up the path and scan the area. I did take a while to open the door, so he could be long gone. Or, he could be in another house, watching me this very minute. I shiver, backing away from the gate. But I keep my head held high as I go inside – I refuse to let him see my fear.

I know I should call DI Walker immediately – and definitely before opening the new envelope as it's clearly from Henry; it's the same type as before with the same block writing – but I'm in no mood to wait, so I rip it open. I pull the paper from inside and unfold it. Two words are written on the top half of the page:

Tick, Tock.

Underneath this, the riddle DI Walker found inside the Tamagotchi is repeated. I frown. Why's he sent me the same one twice? As I read it again, I realise it's written in a different way. I'd scribbled the riddle haphazardly when I copied it down, and in this version the lines are arranged differently, and with the final line now under-lined. My heart begins to race as my memory grapples to make the connection I know is there.

All of a sudden, something clicks into place, and I remember a puzzle just like this one. How could I have forgotten?

I know how to solve it.

Chapter 16

FINLEY HALL CHILDREN'S HOME

Despite the bridge incident, or maybe because of it, Anna continued to play The Hunt with Henry. She wasn't willing to risk her friend getting hurt again. Although they weren't frequent, each one over the past year had become increasingly complex. Henry was becoming even more cocky, doing his best to catch Anna out. Make her sweat more.

Now, a sense of dread fills Anna as she throws her bed cover back, sits up and catches sight of a small, ominous-looking gift box at the end of her bed. She stares at it, her pulse pounding. Henry's been in their dorm again. He's taken to sneaking in when they're asleep – Kirsty caught him in there after breakfast a few months ago and, before Anna could see it, tore the riddle into tiny pieces right in front of him. Anna was beyond alarmed when Kirsty told her, pacing the room, anxiously twirling her hair, then shouting at her friend for taking such a risk. But Kirsty only shrugged; she said that Henry had laughed in her face and called her stupid.

Anna instinctively looks across to Kirsty's bed now. *Shit*. She's not there. Has he done it again? She pulls on a pair of jogging bottoms and a hoody, and rips the box open, snatching the paper from it. With the new riddle in her hand, she rushes down the stairs, asking anyone she passes whether they've seen Kirsty.

With her heart banging, Anna runs outside and casts her eyes wildly around the grounds, silently praying nothing bad has happened. There's movement. She spots Kirsty with her brother Dean, smoking behind the middle cedar tree, and bends over, her hands on her knees, her breath heaving with relief.

'Oi!' Kirsty shouts, then ducks behind the trunk. Anna walks towards them, shoving the riddle into her hoody pocket as she does. Kirsty offers the cigarette to her as she rounds the cedar tree.

'Thanks,' Anna says, drawing heavily on it. 'How come you're up so early?' Anna shoots Dean a cautious look. They seem to have been in deep conversation.

'Couldn't sleep,' she says.

Dean takes the cigarette, finishes it, and stubs it against the bark. There's an awkward silence and Anna senses they want to say something.

'For God's sake,' Dean says, suddenly, looking behind Anna. Anna turns around to see Henry approaching. Her heart drops.

'I'll leave you to it,' Anna says to Kirsty. She begins to walk towards Henry, but Kirsty grabs her arm.

'You've got another riddle, haven't you?' she asks, her eyes narrowed.

'It's fine. I'll do this one alone.' She pulls away.

Kirsty and Dean carry on speaking, their words hushed,

and Anna knows they're talking about her and Henry. Probably about how weird it is that she allows her brother to manipulate her; how weird Henry is full stop. How dangerous he is. A shiver tracks up her spine. How can you be afraid of a twelve-year-old? But then she remembers a news story from a few years ago about a boy killing his sister and mum when he was that age, and realises she has every reason to be. She's too afraid to ignore her brother, and he knows it.

'You need help with that one?' Henry says, his arms crossed as he leans against a tree.

'Nope. I haven't even started it yet,' Anna says.

'Well, don't ask *them*. That's cheating.'

Anna casts her gaze back and sees that Kirsty is watching, listening. 'Whatever,' she says to Henry. 'Leave me to get on with it then.'

'Be careful, Anna.' He winks at her. 'You shouldn't trust them.'

Anna frowns. It's a strange thing for him to say, particularly when it's him she should mistrust the most.

'Kirsty's my best friend. Get over it.'

'Kirsty's a sheep, Anna. She's not special or unique.' Henry's glare focuses on Kirsty. 'Look at her. She follows you around; copies you. It's sad.'

Anna huffs and mutters under her breath. 'That's rich, coming from you.'

'What did you say?' Henry lunges at her, gripping her wrist.

'I said, *whatever*.' Anna snatches her hand away and takes the riddle out of her hoody. 'I need to make a start on this.' She unfolds it, her face intense as she reads it. It doesn't make a whole lot of sense. Henry laughs.

'This one took me ages,' he says, proudly. 'You've got one hour from . . .' He twists the dial on his watch, setting a timer. 'Now,' he says.

Anna lets out a sigh. She's meant to be doing her homework, not faffing about with riddles. She's about to tell Henry this, but when she looks back up, he's already disappeared. She turns around and can't see him, so she sneaks back towards the cedar tree.

'Hey,' Anna says as she approaches Kirsty. 'I know what you're going to say, but I've only got an hour and my mind is a blank.'

'Fine. Right, bugger off, Dean,' Kirsty says, shooing her brother away. 'I'll catch you later.' Dean shakes his head, but does as he's asked. Anna and Kirsty huddle together.

'Thanks,' Anna says. 'I can't risk him doing something bad if I don't do it.'

'He's getting worse, mate,' Kirsty says, her hand on Anna's. 'You're encouraging him by playing along. He needs help.'

'I know. But who's going to step in to do that, eh? It's always been just him and me. No matter how awful things are, he needs me.'

'Until he doesn't.'

'What does that mean?'

'One day, Anna, he's going to go too far. And what's that saying? We always hurt the ones we love the most?' She shakes her head sadly, then turns her attention to the riddle. After a few silent minutes, they both slump down, leaning against the tree trunk.

'Ugh,' Kirsty says, lying down, staring up at the sky. 'Not seeing it.'

'Me neither.' The paper is on Anna's knees – she stares

at it so intensely her head begins to ache. She throws it and it flutters in the air before coming to rest on the grass, then she lies down next to Kirsty. 'Sorry for dragging you into this.'

'So you should be.'

'What were you and Dean talking about?'

Kirsty rolls her head towards Anna. 'This and that,' she says, shrugging.

'My ears were burning,' Anna says. 'I know you think I'm pathetic.'

'No, that's not true.' Kirsty sits up. 'I'm just worried that you're being sucked into his bloody delusions. You're never going to escape him.'

Anna watches the clouds scudding across the sky, tears running down into her hair, a sense of defeat flooding her. Kirsty is right. She's always right. Henry is wrong about her – she's the only person she *can* trust. They're kindred spirits; know each other inside out. If it weren't for Kirsty, her life wouldn't be worth living.

'Hang on. Hold the front page!' Kirsty's excited voice makes Anna bolt up.

'What?' Anna sees Kirsty has folded the paper in half. She points at the letter each new first word starts with.

'He's trying to be clever.'

And then Anna sees what she hadn't before: the letters make another word.

Chapter 17

I remember. The riddle all those years ago had spelled out a clue only when it was viewed differently. I fold the paper in half and look at the words that are now first – ignoring the top line as it's set apart from the rest of the riddle.

> *that's cheated or lied.*
> *regret being the one who fled,*
> *up losing your head.*
> *shall be slit*
> *town shall have a little bit.*

The first letter of each spells out TRUST. The last line, which is now underlined – *All the dogs in town shall have a little bit* – is suddenly meaningful, too. 'Dogs In Town' is the name of a café in Torquay, where outside there is a large garden for dogs to run around in while their owners relax and have a coffee. Not long ago, Ross mentioned that he'd had a meeting there – I can't remember why. It didn't strike me as odd at the time – after all, he quite often meets up with prospective clients. But now I think about it, we don't currently have a dog and usually meetings are held in the properties or office, and together with the highlighted word *trust*, I begin questioning myself all over again. *Is this riddle suggesting I shouldn't trust Ross?*

Taking the stairs two at a time, I rush up to the bedroom and clamber into jogging bottoms and a sweatshirt, then fly back down and sit on the bottom stair to pull my trainers on. I have to go there right away. I should call DI Walker to let him know. With my head in my hands, I run the conversation over in my mind:

Hi, Detective Walker, I got another letter and I opened it.

You did what? Are you mad? I told you to call me immediately if he made further contact, Anna.

Yes, I'm sorry about that, I was overcome with the need to know.

So? What have you learned?

I've worked out the next location.

Stay where you are, the team will be right there.

And that's a problem. I need to go alone. This is between me and Henry.

My mind made up, I snatch my keys and phone and rush outside. At least the next place is close – I'll be there in ten minutes, plus I won't have to lie to anyone to get in. My tummy knots. I might not be lying to gain access, but by failing to inform the detective in charge of the case about my progress, I'm still deceiving someone. But I can't think about that now. I give a quick, cautious glance to the doorstep as I go past. The likelihood of something being there so soon after the new envelope is slim, but I don't put it past Henry to be bold. He's already shown how brazen he can be.

My spine sags as I reach the pavement.

'Oh, my God! Those damned seagulls.' My car looks as though a hundred birds have defecated on it; the windscreen resembles a piece of Jackson Pollock's art. I close my eyes, not to block the sight of it so much as to block the tears from coming. Everyone, and everything, is against me. I'll have to get a bucket of hot water to clear that lot. Anger bubbles in the pit of my stomach. 'Why, why, why?'

'Not your week, is it?' I look up to see the same man who witnessed my previous seagull encounter from the other afternoon, and I huff loudly.

'It would appear not.'

'You should get some hot, soapy water on that quick smart. It'll erode your paintwork if you leave it too long.'

'Thanks.' I smile, tightly. 'I love being mansplained to.' I stomp back to my front door, but something makes me turn around. He's still standing on the kerb of the pavement opposite, watching me. His hands are jammed in his jeans pockets and he's bouncing on his heels. What's his problem? 'Did you happen to see anyone hanging around here about half an hour or so ago?'

He shrugs. 'Just the fella that lives with you – your . . . husband?' he ventures.

I narrow my eyes at him. I don't remember seeing him around Shaldon before this Tuesday; how on earth would he know who lives here with me? I'm about to ask, but my ringing mobile diverts my attention.

'Don't forget what I said,' the man says, as I retrieve

131

my phone from my bag. A lurching feeling gives way to nausea as I read the display – Seabrook. *Great*. I look back up, but the man's gone. The ringing continues and I stare at the phone, deciding if now's a good time to talk to someone from school. It's only been a couple of days, and I very much doubt this will be Craig Beaumont calling to apologise and saying I've been immediately reinstated. But perhaps it will be worse for me if I don't pick up. I jab the button to accept the call.

'Hello,' I say.

'Anna. Craig. I need you to come in for a meeting.'

I recoil at his abruptness and am about to politely decline his offer, but he doesn't give me the chance. 'Right away if you would. It's urgent.'

'Er . . . actually—'

The line goes dead.

I hold the phone away from my ear, staring at the display. No mistake – he terminated it. 'Really? Arsehole.' I ram the key in the lock and go back inside the house, whack a bucket under the sink tap and wait for it to fill. Just how much shit do I have to deal with today?

Chapter 18

Wait a moment; I spoke a lie –
I never really wanted to die.
But if I may, and if I might,
My heart is open for tonight.

FEBRUARY

A year ago

He hadn't wasted any time toying with this victim – he hadn't felt the need to touch her skin or stare at her features, either whilst he killed her or once she was dead. It was business now; he had no particular feelings for, or even against, the woman. She was a means to an end. He wasn't the same as other serial killers; ones who killed because they were compelled to take lives – *needed* to. He didn't do it for the thrill. He didn't fit the profile – the stereotypes perpetuated by the media, on TV, in films and novels, or even by professionals, like psychologists, or profilers who worked with the police. Anger drove him. A need to reach his goal. Revenge. He maybe shared some similarities, but he certainly didn't consider himself a typical killer.

'Wait a moment; I spoke a lie – I never really wanted to die. But if I may, and if I might, my heart is open for tonight.' He smiled as he spoke the words, but took no pleasure when he made the long incision down the centre of her body, then cut through her chest bone; or when he split the ribs open, spreading them wide to access her heart. He did experience a shiver of exhilaration when his fingers encircled it; when he thought about how it had been beating a few short minutes beforehand. How he'd been the one that caused it to cease. He was sure he'd feel so much more when it was *her* life he ended. He was getting ever closer to that goal.

He rested the heart back in the cavity while he gathered the tools. He severed the aorta first, his hands shaking. It was the adrenaline, he assumed, because it couldn't be nerves. Then he sliced through the inferior and superior vena cava, followed by the other arteries and veins he couldn't recall the names of; he'd never really paid enough attention in his biology lessons. It didn't matter; it wasn't as though he was transplanting it, he just needed it out of this body. He didn't want to rush it, though. It couldn't look like a sloppy job or some afterthought; it had to appear as though it was fully intended.

He removed the heart and held it in his hand, surprised at its weight, then he placed it inside the plastic container, snapping the lid on tight. The meaning behind what he'd done wouldn't be easy to decipher – he didn't want it to be. He'd mixed it up a little to keep it interesting. Complexity was required. That way, when the time came, it would all fall into place and she'd know. And he wanted to be there to witness her full horror.

Chapter 19

Pulling into my usual parking space in the school playground feels a bit strange now I'm suspended – like I'm doing something forbidden. It's how I used to feel when I smoked by the lake at Finley Hall. I shake it off. This really isn't the same – it's not some stupid teenage rebellion punishable via the confiscation of contraband and being dragged to Graves's office by Frank. This is my workplace; my job.

I stand tall when I get out, slamming the door hard to signal my arrival. But I don't walk to the entrance immediately. Instead, I lean against the car and look up at the building. It couldn't be more different from Finley Hall. This building is purpose-built, new in 2009. It's one level, with various separate smaller buildings for different activities: a gym, a swimming pool and a library. Until now I've only ever had happy memories in this place. But Mr Beaumont's voice hadn't sounded positive on the phone, and the dread of what's to come swirls like a storm in my gut.

Not able to put it off any longer, I stride towards the entrance and push the doors open, trying to exude a confidence I don't feel. The corridors are quiet – the children are all in class. My own footsteps are all I can hear, which, right now, compete with the thudding of my heartbeat. I come to a halt outside the head's office. Shoulders back, head up. I give three firm knocks on the door and wait. There's a pause that feels like minutes before I hear him tell me to come in. His back is to me as I enter the room – he's standing in front of the window overlooking the infants' play area.

'I came as soon as I could,' I say.

'Sit,' he says, finally turning to face me. His complexion is grey and his demeanour stiff as he gestures to the chair. I sit down. With an exaggerated intake of air, he too takes a seat. I stare at his right shoulder as it twitches upwards towards his ear. I've never noticed this kind of tic before. What's going on? It's like he's nervous. Christ – it must be bad. I wish I'd brought a bottle of water with me because my mouth is dry; my tongue is sticking to its roof. I cross my legs, grip my hands together and lay them on my thigh to stop myself from wringing them. Is this what it's like awaiting an innocent or guilty verdict at a trial?

He leans his elbows on the desk and steeples his fingers, his gaze now intently on me.

'Anna,' he says. He lets out a long sigh. 'Thank you for coming in.'

I chew on the inside of my cheek as I wait for him to inform me of whatever the hell it is that's so urgent that he needed me here during the week I'm suspended. I wish he'd skip the pleasantries, if this is what they are – although

I'm actually getting the sense he's toying with me, stretching this out and enjoying my discomfort, rather than merely being polite.

'No problem,' I say, surprised at how weak my voice sounds. I clear my throat. 'You said it was urgent.'

He makes a strange sucking sound through his gritted teeth.

'Yes, I'm afraid it's not good news. I thought it best to speak with you in person – not nice to do it over the phone.'

My stomach drops. Not nice to do *what* over the phone? Any dream I had that this was a meeting to say it'd all been a huge mistake, that I'm such a valuable and trust-worthy member of the teaching staff that he's decided to forget all about this CCTV nonsense and reinstate me immediately, goes out the window. I glare at him, my mouth taut. I can't trust myself to say anything. His eyes appear dark, almost black – like malevolence lurks behind them.

'The rather unfortunate video is still circulating on the local groups and there's even been an online article about it. And it's made it into *The Mid-Devon Advertiser*, Anna.' There's anger in his delivery; it's obviously been building and now I'm in front of him, he's finally releasing it. I feel myself slumping back against the chair.

'Well, that snowballed, didn't it,' I say, then I mutter, 'Just like he wanted,' under my breath.

'You seem surprised. Haven't you been keeping up? Looked online yourself?'

'There's been a lot going on,' I say through gritted teeth.

'Look, you're an excellent teacher, Anna. One of my best, and you know I think highly of you—'

'There's a but, I assume?'

'It pains me to say, but . . .' I close my eyes and hold my breath. *God, please don't fire me.* He can't fire me, surely?

The pause is too long; the silence deafening. I open my eyes to check he's still in the room. He offers a smile that doesn't reach his eyes. 'I'm afraid I can't have you back in school for at least another month.'

I open my mouth to argue, put up a fight, counter this ridiculous plan, but he continues, dropping the bombshell like it's nothing.

'And I actually think it might be an idea for you to begin applying elsewhere,' he says.

Tears come now and I shake my head. 'No, Craig, please. You know how much I love this job; how much I put into it. This is my life we're talking about. I didn't even do anything wrong; this is insane.'

'It's not coming from me, Anna. It's the board of governors and the PTA. The publicity is bad for Seabrook. We're an exclusive school, and we have to be seen to take action about something so serious. Parents spend a lot of money to send their children here.'

'You can't allow them to bulldoze you into this, Craig.' I leap from the chair and slam my hand down on his desk. He flinches. Losing my temper, together with using his first name in this situation, isn't going to get me what I want, I realise, and I sit back down. 'Mr Beaumont,' I say, ensuring my tone is softer. 'Please get them to reconsider. You're the headteacher – you're the one who knows my worth. I've given eight years to this school; it's not just a job to me.'

'I'm sorry, Anna. Maybe if you'd stopped to think

138

through your actions and the possible repercussions of them the other morning . . . and now, in fact.' His eyes are lost in his furrowed brows.

My cheeks flare as my rage does too. I ball my hands into fists, digging my nails into my palm so as to stop myself losing it. *You'll lose your head* springs into my mind. Henry is behind this. He knew what releasing the footage would do to me.

'You do know it's a smear campaign, right? You're all going to look pretty foolish when the truth comes out.'

'You'll remain on full pay, but you won't be allowed onto the premises until a formal review has been conducted. If there's evidence to prove a . . . a "smear campaign", as you suggest this is, then I'm sure the decision will go in your favour and you'll be allowed to come back.'

I hold out no hope of this, though; not from the way he's coming across – it's a done deal as far as he's concerned. He's only been in post for six months, and he's probably itching to show those who questioned it that his appointment at such a young age was worthy – that he's not afraid to make the more uncomfortable decisions for the sake of the school's reputation. Or maybe he is in on this. I reel at this possibility, but now I consider it, it has merit. Craig Beaumont is a few years younger than me. I know very little about him outside of school. He might've wanted me gone because of what happened – because he felt I'd humiliated him in front of everyone at the Christmas party and might go on to be a threat to his meteoric rise. And now I've given him the perfect opportunity. He knows a lot of influential people; no doubt he has links with the police and the highways. He could have gained access to the CCTV footage and leaked it himself. The timing with Henry could have been a complete coincidence, and I've jumped to the wrong conclusion.

Or Craig Beaumont *is* Henry.

The thought comes from nowhere, and although ludicrous, it somehow makes some sense. I've not seen Henry in so many years – I might not recognise him any longer. When I did see Henry last, he was the same colouring as Craig is now and was a similar scrawny build. Since he started here, I've found Craig to be aloof – a little odd. Creepy even. Is there a reason for that? Something buried in my past that affects my view of him without conscious awareness?

I stand to leave.

'I'll see you soon,' I say firmly as I walk towards the door. Passing the wall of framed photos, I pause. I stare at the one taking pride of place. It's teacher training college – the class of 2009. I focus on each male face in turn, and another thought strikes me. What if Henry is in this group? What if he knows Craig, and that's how he's infiltrating my work life this easily?

'What are you doing?' Craig asks, his voice sharp. I ignore him as I continue to look at the people in the picture. 'Anna? I have to get on if you don't mind.' He stalks past me and opens the door. I move to leave. When I come level to him, I stop, squaring up to him.

'That's a great photo,' I say.

'Right, okay. Er . . . thank you.'

'Which one is you?' As I step away from him and walk back to it, he lets out a juddering breath. With an agitated stride, he jabs his finger at the young man in the centre of the photo and I move up close to see.

'There. I'm that one. Right, as I said, I need to get on.

140

I'll be in touch, Anna.' He lays his hands on my shoulders and physically turns me towards the door. I shrug him off me and head out.

It takes me a while to walk back to my car, my feet heavy, slow. You don't always see what's right under your nose. Has Henry been watching me more closely than I ever thought was possible? Or is Craig Beaumont someone else from my past who wants to see me suffer?

Chapter 20

FINLEY HALL CHILDREN'S HOME

Thumping music greets the girls as they round the corner and they look at each other, eyes wide, then link arms and giggle. Anna has managed to get them invites to what is supposedly going to be the coolest party in Sutton Coldfield by sucking up to Mason Lamar from her English Lit class – offering to do his essay on *An Inspector Calls* in return for getting them in. The kids from 'the scabby home' weren't high on the list of desirables, and certainly very few had ever been invited to social gatherings outside of school time. Mason's status, having been put back a year *twice*, offered their best chance yet at showing the rest of their peers that they were just normal teenagers, wanting the same things as everyone else – to hang out, get drunk and dance. This opportunity had to be snapped up. Anna and Kirsty knew going to a party where there was alcohol was bad enough given they'd only just turned fifteen, but being out after their curfew made it doubly bad and was punishable by a Frank beating, so they had to make the experience a worthwhile one.

'You did hide our backpacks well, didn't you?'

'Kirsty, stop worrying – you watched me stuff them between the rocks.'

'Yeah, sorry. Hope it doesn't rain.'

'If it does, it does. Come on, let's just enjoy the moment.' Anna begins to run towards the house, dragging Kirsty behind her. 'You do want to go, don't you?'

'Course,' she says. Her usual enthusiasm is lacking, though, and Anna turns towards her friend. 'Something's wrong. What's the matter?'

Kirsty pauses, her eyes warily looking towards the house, then back to Anna. She sucks in a breath. 'I know how I come across . . . confident, you know?'

'But?'

She shrugs. 'I'm nervous, okay?'

Anna laughs. 'What? The Kirsty Briggs I know is never nervous. Look, they won't catch us, all right? We've set it all up and Maggie and Paula have our backs. It's all good.'

'It's not that.'

Anna frowns at her friend. 'Well, what, then?'

'Chris is going to be there.'

'Ahhh, gotcha! The gorgeous Chris Connell.' Anna nudges Kirsty with her elbow. 'Well then, we will have to make sure he notices you.'

Kirsty blushes. 'Great, now I'm even more nervous.'

'Maybe you should've worn this outfit instead of letting me borrow it!' Anna looks down at her cropped top and plaid mini skirt with slits on the side.

Kirsty sighs. 'Nah. My clothes always seem to look better on you.'

144

'You do look cute in that outfit. He'd be mad not to want to chat to you.' Anna smiles at Kirsty. 'I'll sort it.'

'Don't make me look a twat, please. I don't want him to know I fancy him.'

'That kinda defeats the object.' Anna laughs again but agrees to be subtle.

The house – a large, detached one in its own grounds – is rammed when they get inside. Nearly all the kids are their age or younger, apart from Mason and his mate from year eleven – and almost all are already well on their way to being drunk. Anna and Kirsty give each other an excited look and head to the table, where every drink imaginable seems to be lined up. Kirsty pours a vodka – half a tall glass – and tops it up with orange juice. Anna sniffs it and recoils.

'Jesus, that stinks.'

'After one, you won't notice,' Kirsty says.

Anna pours some into a transparent plastic cup and necks it back. She gags, covers her mouth and grabs lemonade, swigging it straight from the bottle. Kirsty doubles over, laughing.

'You're not meant to drink it neat, you loon.'

'Maybe I should stick to alcopops,' Anna says, recovering and swiping her hand across her mouth. 'That was vile.'

'Don't show us up – we should at least try and make it look like we fit in with this lot.'

'Good point.' Anna glances around at the others. Thankfully, no one seems to have witnessed her gagging episode.

After a few more, the girls relax and begin to wander through the ground floor of the house, Anna desperately trying to find Chris. Spotting him in the kitchen with a group of lads, she leaves Kirsty's side and saunters over to them.

'Here,' one of the lads says, 'if it's not a kid from the scabby home.' They burst out laughing and Anna turns to see Kirsty disappearing out the back door.

'You're such dicks,' she says, sticking her middle finger up to Chris, then turning on her heel and heading after her. Kirsty would be mad at her for interfering – she'd probably want to leave now, ruin the night. As Anna rushes out through the kitchen, she bangs into someone.

'Hey, you're not leaving a perfectly good party, are you?' The boy puts a hand on Anna's arm, squeezing it. His eyes bore into hers and she feels her legs turn to jelly. He has brown, wavy hair that's longer than most boys wear theirs and he has a leather jacket on, the smell of patchouli wafting from it. She opens her mouth, but no words come. 'Drink?' he says. Anna nods without thinking. He takes her hand and leads her back into the room with the table of drinks. She watches in awe as he pours from a bottle; she doesn't even know what he's giving her. She doesn't recognise him from school.

'What's your name?' she asks.

'Neil. What's yours?'

'Anna.'

Someone turns the music up and the rest of Neil's words are drowned out. She nods anyway, hoping she's not coming across as stupid. Anna allows him to guide her towards the stairs, casting her eyes around to see if she can spot Kirsty. There's no sign of her; she mustn't have come back inside.

'Look, Neil, I have to find Kirsty.' She points to the kitchen. 'She went outside.'

146

'She your sister?'

'No, my best friend.'

'Sure, I'll help you find her.'

The din of the music is muffled in the garden. It's huge – not as big as Finley Hall's, but big for a house. Whoever lives here must be rich, Anna supposes. She calls for Kirsty, then so does Neil. When there's no response, Anna says she must be either back in the house, or she's left. Her chest tightens. Surely she wouldn't dump Anna and sneak back to Finley without her? They came together, they would leave together – that was the deal. Her cheeks grow hot, her breathing shallow.

'She can't have gone. I'm going back inside.'

His hand grips her wrist, yanks her back. 'Leave her. Stay with me.' He pulls Anna towards him, the heat of his body pressing against hers. Her back hits against a wall and in a split second, his lips are on her, kissing her while his hand touches her chest, then grapples with her top. He shoves it roughly up and grabs her breast, squeezing hard.

'Don't . . . please, don't,' Anna says when his mouth leaves hers. Her words are quiet, coming out in a whisper. He looks down, one hand reaching for his zip. And in that moment, the full horror of what might be about to happen dawns on her. 'Enough,' she shouts. 'I said no!'

'Get your fucking hands off of her.'

Anna feels a rush of relief hearing Kirsty's voice. She didn't leave her after all. The weight of Neil's body disappears, and suddenly she's free. Anna regrets the drink, regrets the party, regrets coming outside with a boy she doesn't even know. She just wants to go back to the home with Kirsty and forget this night.

'Thanks, Kirst. Thank God you're still here.'

While her attention is on Kirsty, Anna doesn't spot a group of boys pouring out the back door, heading towards them. And Kirsty doesn't see them until they're on her. Anna lets out a scream, but a hand clamps over her mouth, and other hands push her to the ground. Damp grass presses against her face as she's shoved belly down against it. She hears the usual taunts: 'you're lower than low,' and 'no parents, no future,' and tries to close her mind to them. Anna bucks and kicks out as much as she can, but she's no match for the two boys holding her down.

'Prick tease.' She hears one of them snarl. She forces her head up and sees Kirsty in a similar position on the ground and Neil, the boy that was with Anna, is now on top of her friend. Shit. Where is everyone else? Why aren't people coming to help them?

They are going to be raped.

The inevitability of it speeds her heart up so fast that it feels like it might burst out through her chest. But the thought also gives her a surge of strength. With a roar, she breaks one arm free and pushes her fingertips into the eye sockets of one of her attackers. He gives a roar and falls away from her. The moment gives her enough time to propel herself up, slamming her forehead into the other one's nose, blood spurting from it like tomato ketchup erupting from a bottle. His hands fly to his face, but he manages to push her back down and straddle her. She groans with the effort of pushing him off. Time seems to stand still; everything happens in slow motion.

She hears a low wailing sound and turns to look at her friend. Kirsty's thrashing beneath a body, then she stills; her sobs quieten. Is she dead? The thought gives her a second wind and she pushes with all her strength against the bleeding boy and he slumps to the ground. She's free to go to Kirsty. Anna grasps a chunk of Neil's hair, and she yanks at it hard – a clump remains in her gripped fingers as she stands and pulls her leg back. With a swift kick, her foot makes contact with the side of his head, and he goes down, a dull thud sounding as his body slams against the ground.

Anna grabs Kirsty, pulls her up off the floor and they run, Anna screaming all the way to the back door of the house.

'Those boys tried to rape us,' Anna shouts. Blank faces look at them, while others don't even acknowledge her words. Kirsty takes Anna's arm as they both push through the crowded rooms and reach the front door. Outside, in the cold air once more, they begin to run. They're halfway to where they hid their backpacks before they dare slow down.

'I'm sorry. I'm so sorry,' Anna says, bent over, her breathing rapid.

'They're the ones who should be sorry.' Kirsty's voice is shaky, her face tear-stained.

By the time they've retrieved their backpacks and walked back to Finley Hall, it's past midnight and they've barely spoken – both deep in their own thoughts. To sneak back in, they have to climb the wall to the side of the building. It takes them twice as long to break in as it did to escape, but once they're inside the relief is evident on both of their faces. Careful to avoid Frank's quarters, they go the long way around to reach their floor. Just as their dorm is in sight and they think they've got away with their misdemeanour, a bright light blinds them.

'And what time do you call this?'

They freeze, Anna shielding her eyes from the glare, Kirsty hanging her head. Then Anna realises it's a child's voice, not an adult's.

'Henry?' she whispers. 'Is that you?' She takes a few tentative steps towards the wavering beam, but stops when there's movement and what sounds like a scuffle. Is Henry fighting with someone? As she goes to walk forward again, Kirsty puts her arm in front, stopping her.

'It's okay,' she says. 'It's just Dean.' Her voice is monotone.

The light extinguishes and at the end of the corridor the figure steps out of the shadows. Anna lets out a relieved stream of breath – if it'd been Henry they'd have been in more trouble. He might not have snitched on them for sneaking out and breaking curfew – but he would've held it over their heads and blackmailed them about it, making their lives hell for weeks to come.

'Thought I heard someone creeping around. Found Henry lurking, but lucky for you, I saw him off before he realised it was you two.'

Anna's muscles tense. So Dean *had* been scuffling with her brother. She wonders what he means by 'saw him off', though. She doubted Henry would be scared away by Dean – they're both thirteen and Henry has caught up with him height-wise now. Anna does a three hundred and sixty-degree turn, peering into the shadows. She would bet her life he's still around somewhere.

Dean approaches, and as he reaches them, his face pales. 'Shit, Kirsty – what the hell happened to you?'

'Nothing. Don't worry about it,' she says. She's first to the dorm door and goes in without saying anything else.

Dean's brown eyes are filled with concern and Anna's stomach twists. Is it jealousy she's feeling? Where Henry only wishes her harm, Kirsty's brother actually seems bothered that his sister is in pain.

'It was a party,' Anna says, trying to keep her voice low. 'It got a bit . . . messy. We'll fill you in tomorrow.'

'It is tomorrow,' he says. 'But sure.' Then he looks her up and down. 'Anna – you don't look so hot either. Has something happened?'

'Later, Dean. I promise.'

Anna slips into the dorm and closes the door. She rests her head against it and listens to Dean's retreating footsteps. Then she thinks she hears another set running along outside. She turns to tell Kirsty that she fears Henry heard everything, but in the dim glow offered by the outside security light shining through the thin curtain, all she sees is a lump underneath the blankets. With feather-light steps, Anna goes to her own bed and climbs in, fully clothed, exhaustion making her limbs heavy. What a terrible party that turned out to be.

For the moment, the shock of the event numbs Anna and although her skin crawls with the echo of the boys' hands on her, her main thought as she nestles in her bed is Henry. She wishes her brother was more like Kirsty's – but of course, he *had* been once. They'd been close, always there for each other. Whose fault was it that it had changed?

Hers. She was the one who'd made things different between them. She'd put her friendship before him; she'd neglected her little brother in favour of making her own life easier.

Maybe there was a way to level with Henry. Explain

151

how she'd had to put her friends first. He needed to understand that it wasn't because she loved him any less. She'd try and talk with him tomorrow. It was time to put things right.

Chapter 21

The glass dish cracks under the force with which I throw my keys into it. The line snakes from top to bottom like a branch of lightning. *Another broken thing.* I stare at it and think about how it resembles my life – a hairline fracture that will worsen with additional pressure. I wonder how far I am from breaking.

Making coffee on autopilot is something I do most mornings, but usually once I've started sipping it I'm fully awake – and everything I do is with awareness and purpose. Looking down at my hands now, though, as I feel the heat spread to my palms, I have no memory of making this one. Sitting on the sofa, my feet up on the table, I laugh. And I don't stop. Can't. It's as though hysteria has overtaken and even the release of tears, huge drops cascading down my cheeks, doesn't quell the building frenzy of emotion that Craig Beaumont has unleashed.

I reach forward to pull a tissue from the box on the

table, and I'm reminded of Tuesday morning when Detective Inspector Walker was sitting opposite me and gave me the devastating news. If only he hadn't traced me. I could've continued in ignorant bliss, getting on with my carefully built life. But while that might've saved me from this nightmare in the short term, Henry would have found me eventually. If I know one thing about Henry, it's that he doesn't give up easily.

My eyes are drawn to the words of the riddle. The next location. My adrenaline was pumping when I solved it earlier and I had the urge to leave the house immediately – but Craig put paid to that, and now the adrenaline has been replaced with apprehension. My palms are clammy with sweat. Dark images of Finley Hall, our dorm, the bridge by the lake . . . the party and its aftermath . . . all swarm my mind. All but one of the bad things that happened then, and those happening right now, have a common denominator. Henry. Whatever he has in store for me, the result is bound to include more humiliation, public exposure, punishment. The next killing date is looming, and I'm meant to be working all this out to save a woman from being murdered.

I tried to convince DI Walker – and myself – that I wasn't the intended victim. That Henry was merely playing a game with me, that this was all *for* me, to gain my attention like before. The twisting, gnawing pain that's been inside me since this started, though, suggests otherwise; I really can't be sure if it's me or another woman who is next. I leap up from the sofa, snatch the riddle from the table and leave the house. I have no choice. I have to carry on playing the game.

* * *

154

As I drive over Shaldon Bridge, my phone rings. The display reads 'DI Walker'. I decline the call. I won't be able to lie to him convincingly – he'll hear it in my voice and know I'm doing it again: going off alone to solve the riddle. I check my wing mirror to see if I recognise any of the cars behind me. He managed to follow me last time; he's probably got eyes on me now, too. I know that whatever I find I'm going to have to hand it over to the police anyway, but I want to see it first alone.

I hope to God it's not too late for me to try and protect myself from the fallout. If Henry's agenda includes breaking the final promise we made to each other, he's planning to tell the world my secret. Perhaps getting to the next location first won't prevent that, but I have to try. In the long run Henry might not care about being exposed, given he's apparently committed multiple murders in order to reach his ultimate goal, but for me, the risk is immeasurable.

I'm the one with everything to lose.

I turn the radio up, singing the Sugababes' 'Freak Like Me' at the top of my voice in a desperate attempt to drown out the other voice inside my head – the one telling me my life is about to unravel. As the song ends, the radio presenter informs me that the news will follow. After the dozen or so adverts I check the time – ten o'clock. It feels more like afternoon; the morning has dragged. I'm approaching Penn Inn, about to go across the flyover when the ringtone of my phone drowns out the newsreader. *DI Walker* shows on the display again and my pulse judders. Dare I reject another call from the detective?

With a groan, I tap 'accept' and roll my shoulders, then press my back into the seat, my eyes trained dead ahead. 'Hello.'

'Did I catch you at a bad time?' DI Walker says. I'm about to say something idiotic like I've just got out of the shower, but a speeding ambulance zips past in the next lane, its siren blaring. Damn.

'Not particularly,' I say.

'Where are you going, Anna?' His deep voice is edged with more than just concern; the warning tone makes me shiver.

'Needed to clear my head.' *Withholding information isn't lying.* 'The headteacher at Seabrook just extended my suspension period. I'm all over the place, DI Walker.'

'I'm sorry to hear that.'

'Did the digital forensic team—'

'No.' His abruptness is jarring. I can hear other voices in the background as well as the crackle of a radio. He's with the team of detectives; I bet they're listening in. 'I'm afraid whoever hacked into the feed covered their tracks well, as suspected.'

Although I hadn't expected anything else, disappointment zaps my strength. A horn blasts as I swerve into the overtaking lane, narrowly missing the bumper of the car in front as I correct the steering wheel. I hadn't noticed it slowing down.

'Fuck,' I mutter, flinging a hand up in apology. I hope *that* doesn't find its way onto social media, too. No hacking the CCTV required this time – one of these vehicles is bound to have a dashcam.

'What was that? Are you okay?' Finally, I hear concern in DI Walker's voice.

'Yeah, but I have to go. Must focus on the road.'

'Can you please tell me where you're going? I know you must've figured the riddle out; I'm not an idiot.'

I wonder if, during the time he's had me on the phone, he's traced me – pinpointed my location, or at least managed to gain a radius. He could even have a tracking device on my car. Why hadn't I thought of that before? That's probably why I didn't see him following me yesterday and why he doesn't need to now. He already knows he can easily find me, so he doesn't need to be directly behind me. I'm tempted to pull over, check my car for a small, magnetic box or something. But in all honesty, I don't know what I'm looking for. I'll know if he's attached one soon enough – if he finds me in the next half hour or so.

'No, I haven't.' I scrunch my face up.

'Because I need to know—'

'I promise you'll be the first to know when I do. Have to go, detective.' I disconnect the call, guilt surging through my body at my false promise. Why did I do that? He's not going to trust me once he realises I outright lied.

Not wanting to waste any time now, I park as close to the café's entrance as possible. It's double yellows, but I don't intend to be long. Hopefully the civil enforcement officer will be at the other end of town. I can't see a tell-tale hi-vis jacket as I lock the car and run into Dogs In Town. The underlined part of the riddle has led me to a public place, which seems odd given Henry is on the run. Surely he won't have been in here, much less hidden something in the hope only I'd find it. But it's the only solution to the riddle I can think of.

'Can I get you anything?' a woman asks as I burst in. 'We've got speciality teas and every type of coffee,' she says, beaming at me.

'Oh, erm . . . can I just go through?' I point to the

back of the café, where I can see the patio doors opening onto a decking.

'Of course.' She gives an uneasy smile. I'm probably coming across a bit odd, but I carry on through unperturbed. I've no choice – I have to be here and I have to hunt for the hidden item. I lay my hands over my griping tummy – the thought of what might lie hidden is making my bile swirl.

It's not what I imagined out here. There's seating at park benches and plenty of room for dogs to roam, but in addition, there's a child's play area. The hairs on the back of my neck prickle and I rub my hand over it as my eyes flit around. A serial killer could well have been inches away from innocent children. Imagine if any of my pupils from Seabrook had been on the swings or climbing frame while Henry walked by them, unobserved by the adults. The thought of them being in such close proximity to someone who is willing to take lives purely for attention makes me sick. An awful thought pushes into my mind: if he's been watching me, what's stopping him from snatching a child from Seabrook? The security is good, but some of the older children are allowed to walk to and from school, their parents confident a small village like Staverton is safe.

As I walk around, my mind scrambles to spot something unusual, a hint to where Henry has hidden the next item. I sit on the bench and scan every part of the grounds. He could've chosen anywhere. I swivel around on the bench to look behind, catching sight of the bronze plaque on the back. It's a thank you for a large donation to the dog café: *With thanks to the Walcott family*. The name rings a bell, but the memory floats away as I turn back.

Think, Anna. And then it seems obvious. If someone

were to come here and try to remain low-key, they'd likely sit on this very bench because it's not in direct view of the other customers. I lower my head and my pulse skips as I notice freshly dug earth in front of the rose bush next to me.

Jumping up from the bench, I give a wary look around. There's a couple sitting at a table, their dog lazily slumped on the ground underneath, and two women deep in conversation over their lattes, each with a handbag-sized dog sitting on the chair beside them – but once I duck down, I'm not in plain view. Henry must've realised this too when he chose this spot.

Or, of course, there's a big chance that this area of dug soil is where one of the dogs has buried a juicy bone and I'm about to feel really stupid. I pause, checking around to see if there's anywhere else that could be the hiding place. The earth is neatly laid back, though – a dog would've left it messy. This has to be it. It's worth a try, at least.

I take a deep breath, plunge my fingers into the damp soil and begin scooping the earth into a pile, hoping whatever is buried isn't sharp. With that sudden thought, I slow down, use the side of my palm rather than delving my fingertips in first; I wouldn't put it past Henry to hide something that could cause me injury. With the next scoop, a plastic bag is partially revealed. I pull at the corner and the loose soil slips off as I drag it fully out of its grave. I sit back on my heels, the carrier bag in my hands. Half of me wants to delay opening it – just take the evidence straight to the police. But, no doubt as Henry anticipated, my fearful curiosity wins over and I slowly open the bag. Inside is a large, flat envelope and I'm surprised to feel a snag of disappointment. Is this just another riddle?

After a surreptitious glance around the gardens, I open the A4 envelope and peek inside, my breath held. It looks like it's nothing more than some photos. My adrenaline level reduces – they can't depict anything too bad. Henry didn't own a camera when we were at Finley; I never saw him with one anyway. And even if he did have photo evidence of our shared secret, surely he'd have used them before now – blackmailed me or something.

I pull them fully out. My jaw slackens. I scan through the photos quickly – there are five of them – then I focus in on the first again. A sob catches in my throat and I throw my head back, looking skywards in some vain attempt to rid the images from my mind. My hands start to shake violently as I look through them again, and without warning vomit erupts from my mouth. Green bile pools on the grass behind the bush. I wipe away the remnants with the back of my hand and get to my feet. I only manage a few paces before collapsing back against the trunk of a tree, the rough bark pushing painfully into my spine. But I can't move; I need the support. I survey the area.

'Where are you, you bastard?' My initial shock and sadness is replaced with a hot, gut-wrenching anger deep in my belly. I propel myself away from the tree and stomp around the garden, shouting a string of words I can't even decipher myself – they flow out of my mouth like lava. Rage like this hasn't surfaced for years and I frighten myself. But I've a right to be mad. How could he do this to me? Ross is the last person I'd ever suspect of betraying me.

The woman who asked me if I wanted anything comes out the patio doors, a bemused look on her face, and the other customers are all staring at me. I ignore them and push past the woman to get back outside. To anyone watching, I must look so rude. Is Henry witnessing this?

'Come out, come out wherever you are.' I shout as soon as I'm standing in the street, spit flying from my mouth. 'Think you're clever, do you?' A woman walking by with a toddler pulls them in close, shooting me an alarmed, judgemental glare. Realisation hits me – I'm in a public place, and I've already gained online notoriety; being seen like this will only cement their belief that I'm unhinged and not fit to teach children. I shut my mouth, and hurry towards my car, quickly getting in and slamming the door. I throw the envelope on the passenger seat and sit, motionless, shock seeping through me.

Maybe I shouldn't really be mad at Ross. I don't even know when these photos were taken – although from what Ross is wearing, the way his hair is, it's pretty recent, not years ago.

Henry has decided he will tear down every part of the life I've worked so hard for; the life I love. He's made it blatantly obvious he wants revenge. Wants me to suffer before whatever macabre conclusion he has planned for me.

I can't let Henry win. Or, more to the point, I must not lose – because this isn't just a game.

Chapter 22

I see right through your words in everything you do.
Teary eyes, broken heart: life has torn you apart.

MAY

One year ago

The smell was like nothing he'd known before. Or maybe it was similar to the butcher's, now he thought about it – only much more potent. Overpowering. He stepped away from the bloody mess on the plastic sheets and stuck his head outside the bathroom door, gulping in some fresher air. He should've brought a mask. He'd become cocky, he recognised that. Thought it would be easy now this was his fourth killing. Even a serial killer can be surprised, though. At least there was a human side to him still, he considered. All this murder hadn't diminished that part of him – he wasn't an evil psychopath like he would be portrayed as in the media.

The media attention would be a challenge. They'd think

he'd done it all for the wrong reasons – the pseudo-psychologists and psychiatrists would come out of the woodwork giving their two penn'orth, their theories about why he is the way he is; what traumas in his childhood had affected him and made him into a monster. They'd say that his inability to maintain relationships had turned him into a woman-hater. They'd all be wrong. And that was a hard pill to swallow. He knew there was a small part of him that would want to put them right; ensure they printed the truth.

He just needed to find out what that truth was.

With more neutral air in his nostrils, he went back into the compact bathroom – to the torso with its remaining two limbs – and bent down to retrieve the saw. Sweat beaded his brow and dark patches spread under his armpits. His hands were wet beneath the gloves but he continued to hack away, determined to finish the job. While he worked, he imagined all the ways in which he was going to tear *her* life apart, too. The rush of adrenaline his fantasy created was enough to power him through even the toughest bones.

Chapter 23

My grip is so tight on the wheel that by the time I park outside my house, my fingers are locked and I have to consciously unhook them. The envelope sits beside me and in this moment all I want to do is tear it up or burn it, together with the evidence inside. I couldn't make out the woman's identity because her back was either to the camera or Ross was obscuring her in every image. But one thing is painfully clear: my husband is having an affair. I want to make it disappear; pretend I never saw them. But then, like an erupting volcano, my emotions spill out and I grab the envelope and storm down the road like a woman possessed.

'Go on!' I shout to no one in particular, 'Film this. Put this on fucking social media.' I look around, half expecting to see the man from earlier watching my meltdown again. But the pavement is empty. The Right Price estate agency office is up ahead. I feel sick as I approach and look through the window to see Ross leaning over Yasmin: too close; too cosy. It all clicks together. It's Yasmin – "Yaz", as he likes to call her. Young, pretty, and single. A perfect marriage-wrecker. I launch through the entrance and Ross bolts upright. His face lights up when he sees me, then immediately darkens.

'What's happened? Are you okay?' He brushes a hand through his hair. I wonder how many times it's been Yasmin's hands doing that. Touching my husband. Screwing my husband. I give a sharp laugh.

'Why wouldn't I be okay, Ross?' I glare at him, then shoot Yasmin a look I hope reflects the hurt, anger and betrayal I feel. Ross frowns – the deep one – then his jaw slackens when he spots the envelope in my hand. He looks awkwardly towards Yasmin and she gets up.

'Good to see you, Anna.' She meets my gaze, as though she's challenging me, and smiles.

'Good to know you're fucking my husband,' I say.

'Christ, Anna.' Ross rushes towards me. I bat his arm away as he reaches it out.

'Really? Christ, Anna? *Christ, Anna*!' I repeat, his words causing heat to travel up through me, and I feel like a pressure cooker with the steam trapped inside it. 'What's that meant to mean?' If he's chastising me for saying such a thing, I'll show him just how loud and profane I can be. If he doesn't like how I'm reacting, he shouldn't have caused it.

'Let's talk in private, shall we?' He turns to Yasmin, who's now sitting on the edge of her desk, arms crossed, watching the unfolding drama as though she's merely a spectator – not the reason it's happening. 'Yaz, can you finish up here, please?'

I scoff hearing him call her Yaz. Then a shooting pain

in my chest steals my breath. I rub my clenched fist in a circular motion over my heart, but it doesn't help. Ross hastily bundles me out and closes the door. He gestures for me to begin walking towards home, and we do so in silence – all my anger directed inwards. I run through what I want to say, but I know that once we're behind closed doors none of my rehearsed speech will make it to the final conversation. Things always go so much more smoothly in your mind, when there's only your own monologue and no interruptions or reaction from the other party.

As soon as we cross the threshold, Ross heads for the kitchen and opens the fridge. He pours two large wines, hands me one and then leans against the worktop.

'What's all this about, Anna?' He glances at the envelope under my arm and I pull it out and slam it on the breakfast bar. We stand opposite each other, the evidence between us.

'Guess what's inside there?' I say, tilting my glass towards the envelope, before taking a large gulp.

'I've no idea,' he says. 'Why don't you enlighten me.'

'You first, Ross. Why don't you tell me what's been going on. Get everything out into the open, eh?'

'Nothing out of the ordinary. Aside from your serial killer brother wreaking havoc these last few days of course.' He takes a sip of drink, but his eyes don't leave the envelope. 'Which has affected you rather badly – as it would anyone.'

I laugh. 'I see where you're going here. You're about to tell me that because of Henry and the fact I've been suspended from work indefinitely, that this is all *stress*. That my behaviour is unreasonable, that I've jumped to some wild conclusion about you having it away with your employee. Is that about it?'

'Hang on, you've been what?' Ross straightens, giving me an alarmed look. 'You've lost your job?'

'Don't change the subject – we were talking about you and Yasmin. Answer my question.' I glare at him and he seems to buckle under my gaze.

'I'm not having it away with Yaz,' he mutters, looking down at his feet as he shuffles them like an embarrassed teen caught out by his parents.

'What are you doing with her, then?'

He shifts his weight, and then stretches; his spine cracks. 'What's in the envelope?'

I can't play this game with him – I've been embroiled in enough of those and it could drag on for hours, so I push the envelope towards him. Watch him closely as he sucks in breath through his nose and holds it while he pulls the photos out. His expression remains neutral, but his jaw clenches as he sees himself pictured on the bench at Dogs In Town café with a woman – who I now know to be Yasmin – their bodies close, arms entwined as they're captured kissing.

'This isn't . . . it's not . . .' he stumbles over his words. 'It's not what it looks like.'

'Really? According to you, Ross, the camera never lies. Isn't that what you told me?'

'These are photoshopped,' he says, after staring at them a good while. 'Amazing what they can do—'

'Don't, Ross. Please. At least have the decency to tell the truth now you've been caught out.'

Each second of silence is like a stab into my pounding heart. He's trying to find the right words, I assume. Those that will cause the least damage. To me and to him. I'm reminded of the time we had Beau, our first and last dog. He'd bought her for me as a fifth wedding anniversary present and we'd instantly fallen in love with her – a rescue black Lab who had endless energy and love to give. We'd only had her for four months when it happened. While Ross was walking her along Teignmouth Beach, another dog had run up and attacked her, causing so much damage the vet couldn't save her. It'd taken Ross three hours to tell me what had happened, and even then, he struggled with telling me the outcome, building up to it painfully slowly – dragging out the ending because he knew how upset I'd be. His inability to deliver bad news was endearing in a way. Then, at least. Now, not so much. All he's doing is prolonging the agony.

'Say it, Ross. Tell me the truth. These photos are not fake. But clearly our marriage is.' I shrug, a gesture I know appears more blasé than I feel. I snatch the photos from him, slamming one down. 'You kissing Yasmin on the bench,' I say. Then I put the next one on top. 'You and her around the back of the tree with your hand up her blouse,' I say, my voice rising. Next one. Slam. 'Oh, you've changed it up in this one – moved to your car. Too risky in the *café gardens* for you, was it? Here's you unzipping your trousers . . .' Tears burn my cheeks. I slam the next one down. 'You and her—'

'Stop!' Ross smacks his hand down on top of the photos. 'Yes. Yes. I know.'

'What do you know?'

'I know what comes next. I've done a terrible thing, Anna. I'm so, so sorry.' He drops his head, then puts his hands to his face, covering it so I can't see his expression.

'Well, that makes it all right then. How *could* you, Ross?'

I hear small sobbing sounds. 'I'm sorry,' he says again, the words losing clarity in his cupped palms. Why, when I'm the one who's been hurt, do I have the urge to put my arms around *him*, comfort *him*? But, even with the devastating realisation I've been cheated on, the love we have, or had, for each other is the over-riding emotion, and it's one I've always treasured. I need it, like I need air to breathe.

'Why?' My voice sounds strangled. 'Why have you done this to me?'

He removes his hands from his face and takes my hands in them. They're trembling. He closes his eyes, takes a deep breath, and I know I'm not going to like what's coming.

'I tried so hard, Anna. But as long as I can remember I assumed I'd have kids.'

I withdraw my hands like he's given me an electric shock. Not this again.

'You agreed,' I say, my mouth twisted. 'We both made the decision, *together*, not to have children. You can't push this onto me now, that's not fair. You can't make it the reason you cheated, Ross.'

'I thought I could change what I wanted and be happy as a family of two, but after a few months I realised how deeply unhappy I was.'

'So you should've talked to me. Shared this with me. Not found solace in another woman's arms, Ross. That's not how marriages work.'

'I know, babe.'

I wince at his word choice. 'So now what?'

'I don't know. I do love you, Anna. Always have, always

170

will. But I need more. I should've left when I knew we wanted different things, but I couldn't bring myself to make that break.'

'If these photos hadn't surfaced now, then – when would you have told me? Or were you going to just carry on your sordid affair behind my back? Have your fucking cake and eat it?'

'It's not sordid.'

'Oh, I'm sorry. I thought a married man sneaking around, screwing another woman would be classed as dishonourable. I'm pretty sure if the roles were reversed—'

'Yes, okay. You're right. I'm an awful person. A liar, a cheat. I've been unfaithful and I hate myself for it.'

'Yet you continued.' I'm aware my tone is harsh; I sound nasty. But what does he expect? Forgiveness? For me to give him an easy time and give my blessing? 'How long has it been going on?'

He drops his head again and I put my hands on his face, lifting it up, forcing him to look me in the eye.

'Six months,' he whispers. 'I was trying to find the right time . . .'

'Must've been so difficult for you,' I say, sarcasm mixing with vitriol in my voice. 'There was me thinking things couldn't get any worse.' The tears which were threatening begin to run freely down my face. Ross looks away as I press my fingertips to them.

'I knew time was running out, that I'd have to tell you soon. Then your serial killer brother forced the issue.'

'Ha. Even a psychopath was looking out for me, it seems. I knew when you looked at that riddle that you were worried.'

'When you went out for the walk I snuck out too and

went to the café to try to intercept whatever was there, but there was nothing. He must've been watching the place to make sure it would be you, not me, that found the photos.'

'But how did you know where to go? What was the significance of the riddle to you?'

'The fact it was about lying and cheating was enough to make me think it was about me, but then the last line about the dogs, well, it had to point to the café. And that bench—' he points to one of the photos, '—there's a dedication to Yasmin's family on it.'

I reel. My God, Henry excelled himself with this riddle. I knew the name Walcott was familiar. My nails dig into my palms as questions swamp my mind, then spill out of my mouth.

'Was it where you first had sex with her? Or declared your undying love? Made plans? Discussed the names of your future children?'

'God, Anna.' He roughly runs his fingers through his hair. 'I didn't want you to find out like this, but . . .'

I hold my breath as I witness Ross struggle to articulate what he needs to say. The fact that there's more, something extra beyond what's already been unearthed, throws me into panic. He's about to add another layer to the betrayal. And there's only one thing that springs to mind. My blood runs cold and I know that right now I will not be able to bear what he is about to say. Because I already know.

'You need to leave, Ross. Now.' I walk away from him, go to the fridge and pull the wine bottle from the lower rack. I pour myself a drink, filling it to the brim, and begin gulping it down. I feel his eyes on me, pitying.

'Anna, I swear if it could've been with you . . .'

If it could've been with me? *God, yes – if only*. I lay a hand on my stomach, a deep yearning overwhelming me.

'Go. I can't look at you,' I say, choking back a sob. I sense him moving towards the hallway. I've given him an easy way out by not making him say the words. By not having to speak of his ultimate betrayal out loud.

When I hear the door slam, I pour a second glass and take another glug. My legs tingle, my head spins a little – I don't think I've even eaten today. This won't end well. But then, as an image of Yasmin's swelling belly flashes in my mind, I realise there's no happy ending to this story for me – that much is obvious.

The world is already tilting around me, the edges of my vision fading and growing fuzzy. I stumble through the house and out of the front door.

'Well done, Henry! You win this round,' I shout. I hold my glass in the air in a toast. 'Come out, you fucking coward – be a man and face me.' A mother who is walking past with her child tuts loudly and grabs hold of the girl's hand, speeding up. She glances back over her shoulder, her face filled with outraged judgement. I laugh loudly. 'This is nothing, love. You should meet my *brother*.' I stagger back into the house and drain the bottle of wine, then slide down the wall into a crouch and break into sobs. *At some point, the drink will numb the pain*, I think, as the room goes dark.

I'm floating up, my body light. I open my eyes, snapping them closed again when I only see the spinning ceiling lights of the kitchen. The last thing I remember is finishing the bottle of wine while sitting on the cold tiles.

The spinning sensation continues even though I've closed my eyes. I'm moving. I'm being carried.

I try to speak, but my mouth won't work. Suddenly, I'm falling. Not fast, like one of those awful dreams – it's gentler, and then I feel something firm beneath me. A soft layer of warmth covers me and my mind drifts away. I hear a voice, but it seems so far off that I don't try to respond. I couldn't even if I wanted to.

Is this what dying feels like?

MAY 12th

One day to go

Chapter 24

My tongue is stuck to the roof of my mouth. I pop my index finger in to release it and it comes free with a dry clicking noise. I drag my other arm out from under the duvet and tap my hand over the bedside table, hopeful of finding the glass of water I usually take to bed. My hand makes contact with it and I manage to slowly manoeuvre myself so my other elbow props me up enough to enable me to drink. It's tepid, and as soon as the glug of water lands in my stomach, it contracts to expel it.

'Oh, God.' I practically crawl to the bathroom, stick my head over the toilet bowl and vomit. I feel like someone is ripping my insides out. My heart has been torn out already, so that's one less thing to worry about. Images flash through my mind, like an old cine film. Each one sends a shockwave through me, and each recalled confession from Ross's mouth is like a punch to the stomach. Then the memory of throwing him out surfaces, but it's fuzzy around the outsides. Did I tell him never to set foot in this house again? I groan. He'll have gone to Yasmin's. Did I send my husband directly into the arms of his lover?

I hear my phone vibrating on my bedside table. It might be Ross. I pull myself up from my kneeling position by the toilet, to standing, the pressure in my head intensifying. As I reach the bed and stretch across the mattress to grab my mobile, I have a strange feeling – like a nervous, butterfly sensation – and with it comes the knowledge that I didn't take myself to bed last night. Someone tucked me in, said goodnight. I'm sure of it. Ross must've come back home despite me telling him to leave. I pick up my phone and see that the new message is from Serena.

Are you OK? I heard about the extended suspension. What utter crap, I'm so sorry. Call me. Come over for a Wine & Whinge night. Love you, Sxx

I tap out a quick response saying I'm angry about it all and that I'll call her soon. I end the message with *Ross is having an affair and has left me* – then delete it before sending. I can't do that over text. And besides, seeing it in black and white gives me palpitations, so I can't imagine what talking about it might do. I'll wait until this ticking bomb with Henry is over and deal with it properly then.

If I'm alive then.

I scroll through the other messages. None are from Ross. I clutch my chest – pain crushes it as I remember.

Yasmin's pregnant.

The horrifying reality slams me hard, and I drag myself up and off the bed, bile burning my throat as it makes its way into my mouth again. Giddiness makes me stumble, and I crash my shoulder into the door frame, hot tears bubbling from my eyes. Ross had told me he would rather

178

be with me and not have children, than not be with me but have them.

Liar. Liar. Liar.

I let out an animal-like howl, not bothering to wipe the tears and snot from my face, letting it all run into my open mouth. It's not until after I'm sick again that I clean myself up. It's no good acting like a victim. I'll save that for tomorrow when everything will come to an end anyway, for better or for worse. The thought, dark as it is, somehow bolsters me. One more day to find Henry and stop him. Even though I'm ninety per cent certain I'm going to be the next woman to die, there's still a ten per cent chance I'm wrong and it really will be another woman's life he ends tomorrow. His sixth. That we know of.

But there hasn't been another riddle. No clue, no new location to go to, no treasure to unearth.

'What's your plan, Henry?' I rasp, peering at my reflection in the bathroom mirror and cringing at the sight. I brush my teeth, and with some effort, manage to plaster on some foundation to give my skin some colour – cover the sickly, sallow, hung-over complexion. For good measure, I apply my favourite orange-brown lipstick and immediately feel more myself.

If I'm to face the day – deal with the aftermath of last night and the new challenges in store – I must pull myself together. I make a coffee and break off a slab of chocolate – the best hangover cure known to man. As I stare at my mobile willing Ross to call, it rings and my heart flips. But it's not Ross's name that shows on the display. *DI Walker* flashes up.

I press reject. I'm not ready yet.

My mug clinks against Ross's as I pop it in the dishwasher, and I have to focus hard to stop the tears coming again. It's the little things that cause the most devastation. 'Huh!' I stand with my hands on my hips, a U2 song popping into my mind: 'It's the little things that give you away,' I say out loud, as something tugs on my memory. In a lot of criminal cases you hear that it's something small, seemingly inconsequential, that when put under the microscope gives context or links the pieces of the puzzle together.

Have I missed something else in Henry's riddles? A hidden meaning; an extra clue – something to point me in a certain direction?

I have yet to venture outside, and now I rush to the front doorstep to check if another envelope awaits. Nausea swills in my belly – whether from the anticipation or the hangover, I don't know.

Nothing.

I peer up the street, walk up the path and step out into the road. Seagulls swoop and I'm about to swear at them when I notice a man in the distance. He seems to be looking in my direction, but then turns and goes the opposite way, back towards Ness Cove. I squint, hoping it will give me clearer vision so I can tell if it's the same man I've seen outside my house before. Just because I've only noticed him on two occasions doesn't mean he's not been hanging around for longer. Could *he* be Henry?

Retreating back inside my house, I slam the door and lock it. Then I check the back door and all the windows to make sure everything's secure. By the time I go back to the kitchen and pick up my mobile, I've had three missed calls from DI Walker.

The knock at the back door sends a bolt of fear right through my body and I freeze. I can make out a large, dark mass through the frosted glass panel. My first instinct is to hide – duck down behind the breakfast bar; pretend I'm not here. But the flight response is replaced by fight, and I slide a knife from the block and approach the door with it gripped in my hand, my arm raised. My breathing shallows and the sound of my heart whooshes inside my ears. The knocking becomes more urgent, each rap like a gunshot. I screw my eyes up. It could be Ross, in which case this stress reaction is wasted. And I'd best not attack him for the second time this week.

The knocking stops. Has he gone?

I open my eyes, force my shoulders down, take some slow breaths; then, with the knife held in an attack position, I unlock the door.

Chapter 25

DI Walker's horrified look as I fling the door open suggests he wasn't expecting a knife-wielding maniac.

'I tried calling,' he says quickly, one hand up in defence. 'I was worried when you didn't answer.'

'The front door might've made a more sensible entry point,' I say, lowering the knife, my whole body trembling with the adrenaline. 'You'd better come in.' It's as he's stepping inside that I notice the envelope in his other hand. I frown. 'What, now he's leaving them on the back step?'

'This?' he holds up the thick envelope. 'No, sorry. I thought going through some evidence might be useful.'

I chew on the inside of my cheek. 'Time is running out, I suppose.'

'We are up against it,' he says. 'May I?' He indicates the stool at the breakfast bar.

'Sure.' I push the knife back into its slot in the block and take the stool opposite the detective.

'How are you doing?' he says, his expression etched with an empathy that immediately makes me want to cry.

'Well, let's see. I'm embroiled in some whacko game with a serial killer, I've been suspended from the job I love, and . . .' I suck in air, blowing it out slowly to ease a pang of nausea. 'I've found out that my husband has been shagging his employee.' DI Walker raises one eyebrow and grimaces. To add to his discomfort, I add: 'Oh, and she's pregnant with his baby.' I'd yet to vocalise the words and now I've uttered them, it's become real. Fact. I didn't think your heart could hurt – like proper physical pain – unless you were having a heart attack. I was wrong. Tears blur my vision; I blink rapidly. 'All in all, it's been a great week.'

DI Walker nods like none of this is news. Which mostly, it isn't. He can't know about Ross and Yasmin or the baby, though, surely? *Please tell me I'm not the last to know.* Maybe his interrogation training just means that he is good at masking his reactions.

'I'm sorry you're having such a tough time of it, Anna.' He seems genuine, his eyes sorrowful as they look into mine, and I almost lose myself in the sharp blue irises – they always look so bright, unlike mine, which today I know are dulled by my hangover. I wonder if he sees that now, or whether there's something else he notices, because they narrow ever so slightly. I drop my gaze, worried that he might read what's behind them. In need of a change of subject, I point to the envelope.

'What delights are in there, then?' My voice is mono-tone, weary.

'How about we discuss it over coffee?'

'Sure you don't want anything stronger?'

'It's nine-thirty a.m., Anna. There's one day to go, so we need clear heads.' I smart at his judgemental tone. But making a jokey comment to a detective working a murder case was probably not the best idea.

'Sorry. I tend to use humour as a coping mechanism.' I smile thinly before getting up. I make coffee on autopilot, my attention on DI Walker as he sifts through the contents of the envelope. There's a lot in it, from what I can tell.

'Do you have family, Detective?' I'm not sure why I ask this – maybe to talk about something more normal before the inevitable discussion about Henry and his victims, or to somehow find a connection, something relatable between us. DI Walker looks thoughtful but doesn't answer. 'Or are you told not to share personal information with sisters of serial killers?'

Now he laughs.

'Boundaries are there for everyone's protection, Anna.'

As I place his coffee down in front of him, I catch sight of what he's been looking at. They appear to be crime scene photographs, if the yellow tape cordoning off the entrance to a house is anything to go by. My stomach lurches.

'Do you think you'd be willing to go through these with me?' He taps the top photo, but I don't look down at it again. I want to say 'in a minute' but I'm very aware that every minute counts. 'I know it won't be easy,' he says. 'I'm sorry to even ask, but because of your connection to Henry, you might see something in them that we've overlooked. It's not exactly usual practice . . .'

'I need to know everything, DI Walker. If you want my help finding Henry, I should probably know all the details.' I feel myself blushing. *He* also needs to know all the details, including the fact I went to the riddle's location yesterday without telling him.

'Yes, agreed; but this isn't some cosy murder mystery on the telly, Anna. What I'm going to show you, tell you, is gruesome; it *will* play on your mind.'

'My mind is a mess already. It can't get much worse.'

Miss Graves had a saying that used to annoy the hell out of me, and it comes to mind now: 'famous last words'. The queasy feeling returns after I've seen the first four crime scene photos, and he's only shown me the scenes so far, not the actual women Henry killed. The lifeless bodies, the violated corpses are still to come. DI Walker lays a reassuring hand on my forearm.

'If you want a break . . .'

I glance at the kitchen clock. It's ten a.m. and we're wasting time. 'No. Keep going.'

'You're a brave woman, Anna. We do appreciate what you're doing.'

A shiver tracks up my spine. Am I brave? Or stupid? Either way, hearing a detective saying that gives me pause. The way he spoke those words was like he knows what's coming – that I'm putting myself in the direct line of fire. I lick my lips, my tongue catching on the dried lipstick.

'Are you going to show me the women now?' There's a quiver to my voice – a response I've little control over. I don't want to see, yet I think I need to.

'Yes, selected ones. Not every detail, but enough to give you the idea.' He closes his eyes, taking a deep breath, like he's preparing himself. But he's seen them before, has just been looking through them, so he must actually be preparing himself for *my* reaction.

My pulse races as he places the first one in front of me. Then the next. After about ten seconds, he lays the next on top. I'm reminded how I did this to Ross last night, only I was slamming them down one by one, not gently placing them like DI Walker is doing. He watches for my reaction to each one, seemingly judging whether it's safe to continue. I say nothing as the images are laid out: a close-up of the victim's lips – sewn shut with hideous large, roughly made stitches that look like black wire; a gaping, bloody mouth, the tongue removed; a tongue sandwiched between two slices of mouldy bread; a chest cracked open, ribs spread. I press my hand to my own chest, rubbing the pain away with circular motions. Another photo is a wide-angle shot, taken from further away – hacked-off limbs surround a torso. I snap my eyelids closed. The thought of how these women suffered crushes me. I can't speak. My vocal cords are paralysed, and my throat is so tight I can't swallow. I'm aware of my breathing; how rapid and shallow it is.

'Slow breaths, Anna. You're hyperventilating and you'll faint.'

I do as he says. It takes a few minutes for my breathing to steady. I can see there's another photo and I reach across to take it. DI Walker puts his hand over mine, stopping me.

'You don't have to. I shouldn't have asked you to look. None of this is your fault, Anna.' His eyes bore into mine and I have to look away.

Despite the evidence, it still doesn't seem possible that Henry is a sadistic killer, and my brain struggles to link the two. I couldn't have known he would do such terrible things. Could I? I would've done something – told the authorities, reported his behaviour, had I believed for one moment that after I last saw him he'd go on to murder five women.

You've let people get away with things before.

It's as though the devil is on my shoulder, reminding me of my past mistakes. I close my mind to the voice, push the demons back into their boxes again and concentrate on the here and now. I can't fix the past. But I can affect the present, and hopefully create a better future.

'I'm fine. Show me the next one.' I brace myself.

Chapter 26

Cross my heart and hope to die,
Stick a needle in my eye.

FEBRUARY

This year

He dragged the body to the doorway and let go, her arms slamming to the floor with a thud. Standing back, he looked around at the penultimate murder scene. Adrenaline shot through his veins. One more after this and he'd be done. How would he feel once it was over? A little lost, he imagined. Bored, even. The planning, the execution, the end goal; they'd taken over his life for such a long time, driven his existence, given it meaning. He wasn't sure he'd ever feel as though justice had been done, that his job was truly over. He picked at the tip of his gloved index finger and found a tiny hole. *Dammit.* He went to his kit bag and pulled out another, swapping it and pocketing the damaged one. He couldn't slip up now – he was almost at the final hurdle.

He'd dreamed, fantasised, about finally having *her* in front of him. She'd been the focus of all his hurt and pain, his inability to move on; he could barely wait to punish her. But he had to be patient. Not only in getting to her and ensuring everything was in place, but when he had her, too. Killing her would be pointless before he got what he wanted.

Shaking himself awake from the fantasies of what was to come, he took the Tupperware box from his bag and returned to the dead woman. For the first time since his debut, he kneeled down beside the body and touched it. Took in the details. He hadn't allowed himself to do that for the last three murders. He'd tried to keep any private thoughts, sentiment, out of the process. It was never about them; it was always about her.

The woman was about fifty years old, he guessed. Obviously she looked after herself; she was fit – a sporty type if the photos on her dresser were anything to go by, but not too muscular. Still had feminine curves. She wasn't like those body-building women who were all sinewy and shiny. He appreciated women who made an effort. He also appreciated clever women – a hangover from living at Finley Hall. Miss Graves had drummed it into everyone, sometimes literally, that intelligence mattered. Girls in particular had to be clever, she'd said, to make sure they could fight for equality, like she'd had to do to become manager of the home: because ultimately, it was a man's world. He huffed. Such bullshit. In his experience, women fought for equality, then when they had a sniff of it, they scuttled back into the safety of their stereotypes and let the men do the hard stuff. They picked and chose and that really got his goat. If it was a promotion, more money they wanted, then they would shout from the rooftops, but when it came to security, they weren't so vocal. Who did they turn to when they were frightened, concerned for their safety? Men. Men were the protectors. Men had the real power. He was proof of that.

As he positioned the heart from the last victim next to the freshly murdered woman, he laughed. *Joke's on them*, he thought. He stuck the cross of the necklace into the cold, dead muscle – it protruded from the heart like a tiny headstone. Then, he scooped the woman's left eye out, jammed the needle into it and lay that beside the heart.

'Cross my heart and hope to die. Stick a needle in my eye.'

If she didn't work it out after all that, she wasn't as clever as he'd given her credit.

Given that he was making it so clear who his final intended victim was, an obvious problem was that the police could offer her protection. He enjoyed a challenge, though, and he was resourceful.

He'd find a way.

Chapter 27

'This is the last,' DI Walker says, lifting the photo.

'Hang on,' I say. I don't know why, but I have a sudden urge to tell him about my own photos first. I get up and pull the envelope from the kitchen drawer. I'm reluctant to look at the detective; I don't want to see his annoyance, so I hand it over without making eye contact. His deep sigh about covers it. I stand back, holding my breath as he flicks through them, and listen to his steady respiration. He's good at keeping calm – a useful skill for his job, no doubt. In my own line of work I'm usually able to remain calm, too. But as the past few days have demonstrated, the same cannot be said for my private life.

'This is how you found out,' he says. 'I assume these were found at the location the riddle directed you to?'

I nod.

'You're playing a dangerous game here.'

'Well that's not news, is it?' I lean against the kitchen wall, my hands behind my back, palms flat against the smooth finish. I push myself off then fall against it, repeating this motion, bouncing like a nervous child.

'Seriously, Anna.' DI Walker glares at me, and I stop. 'I can't have you running around the countryside trying to get to the evidence before us. And removing it? Christ, you could be charged with obstruction, or worse, tampering. You could be handed down a prison sentence – don't you get it? This is the second time you've crossed the line. You promised you'd inform me if you worked it out.'

His expression is no longer a picture of serenity. I've really rattled his cage and his angry words hit me like arrows. I've been so focused on protecting myself from past mistakes, I hadn't given much thought to the new ones I was making.

'I was going to hand it over. I'm sorry. I wasn't in my right mind, Detective Walker. I panicked.' I sit back down opposite him. 'This isn't your usual family drama. I'm not accustomed to dealing with family members at all, let alone when they're psychopaths.'

'Not all killers are psychopaths.'

I'm not sure I agree with his view. 'Isn't it more like they can pretend to be normal? Conceal their psychopathy behind a mask?'

'Professionals are more often than not divided about what makes a serial killer. The usual questions are bandied about: are they born, are they made, et cetera. But certainly most have been shown to have had difficult, often abusive, childhoods.'

'By that standard, I should be a serial killer too, then.'

We both fall silent, holding each other's gazes. The silence stretches and I don't feel the need to fill the gap, for a change.

DI Walker breaks first. 'What was the location?' he says, his voice softer.

'It was right there, in the last line of the riddle. Dogs In Town – it's a café in Torquay. Buried beside the bench under a pretty rose bush.' Anger reignites within me as I explain about the significance of the place, about how Ross had known it was all about him and had even gone to try and find what Henry had left before me. DI Walker doesn't appear surprised to hear this – I can't help wonder if it's the type of thing he'd do, too.

'When we're done here,' he says when I finish, 'I'm taking you to the station so you can give me the *full* details – every single one – in a written statement.'

I lower my gaze, embarrassed at being chastised. 'Of course,' I mumble.

He gathers the photos of Ross and Yasmin and puts them back in the envelope. 'I'll take these, thanks.'

'Fine,' I say, looking up. 'I really don't want to look at them again anyway.'

'Okay.' He straightens, jiggles his shoulders and draws a breath. 'Back to the murder cases.' DI Walker puts the final photo on the bar in front of me. 'Every murder has a similar pattern, in that his victims have all been female, and apart from the first, each subsequent killing involved removing a body part.' He gets back into his rhythm as though he hadn't been interrupted. 'The final scene – well, Henry took the heart of his previous victim and put it beside the part he removed from this one.' He taps the image with his index finger.

I lean over and look down to see a heart and an eyeball. The heart has something protruding from it – I move my face closer and see it's a gold cross necklace. My stomach

195

turns to liquid. I've seen it before. Mother's? But it's the needle sticking out of the eye that causes my blood to course through my veins; the adrenaline makes my head woozy.

'I didn't bring the photos depicting the same thing in the other cases for security reasons, but the needle in the eye has been the one constant in every one and we've concluded that's why one was attached to the first riddle. It's his calling card. But we're not sure what it means.'

'I think I know.' I push back from the breakfast bar and on shaky legs, stumble towards the stairs. I make it to the bathroom and throw up – hot, brown liquid splattering the white bowl. When I've expelled the coffee, I continue dry-retching, my eyes streaming, nose running. I go to tear toilet roll off, but there's none left. Probably used that up earlier. I'm about to use my sleeve when a hand comes around me and I jump.

'Here,' DI Walker says, handing me a block of tissue. 'I hate being sick. It's like your throat is being dissolved by the acid, isn't it?'

'Helpful.' I think my stomach has stopped contracting now, and I lean back against the bathroom wall, my knees bent up in front of me. I dab the tissue against my lips. The detective looks at me expectantly.

'Your theory?' He sits down opposite me, mirroring my position.

'Cross my heart, hope to die. Stick a needle in my eye,' I say. Those words haven't been spoken in seventeen years and they feel odd on my tongue; sound even stranger to my ears. It's as though by speaking them, I'll summon a supernatural force, or the bogeyman – like how in *The Candyman* film if you say his name five times he'll kill you.

'What does that mean?'

'You never heard that before?' I say, shocked, as I assumed everyone had heard of it, particularly our age group. But DI Walker shakes his head. 'It's the promise rhyme,' I explain. 'I thought all kids used it to swear they'd keep their promise. No doubt things have progressed – I don't hear the children at Seabrook using it now. But I remember it well. Henry said it whenever he needed to feel secure.' Whenever he needed his big sister to offer comfort or have his back.

'Can't say I have, no. I always swear on someone's life.' He lifts an eyebrow. He says it in a light-hearted way, but tendrils of ice climb my back and twine around my neck. He doesn't appear to notice my discomfort, his mind clearly drifting as he looks towards the ceiling. 'So it *was* all for you, then.' DI Walker seems to be saying this more to himself, like he's confirming his own suspicions.

'I gave up my old life a long time ago, detective. And I tried to put everything behind me. Including my own brother. But some things, however well you suppress them – compartmentalise them – stay with you. Haunt you.'

'You think Henry is haunting you because you abandoned him?'

'Yes. Maybe something has happened in his life more recently that has brought everything back to him. My life was going so well, I hadn't thought about the past for such a long time. But, if Henry hit a low in his own life, he might well have been bitter enough to want to wreak havoc with mine, so he wasn't alone in his pain.'

'Like experiencing a shock, or something? That could trigger his behaviour?'

'Yes, exactly. He always craved stability. If he managed

197

to gain that, but then lose it, I imagine that would set him off on the wrong track. Like it did back at Finley Hall.'

'And his focus would go straight to you. You are the person he blames.'

'Which means,' I say, my voice curiously calm, 'I think you were right from the beginning. I'm his target. I'm the one destined to be his sixth victim. Tomorrow.'

Chapter 28

The car journey to Torquay police station passes in relative silence. We both stare dead ahead, DI Walker focusing on the road while I stare blankly and think. I want to ask more about the women who've been murdered – what their names were, what they did for a living, what family members they were forced to leave behind. Did they suffer? My stomach twists as the images of death flash through my mind. Of course they suffered . . .

As much as I know that it's Henry's deep-rooted issues that made him do such heinous things to these women, I still can't equate the Henry I knew with this one. He hurt people back at Finley Hall, and his behaviour got out of hand, but he was a confused, hurt boy. To think he's done these things now, as an adult, tears my heart in two. After such a terrible start to life himself, why has he then gone on to make others' lives even worse? I went the opposite way, going into teaching to try to impact children's lives for the better.

'You're quiet,' DI Walker says.

I don't look at him, and I don't offer any words of agreement or otherwise. He sucks air through his teeth, then reaches into the compartment between the two seats, taking out a pot of chewing gum. He flicks the lid with one hand and takes a piece out, popping it into his mouth. Then, wordlessly, he shakes the pot in my direction, ejecting a small square of gum onto my lap. I stare at it for a moment, then hold it between my fingers.

'You're meant to eat it, not play with it.'

'Chew, you mean,' I say, my voice weary. 'You can't eat them.'

'Ah. Did your mother tell you it tangles around your windpipe if you swallow it, too?'

'My mother barely spoke to me, detective. Not even to put the fear of God into me.'

'Oh. Sorry. I forgot for a second.'

We fall back into an uneasy silence until he pulls up in the station car park and my tummy flipflops with anxiety. I've not been in a police station for a very long time and I'd prefer not to be stepping inside one right now. Somehow, I feel as though I'll be under scrutiny – that all eyes will be on the serial killer's sister. It's an appellation I'd rather not have. I wonder what other siblings or children of killers feel about such titles. Horrified? Embarrassed? Proud? I'm sure at least one or two will capitalise on it, use their link as a way of gaining attention, maybe even make money from it. Books are written about killers, documentaries and films are made. I shiver at the thought. People are strange.

But before this, didn't I enjoy watching crime dramas? Discuss theories and exchange gossip with people? Does that make me strange too? If this all gets out, if my face is splashed on the front of tabloids, will my Netflix watch-list come under scrutiny? Others will theorise – maybe even suggest that because of our shared backgrounds, I'm like Henry too.

And if my own secret comes out, they may well make documentaries about me.

'I won't keep you long,' DI Walker says, opening my car door for me. I scan the area as I climb out, wondering if there's anyone here to spot me walking inside with a detective. Anyone with their phone camera pointing this way readying themselves to snap a shot to put up on social media.

DI Walker takes me inside the police station with him and we sit in a tiny room while I go through my statement. My hand shakes as I sign it.

'I swear I wasn't trying to obstruct the investigation,' I say, my voice trembling. 'I wasn't thinking straight.' It's partly true.

'I'll do the best I can to limit the fallout,' he says, taking it from me. 'But you *cannot* afford to lie to me again. Understand?'

'I know. I really am sorry. Again,' I say with as much feeling as I can muster, even though the reality is I'd do the exact same even if I had the chance to change it, and I know it. And as DI Walker looms over me, his blue eyes piercing into mine, I get the awful feeling he does, too. Thankfully, he drops it, goes to the door and holds it open for me.

'I'll get uniform to drive you home,' he says, ushering me out into the corridor.

'Oh,' I say, my voice high with surprise. 'Are you not taking me?'

He gives me an incredulous look. 'I haven't got the time to waste taxiing you around.' Then he strides off towards another room. I smart, but then immediately feel sheepish. He's right, of course: not only is there a murder investigation in full swing, but there's a time constraint too. I've likely wasted them enough of that already. I look around for the person tasked with being my driver.

I walk up and down the corridor a bit, trying to spot someone who appears free so that I can ask which officer I should be looking for. Everyone is busy and I feel stupid stopping them at such a time. It'll be more helpful if I get the bus or a taxi.

As I turn the corridor towards where I think the exit is, I see a room with glass doors. A huge whiteboard covering one wall is visible, and I recognise some of the images stuck on it. I stop walking, and keeping out of sight, hover to the side so I can peek in.

DI Walker is standing pointing at one of the photos, and I can hear his deep voice through the doors. Although I can't make out what he's saying, he's addressing a room of people – the attention of the officers I can see in the front row is fully on him. He looks stern, serious and – unless I'm mistaken – angry. Shit. I wonder if he's telling them about me. How I went off without informing him. Removed evidence, made them lose precious time they didn't have. Tears sting my eyes as the reality of my selfishness hits home.

Those poor women – caught up in a game they had no knowledge of, were not willing participants of. Was it bad luck that Henry chose them? Was it merely wrong place, wrong time, or had he stalked them for months beforehand to make sure they were what he wanted? Something that happened years ago for Henry and me has caused these women to lose their lives now, and the fact it's largely down, even if indirectly, to me sits like a heavy stone inside me. As I turn and walk away, I make a promise to myself that I'll be more thoughtful, put others first from now on. If I get the chance.

That promise makes me feel better for all of twenty minutes. Then, as I'm sitting on the bus being jiggled around, numbly watching the buildings and fields whoosh by, I realise I made that very promise before, when I left Finley Hall. Am I really just full of lies and broken promises?

Chapter 29

I step off the bus a few stops ahead of time, deciding a brisk walk along the edge of Shaldon Beach will do me good and help clear my head before going back to my empty house. A chill air whips against my face. May's weather has been hit and miss so far, but even when it's warm, this part of the coast always seems to feel cool as the wind carries across the estuary.

I'm about to drop down onto the beach when I hear my name being called. My first thought is that it's someone who's seen the zebra crossing incident and wants to give me a piece of their mind, but as I turn and recognise the woman whose head is poking out from her wound-down car window, I relax and stride back to the road.

'Serena! What are you doing here?' I smile, a warmth spreading through me at seeing a friendly face, and I duck down so I'm level with her.

She raises her eyebrows. 'Well, seeing as you haven't

called like you said you would, I thought I'd come to you. I've been going crazy worrying about you.'

'Oh, Serena. I'm so sorry, it's been a jam-packed day. I didn't mean to concern you.' I know I owe her an explanation. A full, proper one. I point towards The Clipper Café. 'Why don't you park up and we'll grab a coffee in there.'

Serena looks at me questioningly. 'I may as well come to yours – it's just up ahead and cheaper,' she says.

Of course, we could do that, but rather than attract unwanted attention from whatever police surveillance might be in place at my house, and to reduce the risk that Henry might clock my friend, I'd rather be somewhere else. Plus, it stretches out the time before I *have* to go home. A sadness wells inside my stomach at the thought.

'I'm out of milk,' I say, and walk away before she can object, or offer to buy some for me. I find a table overlooking the waterside and wait for Serena to join me.

'You're not out of milk, Anna. You're never out of anything.' She plonks down opposite me and puts her hands over mine. 'How come you don't want me to come to the house?'

I let out a huge sigh. 'It's Ross.'

'What about him?' she asks.

'He's the reason I didn't call back.' The half-truth is out of my mouth before I have a chance to think. 'He left me.' I really should've started at the beginning, with DI Walker's first visit and how he told me that my brother is wanted for multiple murders. I've skipped a few pages. Chapters, even.

'What? Oh, ha-ha,' she says, laughing. I look into her

206

eyes so she can tell I'm not joking, and her face loses its colour. 'No way!' she gasps, her hand clapping to her mouth.

'It's a bit more complicated than that, but yes, in essence. I was about to order coffee, but do you fancy a glass of wine instead?'

'Oh, no alcohol for me, Anna. I'm driving, remember? Got a date with Tim at eight, too . . .' She twists her mouth into a guilty grimace. 'I could cancel.'

'No, don't do that,' I say quickly. 'Wouldn't want to ruin your night; sounds like it's all going well. Wedding bells soon, no doubt!' I attempt to sound upbeat, excited for her. Her taut expression suggests I haven't managed it.

'I'll ignore the sarcasm, given your news,' she says.

I really hadn't meant to come across like that. I give what I hope is an apologetic smile.

'Hot chocolate, then?'

She nods, shrugging off her coat and flinging it over the back of the chair. We head to the counter and order drinks. When we're seated again, I give Serena the edited details about Ross and Yasmin; how I'd found out about their affair when I went to visit his office yesterday – saw them all cosied up and confronted them then and there. Her eyes are wide as I relay the story, and I can tell she's itching to interject, ask for more details, but I continue so she can't get a word in. I leave the worst till last, waiting until we've finished our drinks then moving to the chairs outside on the patio before dropping the bombshell.

'She's pregnant,' I say, the words spoken sourly, through gritted teeth. I'm surprised at the venom I hear – maybe even jealousy. Serena shakes her head, her earrings tinkling as the movement gets more forceful. I wait. It's as though she's been struck dumb. It feels like five minutes have elapsed before she speaks.

'No, I can't believe that.' She narrows her eyes, crossing her arms as though it couldn't possibly be true. 'Ross? You *must* be mistaken.'

A burst of laughter erupts from deep within me and I can't stop. I laugh until I sob, not even caring about the other people around us. I'm past that. Serena's arms wrap around me and she rubs my back as I rock back and forth, all of the past few days' emotion oozing from me like a river of black, polluted slurry.

'There's no mistake, Serena. He told me himself after . . .' I pull myself up short, almost letting slip that it was after I presented him with the evidence of his affair. I can't face going into all those details right now. 'After I accused him of screwing her.'

'Oh, lovely. I'm so sorry. Bloody men.' She squeezes me again, and I press against her, the smell of her perfume comforting me. It's good to have her by my side, and I wish I *had* called her earlier.

'I thought we'd come through the blip. He agreed about us not having children, then changed his mind without bothering to tell me. All these months, he's been acting like we're the happy married couple, and all the while he's been sleeping with another woman, trying to impregnate her! Well, he succeeded. He's going to get everything he wanted and leave me with nothing.'

'You've got me. You've got your kids at—' She stops abruptly, realising that's another thing I might not have for much longer. 'Shit,' she says. 'Not been a good week for you.' She closes her eyes and slumps. It's like she's feeling all my pain.

And she doesn't know the half of it.

'It's been the worst time I've had for ages,' I say, twisting my wedding band. 'I'm not sure I can pick myself up, dust myself off. If I don't get reinstated at Seabrook . . .' I let the sentence hang.

'The video is still circulating,' Serena says, her eyes cast downwards. It's like she's delivering news of someone's passing. In some ways, I guess she is. 'Have the police found out who hacked the CCTV?'

My head snaps up and I stare at her, my mind scrambling around trying to pinpoint when I told her it had been hacked. As far as I recall, I haven't mentioned it. Or maybe I told Beaumont when I was summoned into his office yesterday and she's heard through him.

No. I don't think I did. I said about it being a smear campaign, that's all.

'Who told you about the CCTV?' I ask. If Beaumont has said something to her, it would be a way to link him to all of this.

Serena frowns. 'What do you mean?'

'The fact it was hacked. I haven't told anyone that.'

Serena sits back, her creased brow deepening. 'Anna. I don't know where you're going with this, but it's obvious that whoever did this managed to access the CCTV. Doesn't take a detective to ascertain that it was hacked.'

'So no one has told you that? About the CCTV?'

'No, I just assumed.'

I take a moment to contemplate her words, before realising of course she's right. Just because she's come to that conclusion without me telling her, doesn't make it suspicious – on her part or Craig Beaumont's. I apologise, blaming the stress of being the local villain for my paranoia.

We talk a bit more about the pages of comments my zebra crossing incident has initiated, Serena trying very hard to make me feel better by saying I have a lot of support as well as haters. There are apparently numerous mentions of how the footage conveniently cuts off with my hands raised in the air making it seem as though I'm about to strike Isobel, with some people saying it's someone with a grudge against me who's posted the footage everywhere. Knowing at least some people are backing me gives me hope.

We settle back into our usual dynamic, my stupid comment seemingly forgotten as we walk back to Serena's car. Serena's a good person; I'm lucky to have her – especially now, when everyone else is against me, or leaving me.

'Thank you for coming over and checking on me,' I say. 'It means a lot.'

'You don't need to thank me, that's what friends are for.' She reaches across and gives me a hug.

Will she remain my friend once she finds out that I didn't fully confide in her? That I lied, withheld the number one reason my week has been so awful? How it's going to get even worse? If the boot were on the other foot, I'd feel hurt thinking she didn't trust me enough to share the truth. Henry's riddle shoots into my mind: *TRUST*. I'd be devastated to think Serena had gone through such turmoil and not reached out. Yet I can't bring myself to open up. It would release a whole can of worms I'm not willing to share. Besides, if I were to tell Serena, it would put her in an uncomfortable position. Not to mention propel her into this mess, too. That would be unfair.

210

I shudder at the thought. 'You should go,' I say, breaking the hug to check my mobile for the time. 'It's getting on and I don't want you to be late for your date. One of us should be getting laid tonight.'

I attempt a laugh, but it comes out as a choking sound. Serena smiles.

'You're one tough cookie, you know that?' she says. 'Are you sure though? Honestly, I can put him off and stay over at yours. I could run to the shop, grab us some wine and we could have a girls' night?'

'I really appreciate the offer. I'll have an early night, though. I'm exhausted.'

'You do look totally washed out . . . if you don't mind me saying.'

'Only you can get away with that level of honesty,' I say, smiling. 'I'll give you a call tomorrow. You can tell me all the gory details about your date.'

'I'll have to make sure it's a good 'un, then.' Serena gives me another hug, kisses me on the cheek and climbs into her car. I stand on the pavement and wave until she disappears from view before walking up the road. As I reach our row of houses, I catch a shadow passing behind my car on the pavement opposite, and goosebumps prickle my skin. Was that him again? I'm relieved I didn't let Serena come to the house now, that I've kept her away from this; kept her safe. I give a furtive glance around then dart up the path, my hands trembling as I try to get the key in the lock.

I'll feel safer when I'm inside, I think. On the third attempt, I jam the key in and the door swings open. The hall is dark, the atmosphere cold, like no one lives here, and I have the urge to ring Serena and get her to turn her car around and come back. Stay with me, like she suggested. But she has someone to go to; I don't want to get in the way of that.

I lock the front door, then slide the chain across. Like that's going to keep me safe.

Chapter 30

Despite the traces of this morning's hangover still making themselves known in the form of an ever-present nausea and a pounding headache, it doesn't stop me from opening a new bottle of wine and pouring myself the equivalent of half a pint now. Speaking to Serena made me realise how important her friendship is. And here I am, keeping things from her, telling her half-truths. I swallow a mouthful of wine, relishing the burn to my throat. If – when – the truth comes out, how will she feel about me then? Way to go to ruin the only good relationship I have left. I've never had groups of friends, always preferring to put all my eggs in one basket. Focus on putting my all into one friendship for fear of spreading myself too thin. Or possibly because I don't feel comfortable opening up to people. My old psychologist would have had some theories about this, saying it has roots in my childhood, that I have an inability to trust people because of being let down so badly by my parents and then those at the children's home. We were supposed to be protected at Finley Hall. Meant to be safe, looked after; loved, even – or at least given the impression of being loved, rather than suffering its withdrawal as a punishment.

It's safer to only rely on yourself, I realise. I laid myself bare to Ross – or as bare as I was able, given my past – and now he has joined the list of those who've let me down. Abandoned me. Serena is all I have. My nose tingles with the onslaught of tears and I rub my nostrils with the back of my hand, sniffling loudly. Sitting in the armchair with my legs tucked up, I gulp down more wine and look around my lounge. All the curtains and blinds are drawn, windows and doors locked. The house is secure, but I still don't feel as protected as I do when Ross is here. The silver-framed photo of our wedding day, with the two of us smiling widely for the camera, stares at me from the bookshelf.

Tearing my gaze from it, I switch the telly on and flick absently through every channel, not really seeing what programmes are on. I stop on one randomly, turning the volume up to create the illusion that there's someone else in the house with me. Then I scroll through my phone, checking WhatsApp to see when Ross was last active. My heart jolts when I see he's online now.

I quickly exit the app. I wonder who he's talking to. Or is he seeing if *I'm* online? I'd have thought at the very least he'd have made contact by now to check if I was okay. However guilty he's feeling – or relieved, maybe? – that his affair is out in the open, surely our years of marriage mean *something*? Enough for him to make sure his wife hasn't been slain – or taken her own life, for that matter. He must know the devastation he's caused. He knew I was already in a state about Henry; adding to that burden by ignoring me feels cruel.

And Ross isn't a cruel person. It was his genuine interest in me as a person, his desire to know what made me tick, that attracted me to him in the first place. He drew me in, enabled me to trust him. No mean feat, considering how damaged I was thanks to my years at Finley Hall. Everyone from there left with scars, either physical or mental – often both. It was a given.

My mind drifts to Henry. Looking back now, it's clear that he had needed help, and he didn't get any while he was there. I doubt he sought it later in life, either. It had taken me a while to admit I needed therapy, having been afraid of it for such a long time. I'd had no idea what a therapist actually did; I'd believed they had a powerful ability to see inside your mind, know things you didn't want people knowing. I'd convinced myself that I was managing the triggers, the awful memories, the trauma all by myself. It took a few 'incidents' before I had come around to the idea that positivity and self-talk could only get me so far. That I would benefit from outside help, and that in fact, therapists *weren't* mind-readers.

Now things are crumbling around me, the coping strategies I was armed with, the cognitive behavioural therapy sessions that covered all the skills to enable me to manage difficult situations, don't seem enough. I'm faced with losing everything I've worked so hard for. Watching everything you care about slip through your fingers is a crushing experience, one that could tip you over the edge. One wrong move, a wrong path taken, could lead to doing the wrong things – illegal things.

Even murder.

The line can be thin; it might not take a lot to cross it.

My eyelids droop, my blinking slows as I begin to fall into the darkness of unconsciousness.

What feels like minutes later I sit bolt upright, breathing fast. I peer around, taking a few moments to gather my bearings. I'm on the sofa, in the lounge. I check my mobile and see I've actually been asleep for two and a half hours.

Something woke me. A noise outside?

Or inside.

I stay stock still, listening, my eyes wide in anticipation – my senses on high alert. I feel comforted by the soft glow of the lamp, which offers evidence that there's no one standing over me with a knife. So, with my heartbeat pelting against my ribs, I start to slide off the sofa an inch at a time, careful not to make a sound. I hear a scuffling noise outside. I move to the window, pinch the curtain back a tiny bit, but I can't see anything, or anyone. I've got a limited view here, though, so I creep upstairs to gain a better vantagepoint, unlocking the bedroom balcony doors. I sneak out, edging forwards on the balcony until I am close enough to see through the glass balustrade, then I keep low to avoid detection. Shadows flit across the road, over the pavements.

Is someone out there, watching? Or is it just nocturnal animals – my imagination?

My unease in Craig Beaumont's office yesterday, and my wild thought about him having something to do with my predicament – or the wilder one that *he* is Henry – come back to me now. Is it as implausible as I tried to tell myself? A few days ago, I'd have said Henry being a

216

serial killer was far-fetched. If someone were hellbent on destroying another person's life, it could be possible they would redirect their own life to make the two paths cross. Infiltrate their target's life. Craig was appointed headmaster of Seabrook just six months ago . . .

Is it Craig who is watching me now?

I shiver – I'd fallen asleep in just my thin shirt – and as I'm unable to make out a figure or anything unusual in the street, I shuffle back into my bedroom, then close and relock the balcony doors. I'm wide awake now; there's no chance I'll be able to drift off again for a couple of hours, so I may as well do something productive. I steal back downstairs, the thought that someone is inside still not flushed out of my system, and I get my laptop to bring it up to bed. I undress, put on my pyjamas and dressing gown, then sit cross-legged and begin searching the internet for anything to do with Seabrook Prep and Craig Beaumont.

It's not long before I make a startling discovery: Craig's brother. He's never mentioned him, but I can't say that's abnormal as I've never mentioned mine, either. However, his brother, Neil, is referred to on an old Facebook profile of Craig's but with a different surname: Holsworthy, not Beaumont. Alarm bells ring in my head; my entire body stiffens.

I know that name.

Chapter 31

FINLEY HALL CHILDREN'S HOME

Miss Graves peers over her glasses at Anna and Kirsty.

'I've had rather a disturbing report that two nights ago you violated the rules laid down by me in order to *protect* you. Sneaking out of the grounds is bad enough; breaking curfew is irresponsible; but attending a gathering and underage drinking is downright inexcusable, and what's more, dangerous. You two have given Finley Hall a bad name.'

Anna scoffs.

'Something to say, Ms Lincoln?' Miss Graves's face turns an even deeper red, her eyes bulging from their sockets as she stands up and leans over her desk.

The girls are waiting for her threat to get Frank to punish them. They are both sitting on their hands, heads bowed, as the manager of the home looms over them like a predator about to pounce.

'No, Miss Graves,' Anna says. 'Sorry.'

'Neither of you will be leaving the premises apart from to attend school. You'll be escorted to and from there by Frank. Is that understood?'

A horrified look passes between the girls as they each privately recall their dealings with Frank. While he beats the boys as punishment, he emotionally torments the girls. They say nothing, though, just nod. They've learned through experience it's better to stay quiet and accept whatever's coming.

'I don't want to see you here again,' she says. Anna and Kirsty share a look that says they don't want to be there again either.

As they slouch out of Miss Graves's office, Anna spots Dean in the 'penalty' chair. Kirsty catches her breath when she sees his face. Both eyes are swollen and black, and one is almost closed.

'Dean,' she says, her voice a whisper. 'Who did that?'

He waves her away. 'Don't worry about it, it's nothing.'

'Back to your dorms, Anna and Kirsty.' Miss Graves stomps across to Dean. 'You,' she says, sharply. 'My office. Now.'

Dean winces as he stands, then follows her in without looking back at the girls.

'What the hell was that about?' Kirsty says as they walk away.

Anna looks over her shoulder, back at the office door, wondering what's taking place at this moment. She remembers Dean's face when he saw them returning from the party – it had been one of concern.

'Did you tell him, Kirst?'

'What? About the party?'

'Yes, about the party.' Anna leans in closer to Kirsty,

lowering her voice. 'About the . . . you know . . . those boys. What they did.'

'Not in so many words,' Kirsty says, giving a shrug. 'And I don't want to talk about it.'

Kirsty hasn't spoken much about the attack, Anna realises. She's skirted around the topic each time it's brought up. They've shared the horror of their near-rape experience, but not shared their thoughts or their feelings about it. They've each been going inside themselves to find a way to cope with it. The trauma of how they'd both ended up in a care home was a story they'd swapped, and Anna was struggling with keeping this latest one as something unspeakable, like it was their fault it had happened. Their secret.

But it had been Anna who had spoken to Dean on the night itself, giving a vague explanation about why they'd returned after curfew looking scared and dishevelled. Maybe Kirsty told him the full story the following morning. Had Dean done something? Had Kirsty's brother sought revenge on his sister's attackers? He's battered – the bruises are fresh. Perhaps he took matters into his own hands to stick up for them; show the bullies they couldn't treat girls that way. A stab of jealousy hits Anna as this plays over in her head, knowing Henry wouldn't do the same. Her own brother's someone she's come to fear, not rely on for backup. Henry hasn't approached Anna for over a week. There's not been a single riddle – The Hunt has paused. Maybe forever. And unexpectedly, Anna feels a sense of loss deep in her gut.

When the night lights are switched off and Anna is sure Kirsty is asleep, she creeps out of their dorm and downstairs, careful to avoid the known hotspots that might signal her rule-breaking to the other residents or carers. It's easy to break into Miss Graves's office – she's done it on a number of occasions – but this time, her palms sweat as she slides in behind the old battle-axe's desk and rummages through the drawer. If she's caught tonight, after the telling-off earlier, she'll be in all kinds of trouble. Anna only finds boiled sweets, some confiscated cigarettes, and an ancient-looking photograph of a group of people she doesn't recognise but who look equally as stern and miserable as Miss Graves. It's the two tall filing cabinets against the back wall that are likely to yield what Anna is looking for; that's where the detailed notes about all the children at Finley Hall are kept, so she should be able to find out exactly why Miss Graves had dragged Dean in earlier. She could just ask him, but something told her he would fob her off with a lie.

Pulling the drawer out slowly, hoping to avoid the metal runner squealing, Anna finds both her and Kirsty's files and places them on the top of the cabinet while she searches through the others. She's about to remove Henry's, too, as she may as well look at all of them while she has the opportunity, when she spots a divider that has the word 'police' written on it, along with today's date. Frowning, she sweeps the rest of the files forwards, plucks the brown folder out and lays it open on the desk. She gulps down air as she sees that it's a police report which details a fight between some boys from Finley Hall and the occupants of a house. Anna's pulse races as she realises it's the house of the party they were at. Bingo. She'd been thinking it would be in Dean's file, so this is an added bonus. Her hands shake as she picks up the report,

222

wondering how on earth Dean is involved. What she reads sends a shockwave through her body, and her legs go weak. There's mention of a serious allegation made against someone who attended the party. Anna gasps, stumbling backwards. One of the boys has been accused of rape.

'What the hell?' Anna's breath escapes in a rush. She rereads it in case she's made a mistake.

No. She read it right. And it clearly states the information came from her, Anna Lincoln. Which is obviously wrong, as she'd have remembered speaking to the bloody police. But she and Kirsty had run through the house in a state afterwards, yelling all sorts. Maybe someone had taken it further? That doesn't explain why the police thought the report came from her, though . . . She scans the rest of the page until she gets to the final part. According to the report, the following day a Neil Holsworthy was set upon in an unprovoked and violent manner and hospitalised from injuries sustained through the attack.

Neil. The name of the boy who'd first attacked Anna, then Kirsty.

'Oh, my God,' she whispers.

Anna puts the paper back inside the file and closes it. Confusion swarms her mind. But through it, the overriding feeling is a sense of karma.

Good. Now he knows what it feels like.

But, no matter how much she felt he deserved a beating, she and Kirsty hadn't been raped by Neil – so why was it reported as such? Or reported at all? She'd mentioned it to Dean, but she hadn't specified names. A twinge of guilt pulls at her insides. It must've been Dean and his mates that had beaten Neil up. Put him in hospital. That's why he was bruised, why Miss Graves summoned him to her office. She should give the proper details, get Miss Graves to inform the police there'd been an error.

They *had* been attacked, though. They'd been lucky to have escaped.

Neil had got what he deserved.

Anna slides the file into the cabinet and shuts the drawer, leaning against it like the wind has been knocked from her sails. Should she tell Kirsty about this?

She'll see in the morning.

MAY 13th

Day Zero

Chapter 32

The second I open my eyes, my stomach is a hot ball of nerves with anticipation of what lies ahead today. My lids feel swollen, my eyeballs gritty from lack of sleep.

At least I *have* my eyeballs. For now.

I roll over to check my mobile. No text messages from Ross. I access WhatsApp and for a split second my hope rises like a tsunami as I read *On my way home* with a smiley face. Then I realise I've accidentally scrolled to a message from over a week ago, and his 'last seen' time was actually 11.38 p.m. yesterday, when I was online the same time as him. It's too late for us anyway. There's no coming back from this. He's having a baby with someone else; we no longer have a future.

My phone pings while I'm in the shower. I speed the process up and skip conditioning my hair. I'm about to step out when a vision of myself on a mortuary slab makes me get back in. I wet my hair again and apply the conditioner. *May as well look my best for the coroner.* If I shared that thought with DI Walker, I'd likely be chastised for making a joke out of something serious. Ross would get it. He's used to me covering my real emotions with humour. Will I ever find someone else like that? Will I even be around to do so?

When I grab my mobile I see that the ping is a voicemail notification, which is strange as I didn't hear it ring.

'Would help if you remembered to unmute your phone, Anna,' I mutter as I tap the volume button. I check who last called and see the name: DI Walker. I take a steadying breath before playing it, knowing it's about today. A stream of air hisses out between my lips as DI Walker's voice informs me he's on my doorstep, waiting. Has the murder already taken place? Neither the police nor I have any idea what time Henry might carry out the killing – it could well have happened just after midnight. I throw on my bathrobe and fly downstairs, opening the door with such force it bangs against the hallway wall, leaving a handle-shaped hole in the plaster. I glance at it, mentally adding it to a to-do list of things I'll have to sort out myself now Ross isn't here, before landing my focus on DI Walker, who's holding a takeaway cup of coffee in each hand.

'Woah. Steady on,' he says.

'What's happened? He's done it, hasn't he? We failed to stop him in time.'

'It hasn't happened. We've not failed, as far as we're aware.' DI Walker's tone is firm, positive, but it doesn't reassure me. I should be glad, as it means an innocent woman hasn't lost her life, yet there's a tinge of dismay lurking beneath the surface that it also means this isn't over.

I swallow, almost choking on the hard lump in my throat.

I could still be the intended sixth victim.

DI Walker hands me one of the cups. 'I got a latte. Everyone likes a latte, right?'

I take it, mumbling a thanks. My attention is on what's tucked under his arm.

'Was that on the step?' I cock my head, trying to see the envelope – checking if it's the same sort that Henry's been sending. DI Walker looks down, then up, his eyebrows raised as if it's a surprise to him, too, that it's there. 'Nope. Henry sent this directly to me at the station.'

My heart plummets. 'Oh, really? Why would he do that? Why change it now, the day he intends to kill?' A sense of panic rises up into my throat, preventing further words, and I take some deep breaths. DI Walker waits patiently while I regain my composure, then tackles my questions. 'Maybe he thinks you might ignore it. Or maybe he wants me to go with you this time?'

That makes sense. Henry wants to expose me in front of law enforcement. Trap me. He can't afford for me to come after what I assume is the final clue – the showdown – alone.

'Let's go and sit in the lounge,' I say, heading back down the hallway. I hear the slow, dull thuds of DI Walker's shoes close behind. He doesn't seem rushed, like he has all the time in the world to figure this all out and stop a woman's – my – murder.

'Go ahead, tell me,' I say, taking the white plastic lid from the cup and sipping the latte.

'Maybe you want to get dressed first?' DI Walker indicates towards my robe, and an embarrassed heat flushes my cheeks.

'Right. I'll be two secs,' I say, passing the latte back to

him and darting out. I pull on the first items of clothes I come across – jogging bottoms and daisy-print t-shirt – and run back downstairs. 'Okay. Go,' I say, retrieving my coffee cup.

'My team have been up all night, but no one saw who dropped this off at the station.'

'No CCTV?' I ask, somewhat sceptically.

'Plenty. Somehow, he avoided it. Or there's a possibility he got someone else to deliver it for him and we missed it. They're still going through the footage though because it would be helpful if we knew what Henry looked like. The only photo available to us is one taken when he was arrested as a teen. And you haven't been able to give us a description of what he looked like from that point either, so we're very much in the dark. He could be anyone – or any bloke could be him.'

'That was my worry,' I say. 'Or my paranoia, you could say. And actually, now I think of it, I've seen a man here a few times. On the street, I mean.' DI Walker's eyes widen. 'Just passing by,' I add quickly. 'But he struck me as a bit odd. I wondered if it was Henry. Now, with what you're saying, it could be it was him, or that Henry's put someone up to it, paid them to deliver the envelopes?'

DI Walker gives an exasperated sigh. 'And you're mentioning this man now?'

'Sorry. I'm not going to tell you about every person that walks past my house, detective. Maybe you should've posted someone on my doorstep if you were that worried.'

He hesitates a moment, then says, 'I've been outside every night, Anna. For the most part, anyway. Once I've finished with the team, I keep a watchful eye on the property.'

This is news to me, and I can't hold back my surprise. 'Even last night?'

'Not until late, so I appreciate I might've missed something. It's the early hours of the morning I feel you are at your most vulnerable.'

'Right, well . . . thanks. I guess.'

Is it DI Walker that I've seen, then? Or heard, at least? I wish I'd realised last night – would have saved the anxiety and insomnia. Although, that time awake did lead to a noteworthy find. One I should probably mention now, before I get chastised for not informing the police of something else.

'I made an interesting connection last night,' I say, getting up to retrieve my laptop. I open the small article I found buried in online archives of a local newspaper. The headline reads *My son took his own life after rape allegation*. DI Walker turns the screen and continues reading it. He lets out a big sigh when he's finished.

'This relates to someone at the children's home you and Henry lived in,' he says.

'Yes. It's more . . . personal . . . than that, though.'

'Oh? In what way?'

'The "young man" referred to here is the brother of Craig Beaumont, the headmaster of Seabrook Prep School.' DI Walker's eyebrow arcs, and he sits forward. 'And the girl . . .' I take a deep breath. 'The girl who accused him of rape was supposedly me.'

The room becomes quiet, like it's been muted. I allow this to sink in before continuing. 'It wasn't me, though. I wasn't the one who accused Neil of rape. I think . . . I think it was my friend, Kirsty. And I also believe her brother Dean took the law into his own hands to deliver

231

justice. Anyhow, it doesn't matter how it happened now, the point is Henry might've used this knowledge and my connection to Neil to convince Craig to create this smear campaign and get his revenge by suspending me. I don't imagine he's backing me with the parents and board. I *will* be fired.'

'It's not actual proof, though – just circumstantial.'

'I guess. And it could be a massive coincidence, I suppose. I admit, I actually thought Craig might be Henry to start with.' I laugh awkwardly.

DI Walker's face is thoughtful, his mouth twisted in concentration. 'It's worth following up – I'll let the team know.'

'Good, thanks.'

He hits a button on his mobile and gets up with it pressed against his ear. He begins to relay this new piece of information as he walks to the kitchen, where his voice becomes muffled. I sip more latte while I await his return.

'Well, anyway,' he says, sitting back down and slapping his hands onto his thighs. 'The clock is ticking; we need to press on. We've only hours left to solve this puzzle.' DI Walker slides out the paper from the envelope. 'What is the point of this final clue do you think?' He hands me the piece of paper. I realise he's not wearing gloves and he hasn't made me either, so I guess this is a copy and the original has been filed in evidence.

I take it from him. It shakes in my hand as I read the short riddle.

Cross my heart, hope to die. Stick a needle in my eye.

It's the last promise you made. It's the first promise
you broke.
Meet me where the lie was spoke.

'I–I'm not . . .' I stammer, reaching forward to put my coffee on the table before my twitching hand causes it to spill. My vision distorts and the walls feel as though they're moving, closing in on me. On my secret. Our shared secret. Just as Henry has wanted. It's what this has all been about. But I still don't know *why*.

The only way to find out is to go where the riddle points to, and confront Henry. My only hope of living through this is to take DI Walker. But once it's all laid bare, the police will learn the truth and my life will still be over. If I go alone and Henry intends to kill me, he'll make up his own version to tell the world.

It all comes down to what I have left to live for.

Chapter 33

'Anna – are you all right?' DI Walker waves a hand in front of my face and I snap back to the moment.

'Sorry, I was just thinking.'

'Are you going to let me in on it?'

'Meet me where the lie was spoke,' I say, my spine tingling. 'He wants to meet me at the place I last saw him.'

He shakes his head. 'Because that's where you lied to him?'

'Yes and no. It wasn't a lie I *told* him. The lie he's referring to is the one we agreed on together.' I look DI Walker in the eye and see confusion. Without telling him everything right here and now, it's difficult to explain. 'It was a secret between the two of us, something we swore we'd never talk of again, never utter to anyone else.'

'I don't understand,' DI Walker says. 'If that's the case, why is *he* trying to expose *you* now? If it's something you both did – agreed to keep quiet, or whatever. I don't get it. What's this really all about, Anna?'

'It's complicated,' I say, avoiding his gaze. I swivel my wedding ring around and around on my finger, lost in the past. DI Walker slaps his hand down over mine.

'You've known all along,' he says, his face contorted. 'Wasted police time. The significance of today's date – the thirteenth of May – all of it – you knew the entire time.' The weight of his anger presses down on me. I feel like a child again.

'I'm sorry, I didn't know what to do. The police haven't exactly made for trustworthy allies in my past—'

'Oh, blaming the police, that's rich. Anything to prevent you taking responsibility for your actions – your *choices*.'

'I'm sorry, Detective Walker. This hasn't exactly been easy.' My voice is thick with threatening tears.

'No. And informing five sets of family members about the brutal murders of their loved ones wasn't easy, either.'

My face burns, and I rake my fingers through my hair. Fine, brown strands tangle between them and I pick at them, unable to bring my gaze up to meet DI Walker's.

'I'll take you there.' My words are quiet, muttered.

'Yes, damn right you will.' He stands, towering above me. He takes hold of my upper arm and pulls me up. 'You're lucky I'm not arresting you.'

I feel a flash of annoyance. 'Well, you need me, don't you. Arresting me would be counterproductive.'

His fingers tighten around the top of my arm. 'When this is over, Anna, you will be hauled into the station. You do know that, right? Just because you've finally decided to help, doesn't let you off the hook.'

'No worries, *Detective Inspector Walker*,' I say, with as much contempt as I dare. 'I don't expect to be alive long enough for you to arrest me.'

His shoulders slump slightly – a sign of guilt for his harsh reaction, maybe? I'm sure that won't last. Once he gets his man, he won't care a jot about me.

'Let's go,' he says, firmly.

I glare at him. 'I need to change into something warmer first,' I say, pulling away from his grip. He nods, but stands at the foot of the stairs as though he doesn't trust me not to make a run for it.

'Hurry up.'

Upstairs, I go into the bathroom and call Serena, but it goes to voicemail. I leave a brief message telling her how much I value her friendship, and that there are things I need to tell her, so could she call back ASAP. I tap out a similar text on WhatsApp too, for good measure. I need her to know that I at least attempted to tell her the truth in the end. I swap my joggers for jeans and grab my favourite FatFace jumper, pulling it over my head as I go back downstairs. DI Walker stares at me, an expression on his face I can't read. I move around him to reach my boots.

'Ready,' I say as I take my coat from the hook.

'Your car keys?'

I frown. 'I assumed you'd be driving?'

'We'll take both cars – go in convoy. I'll follow close behind, but not too close. Don't want to frighten Henry off.'

'But he *wanted* me to be with the police. That's the point of him sending you the letter. Right?'

'And I will be there, just hanging back. In case. If we only have the one vehicle, we've only one means of escape if things turn . . .' He looks up, as if trying to pluck the right word from the air.

'Nasty,' I finish for him. 'Yes. I get it. We will have backup too, though?'

'Once I have all the details, and I've assessed the situation, everything will be set in motion. The team and support will be waiting for me to give them the go-ahead to approach. Trust me, Anna – they'll be close by. We've been after this evil fucker for ages.' DI Walker turns to walk out the door. I quickly check my mobile. The WhatsApp mark remains stubbornly solitary and grey beside Serena's message. I haven't got time to wait for a response anyway, so I pocket it and snatch my keys from the cracked dish.

I hesitate at the door. I take my phone out again and forward the same message to Ross, but add an extra sentence. If I don't return from the location Henry is sending me to, I want to know that I've left this world with as few regrets as possible.

Chapter 34

MAY

This year

Acid churned in his stomach. The build-up of tension, anticipation and excitement all mixed together and he knew it was all about to come to a head. The grand finale was drawing closer. So close, he could smell it; taste it. Truth. Revenge. Justice.

He inhaled deeply through his nose, tilting his head to the sky, then released the breath slowly through pursed lips, controlling it until his lungs were empty. He continued this circular breathing technique until his pulse was slow and steady, countering the adrenaline rush that had swept through his system when thinking about the day's goals.

May the 13th.

Today was the day he'd carry out his sixth murder. The one this had all been for. He'd considered that it might be his last, too. But that would depend. He was prepared for a number of eventualities. Further deaths could well be necessary. He checked the time and mentally prepared himself for the next step.

Tick, tock.

Chapter 35

'I'm going to need to stop off for petrol,' I say when we're on the pavement outside my house. DI Walker narrows his eyes.

'Why, how far are we going?'

'It's a three-hour drive. I've only got quarter of a tank.' I turn away before he can question me further, then climb into the car and click my seatbelt. I don't want to give him an exact location yet. If I simply gave the police the location, they'd know where Henry was going to be. Then they might ditch the middleman, so to speak, and head him off without me even being there. I can't have that – I want to face the man who's brought my life crashing down. I need to see him, understand his sudden motivation to expose me – and himself in the process – because it doesn't make sense. The 'why now?' question still burns within me.

As I drive across Shaldon Bridge, I slow right down. For what might be the last time, I gaze out across the

River Teign estuary, at the fishing boats bobbing on their moorings and gulls feeding in the mudflats, my heart feeling as though it's fit to burst. I swipe at the tears – hot drops that contain all my anger, sadness, regret – and put my foot down hard on the accelerator, quickly leaving my home behind.

'I fucking hate you, Henry Lincoln.'

I yell the words over and over until a calmness washes over me. I check my rear mirror as I approach the petrol station – DI Walker's Audi is a few cars back – then indicate and turn in. My stomach lurches as I realise who is at the next pump and the anger I've just dispelled comes rushing back.

Yasmin. Looking fresh and happy. She would, wouldn't she – she's got a gorgeous partner, a baby on the way – her future is looking rosy.

But Ross is *my* husband.

I avert my gaze as I fill my car up. If I don't look at her, I can maybe ignore my inner voice telling me to aim the petrol nozzle at her. The pump display nears thirty pounds, so I slow it down. The pennies nudge up: £29.90, £29.94, £29.98 . . . I make minute movements of my fingers – abrupt squeezes to ensure the display reads dead on £30.00. The satisfaction when I achieve it is replaced with a burst of rage when I replace the nozzle and an extra penny registers.

'I didn't press it. It was thirty bloody quid dead on.' I kick the bottom of the pump. I'm aware that people are staring at me. 'What? Don't you realise they've got the pumps fixed?' I'm no longer sure who I'm even directing my rant at, but I'm invested now. 'It'll soon add up if they take an extra penny every single time the pumps are used. Don't they take enough as it is? They make billions, they may as well suck the blood straight from my veins.'

'Anna,' a soft voice close to my ear says.

'What?' I turn sharply and my stomach clenches. 'Oh, great. What do *you* want? To take something more from me?' Yasmin, face perfectly made-up, hair twisted into an annoyingly pretty, messy chignon, and dressed in a casual jumpsuit, gives an awkward smile as she lays a hand on my arm.

'Are you all right?' she says, her forehead creasing with concern. For a split second I allow myself to sink into her eyes, and I find myself believing she's being genuine. I shake myself out of the trance.

'No, *Yaz*. I'm not. Strange that, isn't it,' I bark and push her hand away. Her face fills with pity, which makes mine burn with even more rage. I don't need her pitying me.

'I know you're having a terrible time of it,' she says, 'and I know a lot of that is down to me. I'm sorry it's happened this way.' The softly spoken words, oozing with fake compassion, set light to the already smouldering taper and the flame ignites.

'That's okay then. As long as you're sorry that you've stolen my husband, that makes it all good. Excuse me, I've got more important things to deal with.'

'I understand your anger, how you're hurting. He hates himself for it.'

'Good,' I snap. I catch sight of DI Walker's car on the edge of the forecourt. He's leaning against the passenger side, arms crossed, an amused look on his face as he watches me talking to Yasmin. Through the fury that pulsates beneath my chest, I feel a stab of humiliation, but my attention quickly returns to Yasmin, who seemingly doesn't know when to shut up.

'When you're in a better headspace, would you talk to him?'

Who does she think she is, asking that? I blow air from my cheeks. 'When he hasn't even bothered to check if I'm okay? He left me for you, Yasmin. And he hasn't had the decency to speak to me since.'

'Are you sure?' She takes a step back as though I've hit her.

'What do you mean, *am I sure*?' I'm getting tired of this exchange; my restless feet are desperate to get away.

'He left early this morning to go and see you. He's been beside himself with worry, Anna.'

'Well, he must've lied to you then. He's good at that, in case that wasn't obvious.'

Yasmin's face falls, a dark cloud drifting across it. She rubs a hand over her belly. There's no visible bump; I don't know how far gone she is. I imagine she's doing it for my benefit – a middle finger up to me; a "look, I'm giving your husband what he wants" action. But, as she turns away from me, goes back to her car and drives off without saying anything more, a niggling feeling bubbles in my gut. If Ross left Yasmin's to come and see me this morning, it would've been no more than a five-minute walk.

I fling my driver side door open, jump in, and without wasting time putting my seatbelt on, pull away from the pump. Out the corner of my eye, I see DI Walker waving madly at me, but I ignore him and drive off the forecourt onto the main road.

Ross didn't reach the house.

And the only reason that I can think of is that Henry took him.

If I don't adhere to Henry's rules and play the game, he'll kill my husband.

Chapter 36

The satnav isn't required this time. Having only made this journey a few days ago, it's all very familiar. DI Walker still doesn't appear to be behind me; I bet he's cursing me for speeding off without him – and without paying for my fuel. He's likely had to go inside the garage and sort it out. It wasn't actually my intention to do that, I just reacted. I use that garage regularly, they know me – know I'll go back to pay what I owe. Now that I've slowed down, my initial adrenaline spike levelling, I'm sure the detective will catch up. He saw the general direction I was heading, so I imagine he's not far away.

The dual carriageway seems endless as I weave in and out of the lanes, my mind swerving as much as my car does. The gruesome photos of the murdered women scroll through my mind, but now my imagination has added to the reel. Ross, unconscious, bruised, slumped on the ground, his guts spilling from the gaping hole in his lower abdomen, blood pooled around him. My breath judders as I gasp for air, tears hot on my cheeks. I blink furiously, trying to rid my mind of this morbid vision. I hope Henry realises that although Ross has betrayed me, hurt me, he doesn't deserve to be harmed, tortured. I don't want that. Or maybe that's the point.

But then, I don't think Henry is doing this as some kind of punishment and retribution to settle my score for me. He's not standing up for me, and he hasn't got my back. This is different. This is his way of showing me what he's capable of. He's telling me this is who he became. And that it's my fault.

As I near Bristol, my phone rings.

'Stop at the Welcome Break service station and wait for me. You're too far ahead,' DI Walker says, his voice clipped. He hangs up before I can agree. I clamp my hands tighter on the wheel and let out a loud groan. A small part of me wants to ignore his instruction because I'm tired of asking 'how high?' when someone tells me to jump. I turn the volume up on the radio to drown out my thoughts as I continue driving, the signs whooshing by in a blur.

I wriggle in my seat, my bum numb, and glance at the next sign just in time to see that the Welcome Break is coming up and I need to exit at junction 19. Tension pulls my shoulder muscles so tight they feel as though they'll snap, and I struggle to maintain the steering wheel position as I go around the large u-shaped road leading to the services. Finally I arrive, park in the closest space to the entrance and sit rubbing my taut neck muscles. Deducing that DI Walker is at least ten, fifteen minutes away, I get out to stretch my legs and use the bathroom. If he gets here quicker, he can wait for me.

A girl, no more than twenty by the look of her, is washing in the sink when I exit the toilet cubicle. She's wearing ripped jeans, no top – just a grey-looking bra that I suspect was once white. She scoops water with a cupped hand and splashes it under her armpit. As she looks up, our eyes meet in the mirror, and she scowls.

'What?' she says, her voice raspy.

'Are you okay?' I'm standing a little behind her, and so I move to her side.

She gives me a hostile glance. 'What's it to you?'

She is me, seventeen years ago. In a service station similar to this one – it might even be the same one. The lorry driver I'd hitched with dropped me while he was having a comfort break and I took the opportunity to clean up in the bathroom. I remember shivering with cold, using the hot water to bring life to my numb fingers and splashing my skin in an attempt to rid the stale sweat from it.

'Can I get you anything?'

'I didn't realise you got personal service in this place too.' She's hiding her pain beneath sarcasm. I can relate to that. It doesn't deter me, because maybe if someone had asked me the same question all those years ago, I'd have had options.

'If you don't want my help, that's fine. I just thought I'd ask in case no one else does.' She stops drying herself with the paper towels and turns to face me, her expression softening.

'Deodorant would be nice,' she says, her voice small. I smile, and after asking which type, I hurry to the shop and grab roll-on, a toothbrush and a tube of toothpaste, a bottle of water and some snacks, then return to the bathroom.

'Where are you headed?' I ask, handing her the carrier. She shrugs, but tears glisten in her eyes and I have to swallow down my own emotion. 'Has something happened to you?'

'Bad things happen all the time,' she says, rummaging in the bag and pulling out the deodorant. 'That's life.' I watch, my heart aching, as she pulls on her jumper and runs her fingers through her hair. I should've bought her a brush.

'Me and my friend thought like that once,' I say, my mind travelling back to the years at Finley Hall. 'Bad things can happen, but they're not your fault. And you don't have to sit back and allow them to happen.'

The girl's brow furrows, then she walks towards the door. She stops and turns.

'Where are *you* headed?'

I smile at her through my tears. 'A place I won't be returning from,' I say. She nods, like she knows.

'Well, thanks for these,' she says, holding up the bag. 'I hope you give whoever it is what they deserve.' And she leaves.

I think it'll be the other way around.

With a heaviness dragging me down, I walk slowly back to my car. DI Walker is leaning against it as I approach.

'No rush, take your time,' he says.

'It's funny, that, isn't it? How I don't seem to be in a hurry to reach the place where my life is likely to be terminated.'

'Fair enough, sorry. You were in a rush when you left the petrol station, though. What's changed?'

'I bumped into her. *Yaz.* You know, my husband's pregnant lover?'

'Oh.' He makes a face. 'Awks.'

In spite of myself, I laugh at his use of language. 'Could say that.' Then I remember his expression as he watched me talking to her. 'You seemed to be enjoying the show, though.'

He frowns as though puzzled, then shakes his head. 'I can understand why that might cause you to speed off without paying.'

'It was a bit more than that.' I lean back, next to the detective. 'She said Ross had left her place to come to see me this morning. But he never showed.'

DI Walker jolts forwards, alarm evident on his face. 'Shit. That's not good.'

'Oh, great. That makes me feel so much better, thanks.'

He does a strange skip-jump across to the opposite row of cars, opening his door and getting in. I walk across, in time to hear him speaking into his radio about checking the whereabouts of Ross Price, of The Right Price estate agency in Shaldon. Then he rattles off its address. My chest tightens and my heart thuds rapidly as I struggle to catch my breath. DI Walker stops speaking and looks up at me.

'It might be nothing. He probably lost his nerve and decided to go to work instead.'

'It's . . . Saturday, though.' I take a deep breath. 'He rarely works weekends.'

'Officers will check. Try not to worry.' He gets out and lays both hands on my shoulders. 'But let's speed this along, eh?'

I nod. 'Of course.'

As I climb into my car and begin reversing out, I catch sight of the bathroom girl boarding a coach. Her words

251

ring in my ears: 'I hope you give whoever it is what they deserve.' I feel a surge of determination.

I need to alter the narrative. It doesn't have to end with my death.

Chapter 37

This time, DI Walker is sticking so close he's practically tailgating me. When I'm about a mile away from the location Henry wants me to meet him at, I take a left turn. The opposite turning would take us to Finley Hall, but this one leads to a wooded area. Back then, it wasn't frequented a lot by the locals, wasn't somewhere that was mentioned on the maps. I wonder if that's changed. I'm guessing it can't have if Henry is confident to bring me here – he's bound to have checked the place out first.

Unless, of course, that's the point. That he wants this to be a very public affair. My stomach grumbles – it was already unhappy with the lack of food, but now it's cramping from the churning of acid. Why didn't I pick something up at the service station? Eating is the last thing on my mind, but consuming some form of energy would've been wise given what the next few hours could have in store. The thought makes me cold. Every inch of me wants to pull over, stop this madness. Go back to my home and forget Henry's game.

Ross. He has Ross.

I don't make a U-turn, but I do steer the car into a layby, then open the door to expel bile. I cough violently, the burning in my stomach, my oesophagus, my throat, making my eyes stream. A car slows up, I hear its tyres on the gravel behind me. Christ. I can't even puke without an audience.

'Here,' DI Walker says, passing me a pack of wet wipes. I eye him cautiously as I pull out a clump of them. I equate wet wipes with babies, toddlers – messy kids. When I'd asked him before about his own family, he'd neatly side-stepped the topic, but now I wonder if he has, in fact, got children. 'Always prepared for every eventuality,' he says, as if reading my mind.

'Good job one of us is.' I spit the last of the acidic saliva out and drag the wipe over my lips. Then I take another and use it for the rest of my face, the coolness offering a little relief. DI Walker goes to his car, then returns with a bottle of water and thrusts it at me.

'Keep it.'

I attempt a smile, then sip the water. It tastes bitter on my tongue from the remnants of bile. I swallow more in the hope of being completely rid of it.

'Don't suppose you have some mints, too?' I raise a hopeful brow.

'You really aren't prepared, are you? Call yourself a teacher?' He tuts, shakes his head and trudges back to his car again. I think he's genuinely annoyed I'm not as organised as he imagines a teacher should be.

'I used to be,' I say, holding out my hand for him to

drop a few mints into. 'Prepared, I mean. Organised. If you'd met me prior to this past week, you might've gained a better idea of me.'

He cocks his head to one side. 'Oh, I think I've got the measure of you.'

I flush, embarrassed. He's seen me lose my temper with a child on a zebra crossing, he's caught me out in numerous lies and breaking promises, he knows I broke off contact with Henry, which may have led him to murder five women – everything he's seen has been the absolute worst of me.

'There are some good bits,' I say, screwing up my face.

'I'm used to seeing people at their most vulnerable, Anna. You're no different.'

He turns away, calling over his shoulder that we need to get moving again. The fluttering in my tummy subsided after I ejected the bile, but now it's replaced with something else: an ice-cold lump is swelling, filling me up like I'm freezing from the inside out. A violent shiver judders up my spine and I begin to shake all over. There's nothing I can do to stop Henry, I realise. Today will play out the way he wants it to; he's the one with all the power. I thought I was in control of my future, but maybe that was an illusion. From that date – the thirteenth of May, seventeen years ago – it's been Henry who could dictate what happened and when. I was a fool to believe we'd *both* take our secret to the grave.

Once I'm on the road again, I switch the heater on. But it doesn't seem to abate my shakes. They're more fear than temperature induced, I realise. I sing to myself – 'Wonderwall', a comfort song from long ago, forcing my mind to go elsewhere, not to dwell on the destination. The words die on my lips as I spot the small lane branching

255

off to the left just ahead of me. I indicate and check DI Walker is following as I take the turn.

His car has backed off a little, the track becoming rough, uneven. Probably doesn't want to damage the underside of his fancy car on tree roots and mounds of earth, so he's taking it slowly. My car, on the other hand, bumps wildly. I jerk about as if I'm being thrown around during a washing machine cycle, my head knocking against the inside of the car door several times before I reach the small clearing. I park up, but I don't get out, taking a moment for my head to stop spinning.

After some steadying breaths, I scan the area. Is Henry there, in the trees, watching me? The Audi draws up next to me and I see DI Walker doing the same – conducting a visual sweep of the area. He reaches down and I lose sight of him for a few seconds before his head bobs back up and he gets out of the car. I think he's got a gun. A cold trickle of fear runs down my back. I remember that he said he'd ensure reinforcements were close by, and feel a wave of relief.

'You ready?' DI Walker ducks down at my window. I nod, grab my jacket and get out. My legs don't seem as though they'll hold me up; they feel spongy as I walk. DI Walker holds onto my arm, so I'm guessing it's clear just how wobbly I'm feeling. I have to at least *appear* stronger – I refuse to allow Henry to take every shred of my self-worth and dignity.

As we make our way into the woodland, it's like I've somehow stepped back in time. Each tree, each patch of ground has a familiarity to it that makes the hairs on my neck stand up. I even *feel* like I did the last time I was here, the way listening to a certain song can transport you back to the specific time when it meant something to you. I'm charged with electricity. A sense of anticipation. Only this anticipation is for something very different than before.

'Where exactly are you taking us?' DI Walker stops, looking back at the way we've come. 'How far are we going?'

'Not far,' I say, my breathing laboured.

'The cars will still be in sight? We shouldn't stray too far—'

'We have to go where we have to go,' I say, somewhat cryptically, I realise. But he'll understand soon.

'There were no other vehicles. Are you sure he's going to be here?'

'He'll be here.' I don't know Henry any more, if I ever did, but there's a certainty in my gut. 'I've got the right place, detective.'

'How can you be so sure? I know the riddle said *Meet me where the lie was spoke*, but could there be a chance it's somewhere else he meant?'

'Nope.'

I hear him give a huff, followed by a curse as he bats away some low foliage. 'You're the boss,' he mutters.

I stop, turning sharply back to face him. 'That's the last thing I am. Henry is in charge here.' For a moment we are locked in each other's gazes and something behind his eyes shifts. He blinks rapidly a few times and looks over my head, towards something beyond. 'Is that where we're going?'

Turning around I see the gap in the trees ahead. And something solid in the centre. I swallow hard, a sense of dread spreading rapidly through me. I put my hand to my chest; the thud of my heart vibrates against my palm.

'Yes. That's it.' My words, no more than a whisper, are immediately stolen by the breeze sighing through the trees. DI Walker gently moves me to one side, stepping in front of me.

'Stay back,' he says, drawing a gun from his waistband. A breath catches in my throat. I knew that's what he was getting when I saw him reaching down in his car. He holds it out now, sweeping it left to right as he checks the area. He indicates it's safe for me to carry on.

'Why do you have a gun?' I ask when we're level.

'I know it's not routine – and firearms support isn't far away – but I didn't want to risk . . .' He pauses, giving me a look I can't read.

'Risk what?' I prompt.

'I didn't want to risk losing you.'

I'm not sure how he means this – in an entirely professional "I don't want another woman to die on my watch" type way, or a more personal "I don't want you to die because I like you".

'Right, okay. Good,' I say. 'Then we're on the same page.' I attempt a smile.

We're almost where I need to be now, but my feet refuse to move any closer. I stand, rigid, squeezing my hands at my sides.

'Now we wait, I guess,' he says. I look away as he walks up to the stone-walled structure. 'Weird to have an old well in the middle of nowhere, isn't it?'

I don't answer. My vocal cords feel tight, like they'll snap if I try to talk. I take the water bottle he gave me and suck from the sports cap. When I am more confident of speech, I tell him about the woods. How some of the kids from the children's home came here to escape sometimes, but mostly it was deserted.

'This area was likely a farming region, or a settlement thousands of years ago,' I say.

DI Walker leans over the well. 'I wonder how far down it goes.' I half expect him to yell down it, like a child might do. But instead, he delves a hand into his pocket and throws a coin down. I hold my breath.

'I didn't hear it hit,' he says.

'The deepest hand-dug well is in East Sussex and it's 1,285 feet deep.'

He shoots me a curious look.

'I researched it once.' I shrug, giving a cautious glance around. 'Where are you, Henry?'

'It appears we still have some time.' DI Walker sits on the edge of the well.

'Can you not?' Irritation edges my words. He's going on about risks, but then he sits on an old stone well that could collapse at any moment.

'Maybe you should explain why we're here. What's the importance of this place for Henry?'

Now we're at the location and I've accepted this is where it all ends, there's no reason to hold on to my secret.

'You asked what the significance of the second date was. May the thirteenth. Well, this is it. It's the last place Henry and I were at together. It's where promises were made.

'He said it's where the *lie* was spoken, though?'

'I think he was referring to a line from the old poem. You know, the one I was telling you about: cross my heart, hope to die? Well, one of the lines from it is, "I spoke a lie – I never really wanted to die."'

DI Walker nods. Keeps nodding. 'I see. Or, I don't – but I'm guessing that was something between you and him. And each of the murders was a reference to that poem.'

'Exactly.' I take my jacket, and pull out the paper with the poem scrawled on it:

> Cross my heart and hope to die,
> Stick a needle in my eye.
> Wait a moment; I spoke a lie –
> I never really wanted to die.
> But if I may, and if I might,
> My heart is open for tonight.
> My lips are sealed and a promise is true:
> I won't break my word; my word to you.
> Cross my heart and hope to die,
> Stick a needle in my eye.
> A secret's a secret – my word is forever;
> I will tell no one about your cruel endeavour.
> You claim no pain, but I see right through
> Your words in everything you do.
> Teary eyes, broken heart:
> Life has torn you apart.

I pass it to the detective, then lay the jacket on the ground, sitting on it. I need to be comfortable to tell him this story. 'Those are all the verses. I scribbled it down when I couldn't sleep. I'm not sure who wrote it – I think there are a few variations. Point is, the main verse was the one he used all the time. Some kind of comfort blanket, really – a way of feeling sure no one was lying to him.

'I see,' DI Walker says. 'If he wanted to feel safe, that he wasn't alone, he'd make you swear to it. Cross your heart.'

'Yes. If he was really serious, he made you say "stick a needle in my eye". It was the ultimate show of trust, I guess.'

'So, what happened here all those years ago?' DI Walker scans the area, then looks back at me, his eyes imploring; intense.

'On the evening of May the thirteenth, we came here because Henry's clue for The Hunt led to the well.'

'We?'

'As much as she didn't want to be dragged into Henry's cruel games any more, my friend came too. She didn't want me to face him alone. Much the same as you don't want that now.'

There's a pause so loaded I forget to breathe.

'Go on,' DI Walker says. 'It's time you told me everything.'

Chapter 38

THEN

Anna leans over the well, throws a stone down. It doesn't make a sound. Kirsty paces around its perimeter, careful not to trip. They'd left Finley Hall at dusk to walk here, but now it's almost night.

'I don't get it,' Kirsty says. 'How did you know to come here?'

Anna straightens. 'Ding dong bell.' She splays her arms, both palms up, like it's obvious.

'And?' Kirsty widens her eyes at her friend, her patience diminishing fast. 'What's that got to do with this well?'

'It's the nursery rhyme. You know – ding dong bell, pussy's in the well . . .'

'Oh my God – he's killed a fucking cat, hasn't he?' Kirsty thrusts her upper body over the edge, starts calling, 'Here pussy,' and making a kissing noise.

'I don't think so,' Anna says, shaking her head.

'I wouldn't be so sure. He *has* killed other creatures

and left them for you. It wouldn't be a big stretch for him to murder a cat.'

'No, I know that. But if he had, he'd want me to see it, Kirst. It wouldn't be at the bottom of a dark hole.'

She huffs and pushes herself upright. 'He really is weird, Anna. Not right in the head.' She jabs a finger into her temple. 'Once we get out of Finley you have to cut all ties with him, you know that, right? I'm not having that walking danger sign anywhere near us.'

'It's hard. Despite everything he's done lately, the trouble he's got himself in with the police, he's still my brother. You know what it's like. Blood's thicker than water and all that.'

'Tell that to our loser parents.'

Anna bows her head. She knows Kirsty is right, but a part of her clings to the thought that she can help Henry. That his cruel behaviour is reversible.

'If he'd had a better upbringing. . . a better sister—'

'Don't you dare blame yourself for his behaviour, Anna Lincoln!' Kirsty grabs Anna's arm, squeezing it tight. 'You aren't responsible for his choices. Like you, me, and all the other kids at Finley weren't responsible for their mothers' or fathers' choices.'

'Okay, I know. Don't get your knickers in a twist,' Anna says, pulling her arm away.

'Sorry. I'm so tired of watching him torment you like this, is all. It does my head in. Why should he get away with being a bully?'

Anna frowns, suddenly aware her friend isn't herself. 'You seem a bit off, if you don't mind me saying. Is there something you're not telling me?'

Kirsty tucks her hair behind her ear. 'No. I'm fine. It's

nothing.' She wraps her arms around her belly and looks up at the night sky, then around at the trees. 'It's creepy here, I don't like it. And I bet he's in there, somewhere in the shadows, watching us.'

As if that was his cue, Henry crashes through the trees, laughing. '*You're* the pussies,' he jeers. 'Look at you, two dumb scaredy cats.'

'Oh, shut up, Henry,' Kirsty snaps. 'You're such a loser.'

'Whatever. I heard you, though. All creeped out by the rustling and the dark.' He shines a torch in her face, then swings it towards Anna, blinding her. She puts her hands to her eyes to shield them.

'I did what you wanted, Henry. I followed The Hunt, solved your stupid clue, there isn't even anything here – we're done.' With her chin tilted, she goes to walk past him.

'You're done when I say you're done.' He slaps his palm in the centre of Anna's chest and pushes her. She stumbles back a few steps. He lurches towards her again, pushes her again. The backs of her legs whack against the stone of the well.

'Enough,' Anna says, her voice breathy with fear. 'Please stop.'

'Leave her alone, you bully,' Kirsty says, striding up to them. 'I know you get off on hurting her, but give her a break, eh?'

'I could hurt you too, if you like. Change it up a bit.'

'You did that already, didn't you?' Anna shouts, and her words seem to hit a nerve, because Henry backs off.

'Because you didn't play the game,' he says, giving Anna a warning glance.

'Can you hear yourself?' Kirsty says. 'How childish that sounds? I do feel sorry for you. You didn't have the best start but neither did we. You aren't the only one to suffer, you know.'

'Kirst, leave it,' Anna says, putting her hand out to her friend.

'He's pathetic, Anna.'

Henry's eyes blaze. Anna's seen that look in her brother's eyes before – the one where he feels backed into a corner, where memories of how he was made to feel worthless, emasculated, flash through his mind – and Kirsty's crossing a line, triggering him. She can sense the tension; it's palpable. But Kirsty doesn't stop.

'Look at him. Weak little boy who needs to hurt girls to feel all big and powerful.' Her rage-filled words spill from her, and Anna realises this isn't actually about Henry. Not specifically. Her anger is for someone else.

'Kirsty, please. Stop.'

Anna gets in between Kirsty and Henry. 'This has to end. All of it.' She turns to Henry. 'The Hunt finishes here, tonight. Forever.' Then she looks at Kirsty. 'And you need to see someone about what happened,' she says, softly. Kirsty lays a hand on her stomach, and Anna catches the expression in Kirsty's eyes as she does. Her own stomach drops with sudden understanding. Oh, God. Why hadn't she realised? Why hadn't Kirsty confided in her? Anna gasps and takes a step back, leaving Kirsty and Henry facing each other.

'You don't mean anything to my sister, Kirsty Briggs,' Henry says, pushing her up against the stone. Then he turns to Anna. 'And you pretend to care about your so-called friend, but really you don't give a shit. Your friend was raped and you were too wrapped up in yourself to have even realised.'

266

Time stands still – truth and pain, lies and betrayal all mix together, and everything is laid bare. In this moment, they are all seen. Anna's mouth gapes open and her eyes sting with tears.

'It's your fault, Henry.' She speaks quietly, then with more power. 'It's all your fault I didn't realise. I'm always so preoccupied by you! You suck the life from me, I've nothing left for anyone else.' And without warning, something inside her fractures. A lifetime of hurt swells in her brain, pressure building so fast she knows it needs to be released or her head will explode. With a scream as if she's a soldier going into battle, Anna propels herself at her brother as he stands smugly beside the well. Her body slams into his and his feet leave the ground as he is pushed onto the stone wall. They thrash about on the edge, Anna on top of Henry, her fists slamming into his chest. Kirsty is yelling 'No!' but Anna doesn't hear it. There's tugging and pulling. Henry regains his balance and manages to stand up, pushing Anna off him. She stumbles back, falling to the ground.

Kirsty takes a step towards Anna just as Henry lets out a belly laugh.

'On the floor, where you belong.'

'Enough, Henry,' Kirsty says. 'Come on, this has gone far enough.' She stretches out a hand to help Anna up, but Anna smacks it away.

'I'm fine.' She gets up and she and Henry stare each other out.

'Look at me, Anna,' Henry taunts, sitting on the edge of the well again, his body leaning back. 'You haven't got the *guts.*'

And with another burst of energy, Anna runs at him,

her hands out ready to push him. Kirsty thrusts herself between them and when Anna's body makes contact all three of them fall back. The struggle – all arms and legs, grunting and groaning – lasts no more than a minute. There's a scream, a desperate, blood-curdling cry that rips the night apart.

Then silence.

'What the fuck.' The words are weak, shock-filled. Then louder. 'What the actual fuck!'

Henry's face is pale in the darkness.

'What have you done? God, Henry, what did you do?'

Chapter 39

DI Walker's face is as pale as Henry's was that night. I wonder if it's disbelief, shock, or downright revulsion that I've kept this from him. Indeed, that I kept this secret for seventeen years.

'It was a terrible tragedy. It was so dark. Emotions were raging through me. I had this strange super strength – the adrenaline, I guess, and the things Henry said . . . I lost it, Detective Walker. I hated him in that moment and wanted him dead.'

'But Kirsty got in the way. It was her who was pushed to her death.' DI Walker drops to the ground, cross-legged in front of me.

Tears bubble, then fall down my face. 'I've lived with the guilt from that moment on.'

'Well, that makes it all right then.' His head is in his hands, like he can't stand to look at me now he knows what I did.

'No. Nothing will ever make it okay. But I've tried,

since, to do good. Live a life my friend would be proud of.'

His head snaps back up. 'I imagine Kirsty would rather have lived her own bloody life, don't you?'

I let his question hang between us. Nothing I can say now will make this better. Justify it in any way. What's done is done. I can't take it back however much I beg the universe, and I did that a lot in the early days after that night.

'Where is Henry?' I say, as a way to change the subject, but also because I'm guessing he must be somewhere close, watching this unfold. I get up, swivel around, checking the treeline for movement. 'This is what he wanted to expose; it's why he wanted you here – so the police would know what I'd done. So I couldn't wriggle out of it, blame everything on him.'

'Like I assume you tried to do that night? Like you'd continue to do, if you had the chance. You're a piece of work, Anna.'

I stare at him. 'What? It *was* his fault. To begin with at least – he was the reason we were here that night.'

'And he's the reason you're here now,' DI Walker says. 'He got what he wanted, I suppose. You've finally told the truth.'

'Now what, then?' I look into his eyes, wondering what he's thinking. Is he going to arrest me now? Right here? He's not moving, he's not calling anyone. Maybe he's weighing it up. It's not me who's been murdering women for the past three years, I suppose. It's Henry he wanted help catching, not me. If I'm careful, I might be in with a chance of being let off. If I help him catch Henry still, will that buy me my own freedom? All the possibilities scroll through my mind like scenes in a movie. And all movies end with the bad guy being served justice, don't they? Am I the bad guy?

'I'm not a bad person, detective. It was an accident and I freaked out. Henry too. We made a promise to each other that we'd tell no one. What was the point?'

'The point? Are you serious?' His voice is suddenly so loud it rings in my ears, and I cower. I should've expected his anger – I'm sure it's been building, not only the past few days, but during this entire case. He's told me he doesn't want to have to inform any more family members about the death of their loved one. And now, what I've told him means he will have to.

He paces around the well, his hand rubbing his chin. 'Who were you to make that call? Eh?'

'I . . . Well . . . Her parents . . . they gave her up,' I stutter, feeling under fire, but then I recover. 'And yes, she had a brother who loved her, and it killed me to know he was going to suffer not ever knowing what happened to her.'

'Not enough, though, clearly. And it didn't *kill* you, did it. That's a dumb thing to say.'

I cast a wary glance around me. 'I think it's going to.'

DI Walker sighs, then bites on his lower lip. He takes the few steps to the well and leans over. 'So she's down there.'

'Yes, DI Walker, she is.' I hold back the tears because I have a feeling that'll irritate the detective further. 'You might want to make that call for backup now. Get forensics and what-have-you on-scene. I'm not sure that Henry's going to show his face. He's probably been hiding in the trees all this time and knows it's game over for me. He's got what he was after.'

'Do you think?'

I'm surprised to see such sadness in DI Walker's expression. I suppose this isn't the ending he was hoping for. I hold my hands out towards him, my wrists together, but even as I stand with my past mistakes laid out, my vulnerabilities on show, I know it's not everything. There'll be more humiliation to follow.

'Here you go,' I shake my outstretched arms at him. 'I get to go to prison, and Henry gets away with everything. Perfect.'

'Not yet it's not,' DI Walker says. I narrow my eyes at him, unsure what he means. I feel a surge of hope that he doesn't want to cuff me. That he thinks I've suffered enough. That he'll let me go.

'Sit down, Anna.' He pushes my hands down. 'I'm not cuffing you.'

Relief surges through me and I sit, more because my legs have turned to jelly than because he's asked me to.

I close my eyes and all of a sudden I feel exhausted. 'Thank you. Thank you.'

'I'm not cuffing you because I don't have any cuffs.'

My eyes spring open to see him reaching into his inside pocket. My heart skips. What's he doing? I don't have long to ponder, because he's already tearing a strip of duct tape off and coming towards me. Shit. No handcuffs – so he's going to use that instead. He did say he was always prepared – although my mouth is itching to remark that he wasn't *that* prepared, or wouldn't he be carrying a set? I swallow that smart-mouthed comment and instead hold my hands up again.

'Fine,' I say, letting out a deep sigh.

He laughs as he wraps it around my wrists. I wince at

the sounds it makes as it peels off the roll. Another layer wraps around me, tighter than the last.

'That hurts,' I say, trying to pull away from it. 'You can stop now; I think you've made your point.'

'Like you did, you mean? By not reporting a death. That's a hell of a point. If it were an accident, like you said, why didn't you say something?'

'In hindsight, there was likely a better option. At the time, I was young and really afraid and I couldn't see one. And Henry—'

'Oh, Henry, Henry, Henry!' DI Walker blurts out, and I reel. 'If I hear his bloody name one more time. You can't blame him for it all, Anna. He was your younger brother. He looked up to you.' He shakes his head vehemently.

'I – I'm sorry, I don't . . .' I want to say I don't mean to anger him, but I can't finish my sentence. This situation suddenly feels all wrong. His demeanour is different. 'Are the rest of your team going to be here soon? Or are you taking me to the station yourself?' My voice quivers. Adrenaline begins to course through my veins, sensing the fear before I actually *feel* it.

'No one's coming, Anna.' DI Walker brings the roll of tape towards me – but this time, he slaps a piece hard against my mouth.

Chapter 40

I'm usually a nose breather. Very rarely a mouth breather unless I'm congested with a cold. But now, with tape over my lips preventing any intake of air, panic sets in and I can't get enough oxygen through my nostrils. *What is happening? Why is he doing this?*

My trust in the police force was knocked when I was a teenager, but while I may have questioned his tactics, I never once questioned DI Walker's authority, his authenticity. Because why would a member of the police – a detective inspector, for God's sake – be someone to be afraid of? They are there to protect the public – to help, inspire, reassure, uphold the law – not to break it themselves; not to induce fear by binding and gagging innocent people.

I kick out, then freeze. I don't want to give him reason to bind my legs too. I bring them back close to my body. Hot tears sting my eyes as confusion clouds my mind and tendrils of fear wrap around my lungs, compressing them. DI Walker crouches in front of me. I could kick out again now, but I doubt I'd do enough damage to get away. And with my hands taped, even if I managed to make it to my car, how would I drive? He gently sweeps a piece of hair from my forehead and looks into my eyes.

'You don't have a clue, do you? Don't you recognise me?'

I can't breathe. My heart rate doubles in an instant. I see black dots in my field of vision. I cry, try to scream, but can't.

Henry.

DI Walker is Henry? The sky spins as the air in my lungs decreases.

'Don't think that I'll remove the tape if you pretend you can't breathe, Anna. I've seen enough to know when someone is going to die from lack of oxygen.' He smiles, then puts his hands on my upper arms, pulling me into a sitting position from my slumped one. He takes a wet wipe and dabs my nose, clearing it of the snot. 'Slowly breathe in through your nose, Anna. Hold it, and release – again, slowly.'

If I ignore his instruction, I will pass out. I don't know how long it'll take. Maybe seconds if I panic enough, increasing the level of carbon dioxide in my system. If I'm really lucky, perhaps I'll kill myself before he does.

'If you don't calm down and do as I say, then you'll never know the "why", will you? Come on, breathe.'

I begin hyperventilating to spite him. He slaps my cheek.

'Do as I say, or you won't be the only one to die today.' His voice has taken on a different tone. Harsh, angry.

Unrecognisable from the one he used when he first stood in my house on Tuesday.

My eyes widen and a strangulated groaning noise emanates from deep in my throat.

'In through your nose.' He glares at me until I do it. 'Out through your nose.' I continue until I've got a more natural rhythm going. Seemingly pleased with me, he stands and paces around the well again.

Then it hits me. Henry already knew there was a body at the bottom of the well. He had been here. He'd been part of it. I scramble to bring my legs underneath myself and use my bound hands to push myself onto my knees. I make a noise to get his attention.

'Finally,' he says when he catches the look on my face. 'I said it before; I'll say it again: call yourself a teacher?' He shakes his head. 'You're a bit slow, Anna.'

I'm inclined to agree, and if I were able to speak, I'd say so. But I'm still not getting it. Who is this man? Who is Detective Inspector Walker?

'Do you give in?' he says. He walks around the front of the well and bends down so that our eyes are level. 'Hey, Anna. Long time no see,' he says, and pretends to shake my hand. 'You might not remember me; and to be fair, I wouldn't have recognised you either. We've both changed a lot over the years.'

I squint at him. I felt it a few times, I realise now – that inkling, a sense that I'd seen him before – but I hadn't made any links with him and my past life. Why would I?

'I've waited a long time to find the person responsible for my sister's disappearance.'

Sister? I frown. None of this makes sense.

Until it does.

I shake my head. *No. He isn't. He can't be. No, no, no.*

'Yep. It's true – no good shaking your head at me. I was Dean Briggs – Kirsty's younger brother. Remember me now?'

Chapter 41

THEN

'You know this is bullshit, don't you?' Dean paces outside Miss Graves's office. Henry shuffles his feet, not looking at Dean, his focus remaining on the closed door, his ear against it listening to the muffled voices of the manager, Frank the caretaker, and the two officers who were updating them on the investigation into Anna's and Kirsty's disappearance. 'They just can't be bothered, that's the truth of it.'

'Two runaways from the "scabby home" were never gonna gain a whole lot of attention, though, were they,' Henry says, moving away from the door. 'They'll be added to the long list of missing children that no one will ever do anything about. Case closed.' He turns his back and starts walking away.

'That's it? That's all you have to say about this? Our sisters are missing, dickhead. Could be dead in a ditch somewhere. And you're happy to walk away?'

'Look, mate—'

'I'm not your mate.' Dean squares up to Henry, his eyes blazing.

'Whatever,' Henry says, his hands up in surrender. 'They ran away. Left us here in this hellhole. Get over it.' Henry strides down the corridor, but Dean isn't finished.

'Nah,' Dean says, shaking his head and rushing after Henry. 'There's more to it.' He grabs him by the arm, swinging him around to face him. 'And you know it. Don't you? What aren't you telling me?' Dean pushes his face right up to Henry's, the tips of their noses touching.

Henry scoffs and pushes Dean away. 'Just trust me. Your sister's in a better place.'

'What's that meant to mean? What the fuck have you done?'

'Nothing. For Christ's sake, Dean. I'm sorry you've been dumped like me, but face facts – it's not the first time and it won't be the last. Our selfish bloody sisters planned their escape and didn't involve us – end of. They ditched us for a better life. We're on our own now.'

It was the last time they'd speak to each other for thirteen years. Dean Briggs made a promise to himself that he would never stop searching for Kirsty, though. He wasn't going to give up on his sister like everyone else. Like Henry had given up on his.

Henry's indifference had bothered him more and more over the months and years, until he became sure Henry knew what had happened to Kirsty and Anna. Had he helped them run away? Or hurt them? After Dean broke into Miss Graves's filing cabinet and read what she'd written about Kirsty's rape and resultant pregnancy – and her futile attempt to lie and pretend that it was Anna who'd been assaulted instead – he wondered if his sister had been so distraught at what happened to her, what she'd been forced to do, that she couldn't cope with her feelings and had done something drastic.

All his unanswered questions plagued him; gnawed at his brain day and night. When he was old enough to leave supervision and Finley Hall, he did, getting a job with a security firm and renting a room in a shared house. Everyone else who left Finley also scattered; there was no trace of who had gone where. Initially this worked to Dean's advantage, as it meant no one could look him up either. He'd heard about the fire at Finley – all those records he knew Miss Graves kept on the children were conveniently destroyed. For a few years, Dean kept his head down and worked hard until he'd saved up enough to find his own flat.

It was when he lived alone, isolated from others, that he allowed his obsession to take over. Convinced that Henry was the only one who held the answers, he spent every spare moment gathering information and trying to find him. When his means ran out and he was no further forward, he knew he had to up his game.

And whose literal job was it to find missing persons?

Chapter 42

It's as though the world has stopped turning and I'm falling off. Plummeting down, fast, my heart leaping into my mouth. How can DI Walker be Dean? The notion is so ridiculous I laugh, and the restricted, throaty noise sounds alien to my ears. I narrow my eyes at him. My incomprehension must be clear for him to see, because he lunges at me, and I flinch, whipping my head to the side. He sneers, grabs my chin between his thumb and forefinger, and twists my head so his face is inches from mine.

His eyes are wrong – almost everything about him is different. Yet, in my heart, I know. Why hadn't I recognised him? Despite the years without seeing him, I should've known; something should've triggered a recollection.

'Look at you, grasping at every memory you have of me, trying to decide if I'm telling the truth.'

A low groan vibrates against the tape on my mouth,

and I thrash my legs like a spoilt toddler who can't get their own way, frustration at not being able to speak burning my insides. I say the words *Let. Me. Speak.* over and over in my head, then try to verbalise them, but a distressed humming sound, like one of those kazoo instruments we had in music lessons at school, is all I can produce. I bring my bound hands to my mouth and begin rubbing them against the duct tape.

'Bloody hell.' He forces my hands down with his. 'You're not helping yourself if you think creating that noise is going to make me take the tape off. I put it on for a reason. I'm not having you running your mouth off, interrupting me while I talk.' He pats his hand on my coat pockets, then delves into the left one and pulls my mobile from it. 'I'll take this,' he says. He backs away and sits against the tree a few metres away, his legs bent up in front of him, his elbows resting on them. Gun in one hand, my phone in the other.

I don't make another sound, but the thrumming of my heartbeat is loud in my ears.

His face contorts and he bangs the barrel of the gun against his temple.

'I knew something bad had happened to her,' he says. 'There's no way she'd have left me in that hellhole without so much as a goodbye. That runaway story that Miss Graves tried to spin – it was bullshit.' He lies the gun beside himself while he opens the mobile, removes the SIM card and cracks it in half. Placing the phone on the ground, he picks his gun back up and whacks its barrel down onto it. I hear the casing splinter. He strikes it several times until the phone is bent and twisted, then he resumes his position, gun in hand.

I lean, tilting my head to try to get his attention, but his eyes are glazed, like he's somewhere else. Seeing the past. He carries on speaking without looking at me.

'I knew that night, when I saw you both creeping back in long after curfew, that something was very wrong. Kirsty's face – it was like she was wearing a mask. There was no emotion. The light had gone out. Then I found out about the attack.' He shakes his head, wipes at his eyes – and my heart aches. He'd always been good to his sister – she'd never appreciated it enough. My memory of that night forces itself into my mind: the party, its aftermath, and a day later, Dean being dragged into Miss Graves's office, his face bruised. He took revenge on Neil then, like he's going to take revenge on me now. Only, this time, it won't be a beating he inflicts. The five women he's murdered – how he snuffed out their lives – give the best indication of how I'm dying today.

I'm desperate to know, though: *why me?* What about Henry? He had a part to play in all of this – a massive part. I get the impression he's intending to give me the full story, and I hope and pray it's a long one. The sky is darkening – I've no idea of the time but I need to eke this out for as long as possible if I've any chance of being saved.

But no one knows where you are, Anna.

My chest tightens as this reality hits me, and I struggle again to draw enough air in through my nostrils. Given his intentions, I'm guessing he didn't really inform the team of the location. Maybe he hasn't told them any of it. And I have a sinking feeling Ross won't be in a position to come looking for me, even if he is capable of reading my text. A sob catches in my throat and I cough. It's a

285

weird sensation with something covering my mouth. I swallow then take a slow, gentle breath. I can't afford to have a coughing fit, or vomit, or anything that'll cause choking.

Serena. There's still a flickering flame of hope, because my friend is clever and she'll read between the lines of my message. She'll know something is up. Maybe, given recent events, she'll be worried enough to go to the police. DI Walker – Dean – didn't take my phone off me until just now. It must be traceable up to then, surely?

But Dean is a detective inspector. Will the police just assume I'm fine because I'm with him? History might be repeating itself. They did nothing about two runaways back in the day, and maybe they'll do nothing about me being missing now, either. As far as they're concerned, Henry is the one they're after. He's the serial killer, not Dean. Not their very own DI Walker.

Dean's been talking, I realise. I'd lost concentration. I need to keep up.

'You knew she'd been attacked but you only told me half a story. I was her brother – you should've told me everything.'

I should've told – it's a regret that weighed me down for a very long time. But I can't think about that now; there's a more pressing issue. He's not watching me. If I bend my knees up, put my head towards them, I can start picking at the tape on my mouth. If I could just free it enough to get some words out, I could get myself out of this predicament. I need to speak.

'That lowlife raped her.' The tears – of anger or hurt, probably both – are apparent in his voice. 'In hindsight, the beating I gave him was nothing compared to what it should've been.'

There's a pause and I look up quickly. He's staring at me. Did he see what I was doing? I cough, open my eyes wide.

'I'm not removing the tape. Not until I've said everything I need to say. You've had your time. You kept quiet about my sister all these years, kept the whole truth from me – now you're going to keep your mouth shut for as long as I say. Understand?'

I jerk my head, trying to communicate that I understand. But he's seen something. He squints, then stands, coming closer. Then his face is inches from mine.

'Hah! You sneaky shit,' he hisses. He gets the roll of tape, pulls off another strip and presses it hard against my mouth. 'Think you can peel this off?' He wraps it around the back of my head. Around and around, tighter and tighter, and I let out small whimpers with each rotation. Once he's satisfied that I'm not going to be able to pick at it, he stands back.

'No. That's not going to stop you, is it? If nothing else, you've proved you're not to be trusted. You've given me no choice.' He pulls at the tape on my wrists, freeing them. Without hesitation I push my hands against his chest, try with all my strength to get him away from me long enough to use this opportunity to rip the tape from my mouth.

'No you don't,' he says, spreading my arms and wrestling me flat to the ground. He flips me onto my front and yanks my hands back behind me, and I yelp in pain. Then he wraps the tape around them again.

I lie on the ground, sobbing. He's made it impossible for me to save myself.

'Up you get.' His hands are on me again, moving me

to a sitting position. 'Okay, where was I?' He steps away and sits against the tree again. Dean continues to relay how he never got over Kirsty's disappearance; how he had become obsessed with finding out where she was. And how one night, he had broken into Miss Graves's office and searched the files she kept on every child at the home. He'd read about the rape allegation made by Anna, but knew it wasn't right. Then, as he flicked through his sister's file he had made the devastating discovery. A pregnancy was mentioned. He had assumed this was the reason behind her running away.

'It cut, you know? That she didn't trust me enough to confide in me. My sister felt so alone, she thought her only option was to run away – or so I was led to believe. Miss Graves told us – me and Henry – that she had evidence you two had been planning it for a long time and had been waiting for the opportunity to put it into action. You'd left us. Gone without a word. You know, I never even had a photo to remember her by? My own sister. I don't suppose the last image I have of her face is even accurate.' He shakes his head. 'I was gutted, but Henry wasn't at all bothered. And it was his devil-may-care attitude that made me look closer at him. I knew he did those freaky riddles; I heard you and Kirsty talking about The Hunt – she even involved me in one once. I couldn't prove he had anything to do with Kirsty's disappearance, but it niggled away at me, and I kept my eye on that psycho. It was in his eyes – a calmness, a knowing look. I became convinced he'd killed the both of you.'

The ground is hard. Twigs and stones press against my bottom, my arms ache and my face stings. I close my eyes, and my ears, to Dean. I've got the gist. He blamed Henry

288

for his sister's disappearance, possibly her death, and he devoted his life to finding out what happened to her. It's fair enough and actually, very caring in a fucked-up sort of way. I don't need to hear more. His voice drones on, strangely hypnotic in the relative silence of the woodland, and for a moment, I give up and start to drift. Then something sparks inside my skull and my survival instinct kicks in; my mind begins to search frantically for a way out of this.

'Get up!' His breath is hot against my ear. 'How dare you.' The blood leaves my head and I feel strange, woozy, like I've been drugged. His arms are under my armpits, and he drags me to a standing position. My legs are tingly and weak, won't hold me up, and I fall like a rag doll back to the ground. His breath heaves, his face turns a deep shade of red as his anger rises rapidly and he hauls me to my feet again.

'Listen, bitch,' he says, spittle flying from his mouth. 'I've not spent my adult life tracking your brother and you down for you to ignore me like I don't matter.' He props me up against the stone wall of the well and I'm transported back seventeen years to when Henry did the same. This is where it ends. I'm going to be thrown to my death into the dark hole alongside my childhood friend. 'You ready to hear the rest?' he says. I nod, keep nodding, fear surging through my veins. 'Come on, Anna Lincoln. Don't forget your roots. Us kids from the scabby home have a shared history, don't we?'

I'm not Anna Lincoln. I worked hard to escape those roots, become a better person. I scrunch up what little of my face I can still move and shrug, while in my head I repeat: *I am Anna Price. I am Anna Price.* I carved out a good life for myself and until Dean came along, everything was going well. I ignore the nagging voice that contradicts this. Now's not the time to think about Ross and Yasmin. If I'd had the chance – been in the right headspace – I might've been able to deal with that situation, and maybe even reverse it.

'We were all mistreated. Abused. It was something we got used to. Whether we like it or not, it impacted who we were. Who we are today. I had many days when I almost forgave Henry. You. You were both victims of circumstance. Seeing him each day, though, made it impossible. I couldn't let it go. I guess I'm also a product of the broken system. I do see that. I just try to balance it out by doing good, too.'

How much time has passed? Streaks of orange merge with dark grey clouds, and the sun is dipping behind the tall trees. If no one comes soon, we'll be difficult to find. I think we'd hear approaching vehicles, though – we're not that far from where our two cars are parked. If I make enough of a commotion, I might gain attention to lead police to me. I'm thinking this through as Dean explains how Finley Hall closed due to a string of claims detailing negligence and abuse. And, as I told him when he asked a few days ago, the children were all sent to different places – they were scattered around the country. Then Finley Hall had a massive fire, destroying files and ensuring evidence of the wrongdoing never came fully to light. Miss Graves, Frank and all the other carers escaped prosecution.

'I lost track of almost everyone. It wasn't such a big loss. But it did mean finding Henry was difficult. It's one of the reasons I became a policeman: so that I could track Henry down.'

I whip my head around, eyes wide, my interest piqued. Did he find Henry before he found me?

'It was a surprise, I admit, when I finally found him, and things came to light that I hadn't factored in.'

My pulse thumps in my neck, my breaths becoming shallow. I stare at Dean, trying to read his expression.

'He wasn't what I'd been expecting all those years. You'd have been proud of your little brother, Anna. He turned out pretty well considering his past. *He* didn't recognise me either, but then, he was worse for wear. Blind drunk. He said he was celebrating his new job. He was a talker, I'll give him that. Ahh . . .' Dean lets out a sigh, then directs a smile at me. 'Your brother's face is imprinted in my mind. Along with all my other victims.'

My head is suddenly too heavy to hold up, and it drops to my chest. None of what's been happening recently is down to Henry, and a surge of guilt pushes its way through me for thinking it was. Dean murdered Henry. But why, then, did he come after me? If Henry had stuck to the story we agreed, then Dean should've stopped there.

Hadn't he got what he was after by taking revenge on Henry?

Chapter 43

Dean is behind a tree, peeing up the trunk, offering me respite from his story. The next instalment, he has informed me, will be all about Henry. It's the part where I assume I'll find out how he sold me up the river. As I hang my head, my chin on my chest, I go over my options. There is one that would definitely save me, make all this go away, but I'd need to talk to him for that, and my mouth is taped shut. I could scream with the frustration of it. The fact that all of this, everything that has happened the last few days, even years, has been so unnecessary, such a waste . . .

I rack my brain for a way to get the tape off my mouth. My hands are so cold they're painful. I rub my fingertips together, thankful my bound wrists aren't constricting their movement. I must keep the circulation going.

Then I realise. The tape is looser than it felt at first – my hands were warmer when he wrapped the tape around

293

them and now the temperature drop has made them shrink a little.

The hope almost makes me dizzy.

If I'm able to work my hands free, I could remove the tape from my mouth – enough to be heard, at least. It's always what you hear or read about, in situations of kidnap – talking to the perpetrator, relating to them, making yourself human in their eyes, gives you a better chance of escape. But I wouldn't need all that . . .

My entire body shakes. An overwhelming ache – the desperate need to live is sending adrenaline pumping through me. The plastic layer of tape crinkles and gives a little as I twist my wrists and pull them apart a bit. My skin burns as it rubs against the sticky side, but I keep going. I'm sure there's a gap now. Despite the cold, a layer of sweat forms on my forehead and more trickles down my back as my wrists rub against it while I try to work them free.

Keep going. Twist, pull, twist, pull.

Twigs crack under Dean's footsteps. He's finished. My twisting becomes more frenzied and realising I'm almost out of time, I pull my dominant hand upwards to try and release it before he returns. But it's impossible – I haven't made enough of a gap yet. Frustration burns in my chest, and I want to cry.

Crybaby. I hear the mocking words inside my head. A vision of a man's face swims in front of my eyes, and I can even smell his sour breath. *Gonna cry to Mummy, are you? You and that pathetic brother of yours are a waste of space. Can't believe I have to share the same air as you.* I bite down on my tongue, willing the flashback to stop. I repeat the words *I'm strong* in my head, then give myself some positive self-talk: I've successfully put my old life behind me. I survived Finley Hall – I can survive this. Determination burns within me.

I lift my head, my eyes on Dean as he comes closer, and alter my position. With my legs outstretched I rub my feet against the ground so they make a rustling sound. This will hopefully cover the sounds of me twisting and pulling the tape so I don't alert him to what I'm up to. As long as I remain focused on him when he starts talking again, so he believes he's got my full attention, I'll be able to work my hand free and bide my time before attempting to remove the tape he's wrapped around my head. Picking the right time is essential, because if I try too early, and fail . . .

Don't let your mind go there.

His expression doesn't show much emotion. It's like now that he's got me here and revealed who he is, he's on autopilot.

'Oh, I'm sorry. You probably need to go too, don't you,' he says, just as he's about to sit against the tree again. I give a vigorous shake of my head. I can't risk him seeing that the tape on my wrists is loose. He shrugs. 'Whatever. Piss yourself for all I care. You will anyway when I start on you.'

The threat sends a chill through my bones, but I don't let him see my fear. I stare, unblinking, at him until he looks away. *Does he feel shame?* I wonder. Guilt about what he's planning to do to me? I bet he covers my face when he 'starts' on me. The crime photos he showed me flit through my mind's eye. Those women weren't covered, but I read somewhere that often, if a murder is personal – someone known to them – the perpetrator can't look at them.

It's unnerving how he's changed since revealing his true identity. His mannerisms, speech, movements, have all altered. Even his facial features have taken a different shape – harder, sharper. He rubs at his eyes, then with his thumb and forefinger, he pinches his eyeball. What's he doing?

'These have driven me mad every day,' he says, flicking something onto the grass. 'But it's surprising how a change of eye colour makes someone look so different.'

Of course. I knew the azure blue was too intense; the shade never altered, no matter what the lighting, no matter what he wore. And now I remember how I thought something had shifted behind his eyes earlier, but that must've been the lenses moving. I can't be too hard on myself for not noticing, though, because even if he hadn't worn coloured lenses, I still wouldn't have ever suspected he was Dean. Knowing who he is now, and seeing him in front of me, he is still too unfamiliar, like the passage of time has stolen my memory of his face the last time I saw it. I can't picture him as a child, either. With no photos of my past, and from years of burying everything about it, I've no frame of reference.

DI Walker could've even told me his name was Dean when we first met and I probably wouldn't have made the connection.

'Where was I?' he says now. 'Henry, yes. Twelve years on the force before I finally found your brother. It was a bizarre twist of fate. I suffered a mix of emotions: relief he was still alive, hatred that he was still alive, a sense of success, a sense of failure – every juxtaposition you can think of, really. The strangest thing was seeing him for the first time since we were teenagers. In my head, my image of him was as a thirteen-year-old boy, not a thirty-year-old man, and to be honest it threw me. I contemplated walking away. But when I was face to face with the man I knew was key to finding out where Kirsty was, my passion to bring it all to an end was so overwhelming. All I wanted to do was kill him.'

I flinch at the intensity of his voice. It's how he feels about me, too; I can feel it.

'Course, I had to manage my deep-rooted rage, for a while at least, so that I could get what I needed from him. So, there at the bar in a pokey pub in the middle of nowhere, I struck up a conversation, safe in the knowledge he wouldn't recognise me.'

I raise my eyebrows.

'Because, Anna, your brother was blind drunk. Which was good in a number of ways. He didn't ask why I offered him a beer, wasn't bothered who I was, where I came from, what I wanted with him – he was celebrating, he said. Needed a partner in crime to drink with because he had no mates.'

A sadness swoops through me. Henry was a broken child, grew up broken, and it sounds as though he stayed that way until his life was stubbed out.

'He gave me an inroad, if you like. A way to talk about the past. He told me all about how he and his sister were taken into care, how they grew apart and that he reacted badly. He became mean, spiteful, out of control; he admitted that. I imagine we both agree with him there, eh?' Dean looks up at the sky, then gets up. 'Getting dark. I need to see your face clearly for this.' He brushes himself off, walking towards me. I stop twisting my wrists for the moment, afraid he'll catch me. I shut my eyes, say a silent prayer that he doesn't sit next to me, then open them. He's close, but opposite me. I should still be able to move my hands without attracting his attention, but it'll have to be more subtle to prevent him hearing the crinkling.

'Henry was keen to explain The Hunt to me – even recounted some of the riddles, which was super helpful of him – and how he'd gone through a few rough years at the home, followed by even rougher years outside of it, but then got himself straight again. Your brother came good in the end, you'll be pleased to know. He trained and qualified as a plumber.'

It's almost too much to bear. It's like watching the film *Titanic*, knowing no matter what else happens, the ending is inevitable – there is only one outcome. Poor Henry. Years of disliking him, being afraid of him, melt away. Dean is clearly relishing building up to the finale of his time with Henry. His now-brown eyes are filled with excitement as he recounts the last moments.

'Then I asked him about you – how you must be proud of his achievements – and at first, he crumbled, became a quivering wreck. But then he got angry. Began blaming you for his nightmares, the fact he was never able to fully let go of his past – how the secret would end up being the death of him, saying, "It was an accident, but we did it."'

My eyes hurt from holding them open so wide. Waiting for the punchline, for Dean to deliver the twist in the tale so that he can get to the part he's spent the past three years planning, fantasising about: killing me.

'You know what's coming, don't you?' As his breathing shallows, I speed up my efforts at loosening the tape. He's so lost in his retelling of his story I don't think he'll hear my attempts. I'm so close, I'm sure of it. If he gives me just a bit more time, I can do this.

'Unfortunately, this is where it goes south. Drunk Henry was already a bit confusing, but a drunk and unstable Henry made my task all the more challenging. He kept repeating "It was an accident", but when I pressed him on the details, he clammed up. He did let some titbits of information slip, though. And despite his drunken gabbling, I finally figured out the secret you and Henry swore to keep.'

Dean stands now and moves to the well, leaning over it as he carries on speaking.

'You were the one that pushed my sister down there. Left her alone. Shit,' Dean says, peering down. 'She might've still been alive. Did you even consider that?'

He pushes himself away from the well and grabs a chunk of my hair, yanking my head back. I let out a muffled scream.

'"She died, man. We killed her"', Dean yells in my face. 'That's what your brother said. Can you imagine hearing those words, Anna? I can tell you, Henry finally confirming my biggest fear was like someone ripping my heart out with their bare hands.'

I whimper, and plead with my eyes to try and make him take the tape off. But he's deep in his memory of when he met Henry now, I don't think he's even really aware of me – he's talking at me, through me. I'm merely a conduit for his anger.

'In those moments after you did it, Henry finally decided to be the good little brother because, no doubt, he felt guilty for the way he'd treated you. So he stepped up to the mark, and once he realised what might happen to you if the truth were to come out, he told you to run away. That he'd stay, make sure everyone believed you and your friend had done a runner. That's about the size of it, isn't it? He didn't give all the details, because once I realised my sister was dead, I couldn't keep the years of anger that had been building contained. My bad.'

A muffled groan emanates from behind my taped mouth as I realise he's about to tell me what he did.

'I lost my composure, took him outside and killed him before I got the location of her body. I've never hated anyone more than I hated myself when I realised that. But once I'd calmed down, it dawned on me that I had enough to be able to make sure *you* would lead me to my sister. I just had to find you. Took some years, but here you are.' He glances at the well again, shaking his head, his face falling and his voice softening. 'Here she is. I can grieve properly now. You were happy taking that opportunity away from me. Didn't even give me a second thought when you left your past behind, did you?'

He pushes me back down, then ducks down to roughly wipe the tears from my face.

'Henry did his best to protect you over the years, Anna – and he took the secret to his grave, as the saying goes. Like you're going to take mine to yours.'

Instinct tells me to get up and run. I know I won't get far, but my legs kick against the ground as though of their own accord, a cloud of dirt billowing into the air around my feet as they scramble and slip on the earth. It's like they are disconnected from my body, no longer controlled by my brain. Dean lays a hand on my thigh and laughs.

'Don't panic, Anna. It's not your time yet. Like it wasn't the other night.'

I frown. The other night?

'You were really out of it, weren't you?' He tuts, and a shiver runs the length of my spine. How would he have known that? 'Anything could've happened, Anna, without your cheating, lying husband there to save you.' He's clearly enjoying this moment. His face is bright, his movements animated as he goes on to describe the evening after Ross left and I got drunk. How he'd managed to get inside my house. My skin prickles, goosebumps rising as though ice-cold water has been poured over it.

'You had no clue it was me who carried you to bed and tucked you in?' He seems genuinely surprised. 'All that time I knew you were coming on to me. You wanted me, I could sense it.'

Disgust turns my stomach. I screw my face up so he can see how that thought makes me feel.

'Liar,' he says, pushing his face up close to mine. 'You thought I liked you. Wanted to protect you. And all the while I was getting you where I wanted you so I could kill you.'

I flinch unconsciously, and he laughs. 'But! I'm not quite ready yet. You've a little while longer.' He jerks up, suddenly, like he's just had an electric shock. 'I've got one last surprise for you,' he says, then gives a quiet laugh. 'Wait there. Don't. Move.' He points the gun at me. 'I don't want to have to put a bullet in your leg. Yet.'

He heads into the trees, the way we walked when we got here hours ago. My pulse judders. He's going back to his car, and I have a dreadful feeling I know what this means.

Chapter 44

I frantically twist, pull, and yank my hands, desperate to get one free. It took a few minutes to walk to this spot from where we parked the cars. By my calculation, I've got at least five minutes until Dean returns. My mind is muddled, blind panic blurring my thoughts.

Run. Get up and run into the woods. I could find a place to hide, maybe. Wait it out, then circle back around to my car. What did I do with the key? Which direction is the road? I turn my head, trying to get my bearings. The edge of the woodland runs along the road. All I'd have to do is reach it, pray someone drives by and sees me in time to save me.

But I've already wasted a minute or more thinking, not acting. Dean will easily catch up to me and shoot me in the leg as threatened. No, my only real option is to escape the binding, remove the tape from my mouth. I can't feel my lips. An awful thought occurs to me: what if I can't speak even if I do manage to get it off?

My breathing is erratic, pushing my heart rate up too. Regrets and thoughts of things I still want to do in my life swamp my mind, and all I can do is cry. The tears settle on the tape before rolling down over it, and I experience a thrill of hope. Will getting it wet affect the stickiness? I allow the tears to come, all the while twisting my mouth against the tape, forcing my lips to part enough to push my tongue through them. The adhesive tastes metallic – or maybe that's blood. I groan, and the realisation it's more audible than before makes my pulse race. This small success reignites my desire to get free. I suck in a tiny bit of air through my mouth, the first I've managed. It's nowhere near enough, but it's a start, and the tears turn to ones of relief.

I freeze at the sound of breaking twigs and direct my gaze to the source. *He must be coming back.* A figure slowly emerges from the clearing, but Dean's movements are hampered. He's dragging something.

Someone.

Oh, my God. It's Ross. Has to be.

What have you done?

My heart nearly stops when I see who he's got.

Not Ross.

Serena. Her body is limp, her arms hanging loosely, her legs trailing. She's not reacting to being hauled across the forest floor. Is she dead?

'It was you and your friend here seventeen years ago,' Dean says, his breathing rapid from his exertion. 'I thought it only fitting you should have a friend here now.' He drops Serena to the ground, swipes at his forehead and whistles. 'That was farther than I realised. You are challenging me, Anna.' He smiles. 'I made sure I didn't have to move the other women too far for this very reason, after the first.'

I smack my heels into the ground, thrash my body as much as I can – anything in an attempt to release the burning rage and frustration inside me. I hear Dean laugh. I'm giving him exactly what he wants. I clamp my teeth together, screw my eyes up tightly and take a noisy, ragged breath in through my nose. How can I make him see? *Think, think!*

Serena lets out a groan. She's alive. Instant relief is replaced with the gut-wrenching realisation that things are about to get a lot worse – that the end result will be a painful, horrific death for both of us unless I do something drastic. I use my legs to scoot myself closer to Serena. I lean down towards her face as her eyes spring open and I see the absolute terror reflected in them. She opens her mouth wide to scream, but I shake my head, my eyes wide and begging – *don't make a sound – please, God, don't make a sound.* She seems to understand and clamps a hand over her mouth. Her skin is pallid. A tender-looking red lump sits below her left eye and the lid of her other eye is swollen. Blood is caked beneath her nostrils, and splatters of it cover her pale blue jumper.

'I'm sorry, Anna,' she says, her voice a whisper.

I narrow my eyes, questioningly. *Why is she the one apologising?* I look towards Dean, who's standing with his arms crossed, watching with a satisfied look on his face. The cat that got the cream.

'Go on, Serena. Do let Anna in on it,' he says.

A shudder jolts my body. *Let me in on what?* My mind scrambles with a sudden influx of thoughts. When I'd found the link between Craig Beaumont and Neil

305

Holsworthy, I'd jumped to the conclusion that Henry had used it to his advantage to get to me. Or that Craig *was* Henry. And yesterday, when Serena had mentioned the hacked CCTV, I'd felt a pang of unease because I knew I hadn't told her about it. I explained her knowledge of it away, thinking that she must have seen it on the Facebook group . . . but was I too quick in dismissing my concern? I stare at my friend, searching for a hint of betrayal in her face. Henry is dead and it's been Dean tormenting me. Now he has Serena here, but apparently not as an ally. So what *is* her involvement?

Has my friend really been my enemy all this time?

'She's slow on the uptake, Serena. You're going to have to help her out.' Then he turns to me. 'As you can see, she's a bit dazed. Give her a second.'

'I didn't mean to help him,' she whimpers. My heart drops, her apology now making sense. But she was tricked – has to have been. Tears stream down Serena's face as I glare at her. 'He manipulated me. I should've known he was too good to be true.'

"He was too good to be true?" What? A wave of nausea crashes through me as realisation hits. *He* was who Serena was seeing. The new man in her life, Tim, was DI Walker. Dean. My head reels. Unwittingly, Serena was feeding Dean information he needed to get close to me, play with me. He kept her close so that he could use her until, like me, she was surplus to requirements.

'Just as you took the person I loved the most from me, ruined any chance I had at living a normal life, I set out to destroy yours by taking away what you've gained through your lies and deceit. I wanted you to suffer, so I instilled fear, drove you to behave erratically, tarnished your good – *fake*, by the way – reputation. You made it pretty easy for me to take your job – the zebra crossing incident was perfect, thank you. I was following you, and saw it all happen. Being a detective gave me all the access I needed to utilise it quickly. And then I took your husband from you. Now I'm going to take the only real friend you have left, after you killed your other one.' My heart sinks as I see Serena's eyes widen at this. She flashes me a confused look. 'Yep, that's right, Serena.' Dean bends down between us, takes the roll of tape, and wraps it around Serena's wrists. 'Your friend here, she's a killer.'

'Anna?' Her expression is one of incredulity, and there's nothing I can do to convince her he's lying. One, because he's not, and two, without the ability to speak, I can't convey what's needed in a mere look.

'Anna,' Dean says, putting his index finger under my chin and tilting it up. 'You're both going to die today, the thirteenth of May – the date you tried so very hard to keep from DI Walker. It was amusing at first, watching you squirm when I asked about the significance of it. But your repeated denial of any knowledge of why Henry might be killing a woman on that day each year began to really piss me off. Like you were denying any existence of my sister. Pretending you didn't kill her then run away and leave her to rot. I hope you feel bad that you never once questioned Henry's guilt during your involvement in the murder case. You wanted him to be responsible, didn't you? Then, when it eventually came to light, you could pin Kirsty's murder on him, too. Some sister you are.'

I let out a howl, like a dying animal, and stamp my feet again. I get as close to him as I can and stare at him, trying to force eye contact. He rolls his eyes while I plead with mine.

See me! Let me speak!

'Stop with the dramatics, Anna. That's my domain. I'm killing her first,' he says, kicking Serena's leg with the tip of his boot. 'I need to know that as you lie dying, it's filled with the pain of knowing it's your fault your best friend died too.'

Serena's breaths grow loud, more rapid, and I'm desperate to wrap my arms around her, protect her from him. She tries to scuttle away, but Dean grips the back of her jumper. Her legs flail frantically but she gets nowhere and gives up. Tears glisten on her cheeks. 'Why are you doing this, Tim – *Dean*?' she rasps. Is she genuinely interested in the answer, I wonder, or is she trying to buy us time now that she fully realises the predicament we're in?

Dean either doesn't consider the possibility or doesn't care either way, and seems to embrace the opportunity to rattle off the highlights. While his attention is on her, I work on loosening the tape on my hands and mouth.

'After I killed Henry I hid his body in a panic, but when I realised how I could use him to my advantage I went back and took samples of his hair, even his fingerprints, so I could leave trace evidence at each scene. Turns out I only needed it for the first one, then as I used similar stage-setting and of course, the pièce de résistance – the needle in the eye – each subsequent murder was linked to Henry Lincoln, anyway.' He pauses, glancing at each of us in turn. 'Genius, don't you think?'

Serena stares at him, her head nodding. 'You used your position in the Major Crime Unit to your full advantage, then.' Her voice is quiet, and she speaks the words like she's impressed, which pleases Dean, but I know her better – she's only trying to tell him what she thinks he wants to hear.

'Exactly. Being centre stage on this investigation gave me all the insight I needed, and I was able to plant my ideas, theories, evidence – manipulate the case so it fitted what I needed it to. Trust me, when there's a killer on the loose, especially a serial killer, there's a shitload of pressure to arrest someone – it's so easy to make the evidence fit with the suspect rather than remain open-minded and allow the evidence to lead you to the right person. No one, literally no one, suspected I was pulling the strings, that it was me committing the murders.' His face twists with a chilling smile. 'Ah, God. It's both hilarious and depressing at the same time, isn't it?' He grins at me and even though it's disdain that I feel, I give him a beseeching look in the vain hope he'll remove the tape so I can speak.

Serena's fearful expression changes, as though a switch has flicked, and she frowns. Shakes her head. Dean narrows his eyes, his face darkening.

'What?' he snaps.

'And you're sure you've covered your tracks?' she asks. I hear the shake in her voice, but then she sits more upright, jutting her chin forward. She continues, more confidently, 'You believe you'll never be suspected of any of this, even when police find our bodies here?'

'I didn't say I'd be leaving your bodies here to be found, did I? The other women were staged, meant to be seen. Otherwise I'd never have got to Anna. I'm done now, once you're both dead. I don't need anything from you. No one will find out.'

Serena's breath hitches and I watch on, helplessly, as her fear returns, her face contorting. 'People will report us missing,' she says, desperately. 'You've been seen at both our houses. There's only so much more you can manipulate before all eyes and theories turn to you.'

'I know what you're doing.' He paces, waving the gun around. 'My plan is sound. There's no hard evidence linking me to anything. Try harder.'

'If Henry's body is found, that will change everything.'

Dean's jaw tightens and his lip twitches violently. I can see it even in the diminishing light. She's angered him by questioning his ability to hide his crimes.

He lunges at her, ripping off more duct tape and covering her mouth too now.

'Enough talking.'

Serena's eyes are wide, desperate, as he moves towards her feet.

This is it. He's making sure she can't run. Can't lash out with her legs when he's killing her. My heart hammers hard against my ribs. If I don't do something now, it's going to be too late. I've only released the tape on my mouth enough to take tiny breaths, but I push my tongue as forcefully as I can against it and cry out.

'Stop. Wait.' The words don't form the way they sound in my head – they're distorted, muffled. Unintelligible. Dean grabs my ankles and jerks me towards him. The skin on my back is exposed and burns as it skids across the ground. My shoulder joints feel like they're being ripped from their sockets as my arms are pulled in the wrong direction. I yelp, sob, but Dean ignores me as he binds my legs. When he's done, he drags Serena over to the well, pulls her up and forces her to sit on the edge.

My ears fill with a pulsating, whooshing noise like the sound of crashing waves at Ness Cove and I wish above all else that I was there now, with Ross, living out a quiet, uncomplicated life.

As he hauls me to my feet and places me next to Serena, I know it's too late for any of that.

Chapter 45

Despite the tape on our mouths, our combined, panicked sobbing is so intense now it drowns out Dean's voice. I see his lips moving but I can't hear what he's saying. He stomps back and forth in front of us, his fingers dragging through his hair. Eventually, Serena becomes quiet and still, as though the inevitability of the situation has muted her. But my wails grow louder.

'Shut up, shut up. Shut. Up!' Dean aims the gun at me and my cries extinguish as quickly as snuffing out the flame of a candle. I hold my breath and turn to look at Serena. My fear is reflected in her expression. She blinks, moving her eyes towards Dean. She's desperately trying to communicate something to me. She indicates towards my legs, then hers. Nods her head three times.

Okay. I've got it. On the count of three, both of us kick our legs out at Dean. Maybe with enough force, he'll fall to the ground. *But then what?* Even if we both jump on him, putting all our collective weight on him, without the use of our hands he'll soon recover and use the gun. It'll be futile.

Better than giving up and letting him kill us both easily, though. At least we'll die with the knowledge we put up a worthy fight. There's some dignity in that.

'Hey. Hey.' Dean slaps the barrel of the gun across Selena's head. 'Stop with the communication.' He takes a few steps back until he's far enough away that neither of our legs can reach him. I should remember that he's a detective – he's perceptive and has likely seen all the tricks in the book. Hope collapses in on itself and I start to pray for a swift death. That's not his aim, though; I know that. He wouldn't have gone to these lengths if he were merely going to put a bullet through my brain.

I twist around on the stone wall of the well and peer down into the abyss, my stomach dropping.

Dean thinks he has the control – thinks he can choose how I die. If I take that away from him, he'll lose. If I fling myself backwards it'll ruin his plan. I could end this now, myself.

And one day, when he's caught, and our bodies are found – the truth will all be revealed.

That'll teach him.

My eyes sting with tears as my plan plays out in my mind, my heart fluttering like a trapped animal. I've run out of choices. I'm about to make peace with my decision – after all, what have I left to live for anyway? – when a voice in my head screams: *You saved yourself before – you can do it again.* I wriggle my hands, furiously twisting and pulling them. Serena clocks what I'm doing and gives me an encouraging nod. She shuffles to the left, away from me, drawing Dean's attention to her in the hope I can get my hands free without him realising.

'Where are you going?' he says to her. He presses his hands down on Serena's thighs, preventing further movement. I keep an eye on them, while I manipulate my hands to create more space. I feel the tape give some more, the progress increasing my adrenaline so much my body seems to vibrate with it.

Nearly there. I've almost got enough room to slip my hand out.

Dean's full attention is on Serena. He's telling her how he did like her, how it wasn't all fake. The sex was good, he says, and in a different set of circumstances he reckons they'd have been a great couple had they been able to continue dating. Had she lived long enough. I hear Serena make a weird sound in her throat and assume she's disagreeing with both his evaluation and his prediction.

'But no point crying over spilt milk, eh?' he says, putting both hands on her chest. My stomach flips. He's going to kill her first. And he's going to do it now. I give one almighty tug and my right hand releases with a loud tearing noise. Dean's head snaps around and he glares at me, but in the split second it takes for him to see I'm free of my binding, I'm on him, my hands grasping his hair and yanking hard. For a moment, my entire body weight hangs from the clump of it gripped in my fist, then I bring my other arm up and wrap it around his neck. Serena flings her legs out and directs her bound feet upwards. With a sickening blow, they make contact with his groin. He drops the gun and doubles over, the air expelling from his lungs in one loud *umph* noise. At the same time I land hard on the edge of the well. A sharp pain jabs at my ribs, stealing the air from my lungs, and I struggle to catch my breath. I gasp through the gap in the tape and put my hands to it to rip it off, but I'm not quick enough. Frustration burns in my chest as my hands are yanked away. Dean's on me, flipping me over to face him. I force my head to the side, but I can't see Serena.

Where's Serena? Oh my God – did he push her down the well? Did I knock her while I was grappling with Dean? Panic rises along with my heart rate, the frantic beating making me giddy.

'You're just like your brother,' Dean rasps. 'He put up a fight too.'

He pushes me, and I thrust my hands to his chest, holding on with all my strength. He forces me back until I'm teetering on the edge of the stone wall, the top half of me floating in the air above the drop. I attempt to speak, but now with little air and the tape still restricting my mouth, I fail to eject a single recognisable word.

'Looks like it's your turn,' Dean says, his words forced through gritted teeth. I sense he's weaker than before, the kick to his testicles maybe rendering him less powerful. I have to make the most of this moment, strike while he's not at full strength. Our bodies are touching, grappling with each other, muscle against muscle, skin against skin in a desperate battle for survival.

In my head, the words I want to shout play out unheard.

It's said that your life flashes before your eyes in the moments before death, and as I inch towards mine, images of my parents, my brother, Finley Hall, my only real friend there, and now my only real friend here, fly through my mind as the darkness of the hole envelops me.

Survival.

The word illuminates inside my skull and something deep within me gives me the strength to give one final push. I grab the front of his shirt and use it to regain my balance, taking him by surprise, then with a roar I pull him around so that his back is to the wall. I stagger away from it and, seeing Dean struggling to keep his balance, I realise this is my chance.

I know it, but I hesitate, my conscience questioning what I'm about to do. It's a millisecond decision whether to use the opportunity to tear the tape from my mouth and take the chance that I will have time to say what I need to, or to put an end to this right now.

As I reach for the tape, he thrusts his hands towards me, and I know I can't take another risk.

It's him or me.

With everything I have, I lunge at him.

His hands flail, clutching at the air, desperately trying to grasp my clothes – he wants to take me with him. But the momentum takes him away from me. He yells and swears, understanding hitting him. Our eyes meet and I've the urge to try and catch him, my hands reaching to clutch his – it must be instinct – but my fingertips merely brush his as he disappears from view. There's a few seconds of silence, then a blood-curdling crunch and I flinch as it echoes in my head – in my memory.

Then, silence.

I tear at the tape around my head, my lips, crying out as it pulls at my skin. I twist my mouth, open and close it to get the feeling back, then, with my pulse pounding in my ears, I scour the area for Serena.

Please be here, I pray silently. The thought of three bodies in the well is too much to endure.

317

I hear a low, deep moaning and let out a relieved breath. I run around to the other side of the well, where Serena lies on her back, her chest heaving.

She's breathing. I'm not responsible for another death. I go to her and begin stripping off the tape.

'He's got to be dead, right?' she gasps when I've freed her mouth.

I close my eyes and continue to suck in huge breaths of air through my mouth now I'm able. Dead. Dean Briggs is dead.

'Even if he isn't,' I say, my voice breaking, 'there's no way he'll climb out of there.' It's dark now, even darker down the well. I'm drawn to the edge, compelled to check he's not somehow halfway back up. My pulse thrums as I lean forwards an inch and extend my neck so I can just peep over. I can't see him clinging to the wall; I can't hear any effort to escape. There's no sound at all from down there. 'Hello?' I call. The single word, loudly spoken, scratches my throat. I allow some saliva to build, swallow a few times, then I shout, 'Dean!'

I have to be certain.

Nothing.

A deep, guttural cry erupts from me, and I fall to the ground and sob. Serena sits beside me and wraps her arm around my shoulders and cries too. A few minutes pass with us huddled together, and when Serena's tears stop, mine keep flowing. It's like years' worth of pain and anger is being let out, together with relief, regret, grief, and guilt.

Serena pulls me up, and holding me at arm's length, she locks eyes with me.

'Are you okay?'

I'm not even close to being okay, but I nod all the same.

It's easier than telling her the truth. There'll be time for that later. There's a confused expression on her face and I wonder if that's in response to my own. I drag my hands down my face, my fingertips snagging on the sticky residue of the duct tape.

'I'm fine. I will be fine.' I say it not just to Serena, but to the universe – if I repeat it enough, it might become the case.

'I'm so sorry,' Serena says, tears swimming in her eyes again. 'I *swear* I had no clue who he was.'

My eyes feel like they're the size of golf balls, my lids swollen with tears. I shake my head. 'I had no clue, either, Serena. And I'm the one who should've.'

Her brow creases. 'I know now isn't the time, but I think we'll need to have a full and frank conversation soon.'

'Oh, Serena – what a mess.' I sweep an arm around her. 'How are we going to explain all this? There are two dead people in a well, seventeen years apart – one of whom is a detective inspector – and I'm responsible for both, in different ways.' The repercussions are beyond my comprehension and a wave of panic crashes over me.

'Breathe, Anna. Come on, we've not survived a madman only for you to die of a heart attack.'

'How can you be so calm?' I gasp. Maybe, I realise, it's because now the immediate danger is over, she knows she's the innocent party in all of this and there are no criminal consequences for her.

There are plenty for me.

I have the uncontrollable urge to leave now. I start walking towards the path between the trees that we came through.

'Wait up, Anna. Shouldn't we stay a while longer to, you know . . . to make sure?'

'What, you think he'll come back to life, like in the *Scream* movies?'

'It would be your luck.'

She has a point. I move to her side and together, we both lean over and stare down into the black hole again. I absently rub at my wrists to relieve some of the stiffness and stinging.

'It's over,' I say, tears clogging my throat. I bend to pick up Dean's gun, then toss it in the hole. 'Let's go.' I turn my back on the well. Turn my back on the past, once again.

This *will* be the last time. No one else will come after me, because there's no one left to care.

Chapter 46

As we make our way to the cars, shadows lend the woodland an eeriness that makes my skin creep with a feeling like we're being watched. But there's no one left to observe us now. Serena's arm loops through mine and we stumble over the uneven ground in a subdued silence. We're each trying to process the past few hours in our own way.

Seeing the cars side by side forces me to face uncomfortable questions. The immediate danger is over; Dean is no longer a risk to us. But what we've done – what I've done – is. I might've got away with my life, got away with the death of my childhood friend up until now, but with a dead detective in the mix, how long will that last? My life has already flashed in front of my eyes once today, and now it does so again.

'The key's in the ignition,' Serena says, ducking inside Dean's Audi. 'What are we going to do with it?'

'We can't leave it here to be found,' I say. 'If this is the last known location of his vehicle, they're bound to search this entire area. It won't take much to figure out his body is in the well.' My heart flutters furiously at the thought of him being found and, worse, what lies beneath him. I can't have gone through all of this only to be thrown into prison. I give Serena a pleading look. 'If maybe you drive it somewhere else, I'll follow, then we can dump it and I'll take us home?'

'Why can't we simply tell the police he was the real killer – the one that they've been after? This was self-defence, Anna.'

'Yes, *this* was,' I say. 'He might be the person responsible for the murders of five women – but he's not responsible for the death of the girl they'll unearth at the same time.'

'Look, I know you've got a lot of explaining still to do, but I know you, Anna – and I know full well that whatever happened here all those years ago can have been nothing more than a horrific accident. Surely between us we can formulate a feasible story where his sister's death can be pinned on him, too? The police are more likely going to believe us given what they're going to find out about one of their own detectives. Or we say it was your brother who killed Kirsty, Dean killed him in revenge, then went mad and started targeting you.'

'What if they don't believe it, though? Think about it, Serena – all we have is what Dean told us. His confession was to us – and there's no evidence of it. As he said, the only evidence at the scenes of the murders is what Dean made sure was there. And all of that pointed to Henry, not him. I'm not even sure the timings of your suggestion match up and without Henry's body, there's unlikely to be a smidgen of proof that successfully ties Dean to any of this.'

'He *abducted* me, Anna. He bound the both of us. There'll be evidence of that.' Serena's eyes are wild, determined. Is she right? 'Of course, that does entail us reporting it straight away.' She draws in a deep breath, then releases it forcefully.

'I can't . . .' I struggle to catch my breath, anxiety crushing my lungs as the options swim around in my head. I lean against my car, breathe slowly until I recover my composure. 'I'm not certain enough to take the risk.'

'Once we move his vehicle, the opportunity to go down the self-defence route will be lost, though, Anna. There's no way it'll look like we're innocent if we drive his car away from here.'

'Yes, you're right. Whatever decision we make now will impact us forever, either way.'

And I know this to be true, because my life changed completely the last time I was in this cursed place.

Chapter 47

THEN

They stare at each other in horror, the reality of what's just happened plastered on their faces.

'You . . . you—' Henry stutters. 'God, Anna.'

She calls down the well, but there's only silence. Tears blur her vision and her legs buckle.

'We can't tell anyone.'

'What? We have to. We can't . . . just . . .' His breathing is rapid and further speech is impeded.

After minutes of shocked silence, panic floods each of them and survival instincts kick in.

'You did it. It's your fault.' He begins pacing around the well. 'I'm going back to Finley – I'll get Frank.'

'No! Don't be stupid. Look, we have to think this through. It's no good panicking and ruining the rest of our lives.'

'I think you'll find they're ruined already.'

'You'll go to prison, Henry. You think Finley is bad? Jesus,' she says, taking hold of him, giving him a shake.

'If you tell, I'll be forced to blame you and we both know I'll be believed. Your track record isn't exactly angelic, is it? And what with your weird behaviour, they'll automatically point the finger at you, not her best friend.'

He collapses to the ground, head in his hands, and begins rocking.

'I'm sorry,' she says. 'We're both hurting here – we've both contributed to her death – and we both need to make a promise here and now that this stays between us.'

'How can you be so callous?'

'Shit, really? You're asking me that, after all you've done?'

Accusations fly until exhaustion takes over.

'What are we going to do then?' he asks eventually.

She suddenly looks shifty – sheepish. 'We had a plan. To leave Finley, run away. All we need to do is stick to that plan.'

'You were both going to leave? Without a word to me and Dean – your only fucking relatives?' Anger swells inside him.

'Only to begin with, Henry. We'd have come back for you both, I promise.'

His brow furrows in disbelief. 'Yeah, course you would've.'

'You need to sneak back to Finley. Go into our dorm and under each bed is a backpack all ready with our runaway clothes, purses and fake IDs.'

'You're leaving me behind in this shithole to cover for you, make sure they believe you both ran away? I can't.'

'You have to. Please, Henry – it's the only way.'

He gets up, brushes himself down and swipes at his tear-streaked face. He leans over the stone wall of the well. 'No, no, no.'

'Please, Henry. For me?'

He closes his eyes, shaking his head. Everything has changed in the matter of an hour. Their game, The Hunt, ended in a way that he'd never intended. With the dire consequences stretching ahead, something inside him gives.

'Okay. I'll do it for you, Anna,' he says, then finally moves away from the well and stomps back through the trees. 'Stay right there,' he calls back over his shoulder.

Chapter 48

After another hour of anguished discussion, Serena agrees to drive the Audi away from the woodland along a route of minor roads to avoid traffic cameras.

'Thank you,' I say. 'I'm not sure how I'll ever repay you, but I promise I'll spend the rest of my life trying.'

'Let's just get through the night before you make any further promises, Anna.' Her tone sounds harsh, unforgiving, and I can't blame her. My promises don't count for much. Her shoulders slope, and she takes me in her arms. 'It'll be okay. *We'll* be okay,' she says, more softly. If I escape punishment for this, I'll owe her my life.

'You best go first because you know the area better.' Serena says, backing away from me and walking to Dean's car. I'm also the one who's going to choose the location to ditch the Audi. I seem to remember talk of a disused quarry around here, which might be the best bet. Even if Dean's car is found at some point, the quarry is far enough away from the well that the two are unlikely to be linked.

If anything, police will assume DI Walker's vehicle was stolen by joyriders and dumped – or that he must've been in this area trying to locate Henry Lincoln single-handedly, and Henry is the person responsible for the detective's disappearance.

It's the best hope I have.

There are no lights along the lanes leading to the land where the quarry is; only my headlights and those of Serena's in the Audi behind illuminate the path ahead. The lane narrows so much that the hedges scratch against each side of the car, the high-pitched squealing sounding like screaming. I feel a moment of panic. Have I taken a wrong turning? I'm afraid I'm about to end up in someone's farm when it suddenly widens and the ground changes, becoming smoother; sandy, and I let out my held breath in a rush. After a few minutes, I brake and get out, indicating to Serena to pull alongside me.

She doesn't get out immediately, and I can't see her face. My pulse skitters. Has she changed her mind? I couldn't blame her – this is going beyond the call of friendship. I lay my hand on my chest, feeling the beat of my heart drumming against it. I'm allowing her guilt that she was suckered in by Dean to ensure I get what I want. I swore I'd never be this selfish again, yet here I am. It really will be the last time, though. I'll make sure I'm the very best friend to Serena. And here and now, I make a new resolution: I'm not going back to Seabrook Prep. I look up to the night sky, tears pricking my eyes. I'm going to find a new teaching job at a more disadvantaged school, just like I'd intended all those years ago. I'll prove my worth by contributing to the wellbeing of kids who aren't as fortunate as those at private schools. And I will lead a good life.

Even if that means leading it alone, without my husband.

The car door opens, and Serena steps into the beam of light created by the headlights.

'You okay?' I walk towards her, my hand out. She takes it and I feel its clamminess against my palm.

'When it's over I will be,' she says. She lets go of my hand and edges forwards.

'Careful.' I tug at her jumper sleeve, fear sweeping through my veins. The last thing I want now is for her to accidentally fall into the quarry.

'I'm getting a little tired of deep, dark holes,' Serena says. 'Can we make this the last?'

I can't help but smile. It's comforting to know someone else who uses humour in stressful situations. 'With pleasure.'

We go through the plan again, and when we're both as certain as we can be that we've thought of everything, Serena gets back into Dean's car and uses the wet wipes from his glove compartment to remove her fingerprints. They'll find her blood in the boot, if the car is ever retrieved, but that can be explained with the abduction story, which she'll say she was too traumatised to report at the time. Finding her fingerprints on the steering wheel would be trickier to explain, so a few minutes eliminating those is time well spent.

When she's finished, Serena pulls the sleeve of her jumper over her hand and releases the handbrake. We both get behind the car and with our hands covered, we begin pushing it closer to the edge. It's hard to begin with, then it gains momentum, moving more easily. Within seconds, I feel a release of pressure, and the car is falling into the black void beneath us in a cacophony of crunching, scraping metal and shattering glass.

Once the noise abates, Serena takes my hand in hers and we stand in quiet contemplation at the edge of the quarry, looking out across the skyline. Twinkling lights in the distance are the only reminder other people exist in this moment. I close my eyes, giving a silent prayer to poor Henry and to all those who've been hurt by, or had their lives taken by, Dean Briggs. And as I tilt my head to the heavens, I pray for him, too. That he may be at peace, now.

Shivering with the cold air and shock, we climb back into my car and I whack the heater on as we begin the drive home. There's still a lot to talk about, decisions to be made about what to say, to whom, and when. But we agree to keep the truth between ourselves.

I've replaced one secret for another.

But what's a secret between friends?

Epilogue

THEN

Avoiding public transport, at least while still in Sutton Coldfield, was a must – I couldn't afford to be traced that way. Now, two days' worth of hitching has left me grubby, and my face shows every bit of fear, guilt and exhaustion – my skin sallow, dark circles heavy under my eyes. I stare at myself in the mirror of the service station toilets, loathing the person I see. I splash water over myself, rub my face hard in a vain attempt to rid it of the evidence. Nausea swells in my belly. I've had no food to speak of and I've already vomited twice, so there can't be anything left to bring up.

A woman coming out of a toilet cubicle side-eyes me. She's weighing me up; judging me. I should be used to it, but today irritation is quick to surface, and I glare at her.

'What?' I say, my voice harsh with aggression. She opens her mouth to say something, but thinks better of it, and leaves, the door slamming behind her. A knot of regret gripes in my gut. I shouldn't have been so snappy; she was likely only concerned at seeing a dishevelled-looking girl alone in a service station toilet. I look intensely at the closed door for a moment, willing her to come back through it and ask me if I'm all right. When she doesn't, I turn back to the mirror with a sigh. *Maybe I look older than fifteen*, I think, touching my face. Maybe I won't need that fake ID after all.

Outside, I spot a group of people, touristy types by the look of them, about to board a coach. I spot its destination lit up on the front. It's bound for Devon. I've always wanted to live by the sea. I edge closer to the group, then mingle in with them as they jostle to get up the coach's steps, my pulse skipping when the driver glances at me. I wait for his barked demand of *what do you think you're doing?* but it doesn't come. I find an empty seat near the back and quickly take it. For the next ten minutes, sitting with my eyes averted from the other passengers, my nerves jangle and I fear people can actually hear my legs as they knock together. Then, I feel the vibration of the engine under my feet and allow myself to relax back in the seat as we move off.

I'm finally heading for the coast.

Five hours later I glimpse the expanse of glistening water for the first time in real life and emotions overwhelm me. The strongest, guilt, takes centre stage, along with regret for what I've done. But as I gaze out of the grimy coach window at the distant horizon, a calmness settles within me, mirroring the silent ocean. I can't change what happened, but I can try to live a good life and make sure I give back as much as possible.

A sign for Torquay flashes by. I read up on this area

before leaving – it'll be a good starting point. Plenty of touristy places offering seasonal work to see me through the first weeks and months, with luck. I trudge from the coach station to the tourist information centre and get a list of nearby accommodation. There's a hostel – cheap and cheerful looking – that has a view of the sea, and it states that the rooms are single with a private bathroom. I can't remember the last time I had that. A flurry of excitement is quashed by the stronger sense of trepidation, and the words flying through my mind: *you don't deserve this*. I push them away.

I have no choice.

The building isn't how it looks in the photo. It's tired-looking, dirty, with flaking paint that reminds me of where I lived before Finley Hall. A swishing sensation deep in my belly stops me, and I grip the metal railings outside. Is this the best place there is? It's not as though I have a whole host of options. Beggars can't be choosers, as my mother would say when she slopped beans in a bowl for dinner, or dressed me in clothes she'd found on the steps of charity shops.

If I'm to survive on my own, I have to be brave. With a huge intake of the sea air, I push the doors to the hostel open and walk inside, striding with fake confidence up to the reception. The middle-aged man gives me a cheery greeting. He has kind eyes – a honey-brown colour – that look knowingly at me as he asks my name. I pause, with my purse containing the ID with the falsified date of birth in my hand, my knuckles white with anxiety.

I told Henry we'd planned to run away, that we'd secured everything we needed to ensure we weren't found, but the IDs aren't exactly high quality – just good enough to make ourselves sixteen, so that legally we were free to leave the home and gain our own accommodation. We figured Miss Graves wouldn't involve the police – it would look bad for them, and they wouldn't want the attention for fear the police would dig further into Finley Hall. Going all out with fake names was far too risky according to Dodgy Dave, the guy who hooked us up with his mate who only usually forged IDs to get underage kids into clubs. Proper kosher-looking ones would cost more than we'd ever get our hands on. These would be good enough, he'd assured us. As an extra precaution, Henry had said he'd set fire to the files in Miss Graves's office to make sure there was no record of Kirsty Briggs or Anna Lincoln.

Doing this alone, now, though, makes me edgy. My hands shake violently as I reach into my purse, aware of the guy's eyes on me. I can almost hear him weighing up whether he should call the police or not, and my paranoia makes me fumble. I pull out both the IDs and as I do, a scan photo comes with it. My breath hitches as I look at the grey and white grainy image of the five-week-old foetus, and my surroundings melt away as the worst moments of my life come back to me.

Tears stream down my face. The journey has been an incredibly long one – the botched abortion thieving me of the chance to ever have children. Maybe that was a good thing – it's my deserved punishment for what I did. I'll try and tell myself it's my choice – because let's face it – who'd want to bring children into this world? With my genes, no doubt I'd make a terrible mother anyway. I can't chance ruining another life. I want to run as far away from my own as I can.

It's suddenly clear what I should do. I look down at

the two IDs, putting the one saying Kirsty Briggs back in my purse. Then, with a smile, I hand the man Anna's.

'I'm Anna Lincoln,' I tell him. It feels odd saying her name – it's the first time I've uttered it since the other night, since Henry and I yelled it after she fell into the well.

But I'm sure I'll get used to it.

Acknowledgements

I am truly grateful that I'm able to do what I love. Thank you to all who have helped – and those who continue to help – me achieve my dreams. I have a fantastic publishing team behind me – I'm thrilled and proud to be a part of Avon, HarperCollins. Thank you to **all** of Team Avon, in particular my amazing (and ultra-speedy!) editor, Thorne Ryan, who helped make this book something to be immensely proud of, and Helen Huthwaite whose belief and support in me means the world. I've also had the pleasure of working with the wonderful Elisha Lundin and editorial assistant Raphaella Demetris, as well as Gabriella Drinkald, Maddie Dunne-Kirby and Ella Young who run the publicity and marketing team. Also, a huge thank you to Samantha Luton for getting my books onto the supermarket shelves. Everyone at Avon is professional, enthusiastic and a joy to work with and so many people are behind the scenes working hard to ensure books get into the hands of readers – THANK YOU. Thank you to my copy editor, Felicity Radford for her diligence and brilliant suggestions. I'm lucky, and grateful, to have a fiercely talented and supportive agent in Anne Williams, of KHLA who goes above and beyond – I couldn't be in better hands and I'm looking forward to an exciting time ahead.

As ever, I owe a debt of gratitude to my family and friends for their unwavering support and dedication to spreading the word about my books – I have my own little-but-mighty promotional team! For everyday support and being brilliant friends, not to mention therapists, I thank the lovely Libby, Carolyn and Caroline – you're all blinking amazing!

I had an extremely busy time during the writing of *The Serial Killer's Sister,* including two weddings and a birth (thankfully I was not the one marrying or birthing!) so last year passed in somewhat of a blur – but our family grew, and fond new memories were made, all of which I know my dear mum and dad would've absolutely loved. I thank you both every day for what you gave me.

Thank you to my fabulous readers who make all of this possible and helped get my previous books onto bestseller lists. You make everything worthwhile. To the brilliant bloggers and reviewers who share their book love – thank you – it is most appreciated.

To you, my reader – thank you for picking up my book! I hope you enjoy *The Serial Killer's Sister* – and while the title is a good indicator of what you can expect, there are, as is usual in psychological thrillers and crime novels, some dark themes and sensitive topics which some may find triggering.

Is murder in the blood?

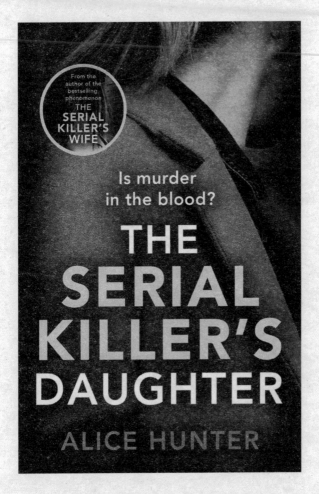

Is murder
in the blood?

From the
author of the
bestselling
phenomenon
THE
SERIAL
KILLER'S
WIFE

THE
SERIAL
KILLER'S
DAUGHTER

ALICE HUNTER

The shocking killer thriller with a
breathtaking twist.

Every marriage has its secrets. . .

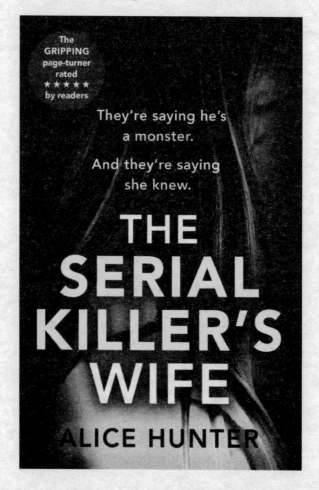

The
GRIPPING
page-turner
rated
★ ★ ★ ★ ★
by readers

They're saying he's
a monster.

And they're saying
she knew.

THE
SERIAL
KILLER'S
WIFE

ALICE HUNTER

The addictive and chilling debut crime
thriller from bestselling author Alice
Hunter.